"I am not afraid of cops. And despite what you're implying, I am not some snob who looks down on them because I'm a judge's daughter and you're an officer who serves the court."

"So why don't you want me here?" Mitch demanded, the top of his nose nearly touching hers.

"Because I'm afraid of..." Of what? Him? Men? What he reminded her of? What he made her feel? That he made her *feel*, period?

"What scares you, princess?" he whispered.

Casey zeroed in on the mouth that spoke such a challenge. *Sexy.* Firm and flat and as unerringly masculine as the breadth of his shoulders or the timbre of his voice.

He liked to argue. He seemed to bring out the worst in her red-haired temperament. Sparring with him made her feel strong. Opinionated.

What if he simply silenced her with a kiss?

Dear Harlequin Intrigue Reader,

It's autumn, and there's no better time to *fall* in love with Harlequin Intrigue!

Book two of TEXAS CONFIDENTIAL, *The Agent's Secret Child* (#585) by B.J. Daniels, will thrill you with heart-stopping suspense and passion. When secret agent Jake Cantrell is sent to retrieve a Colombian gangster's widow and her little girl, he is shocked to find the woman he'd once loved and lost—and a child who called him *Daddy*....

Nick Travis had hired missing persons expert Taryn Scott to find a client, in Debbi Rawlins's SECRET IDENTITY story, *Her Mysterious Stranger* (#587). Working so closely with the secretive Nick was dangerous to Taryn's life, for her heart was his for the taking. But when his secrets put her life at risk, Nick had no choice but to put himself in the line of fire to protect her.

Susan Kearney begins her new Western trilogy, THE SUTTON BABIES, with *Cradle Will Rock* (#586). When a family of Colorado ranchers is besieged by a secret enemy, will they be able to preserve the one thing that matters most—a future for their children?

New author Julie Miller knows all a woman needs is *One Good Man* (#588). Casey Maynard had suffered a vicious attack that scarred not only her body, but her soul. Shut up in a dreary mansion, she and sexy Mitch Taylor, the cop assigned to protect her, strike sparks off each other. Could Mitch save her when a stalker returned to finish the job? This book is truly a spine-tingling pager-turner!

As always, Harlequin Intrigue is committed to giving readers the best in romantic suspense. Next month, watch for releases from your favorite special promotions—TEXAS CONFIDENTIAL, THE SUTTON BABIES, MORE MEN OF MYSTERY and SECRET IDENTITY!

Sincerely,

Denise O'Sullivan
Associate Senior Editor
Harlequin Intrigue

ONE GOOD MAN
JULIE MILLER

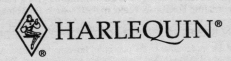

HARLEQUIN®

TORONTO • NEW YORK • LONDON
AMSTERDAM • PARIS • SYDNEY • HAMBURG
STOCKHOLM • ATHENS • TOKYO • MILAN • MADRID
PRAGUE • WARSAW • BUDAPEST • AUCKLAND

ISBN 0-373-22588-1

ONE GOOD MAN

ABOUT THE AUTHOR

Julie Miller attributes her passion for writing romance to all those fairy tales she read growing up, and shyness. Encouragement from her family to write down those feelings she couldn't express became a love for the written word. She gets continued support from her fellow members of the Prairieland Romance Writers, where she serves as the resident "grammar goddess." This award-winning author and teacher has published several paranormal romances. Inspired by the likes of Agatha Christie and Encyclopedia Brown, Julie believes the only thing better than a good mystery is a good romance.

Born and raised in Missouri, she now lives in Nebraska with her husband, son and smiling guard dog, Maxie. Write to Julie at P.O. Box 5162, Grand Island, NE 68802-5162.

Books by Julie Miller

HARLEQUIN INTRIGUE
588—ONE GOOD MAN

THE TAYLOR CLAN

Sid and Martha Taylor:
butcher and homemaker
ages 63 and 62 respectively

Brett Taylor:
contractor
age 38
the protector

Mac Taylor:
forensic specialist
age 37
the professor

Gideon Taylor:
firefighter/arson investigator
age 35
the crusader

Cole Taylor:
the mysterious brother (the family's not quite sure what kind of work he does—undercover)
age 30
the lost soul

Jessie Taylor:
the lone daughter
antiques dealer/buyer/restorer
age 29
the survivor

Josh Taylor:
police officer
age 27
at 6'3", he's still the baby of the family
the charmer

Mitch Taylor:
Sid's nephew—raised like a son
police captain
age 39
the chief

CAST OF CHARACTERS

Mitch Taylor—Captain of the Fourth Precinct. Gladiator in a suit and tie. He was once a kid of the streets, and the last thing this veteran cop wants to do is baby-sit a Plaza princess.

Cassandra (Casey) Maynard—She lost her family and her future in one horrible act of violence. She knows it's just a matter of time before her stalker returns to finish what he started.

Commissioner James Reed—Uncle Jimmy is the only family Casey has left. But is he too busy with his reelection to listen to her fears?

Iris Webster—She's been James's right hand for years. She'd do anything to protect him.

Emmett Raines—A master of disguise. Toying with his victims is all part of the game.

Darlene Raines—Emmett's twin. Together, they devised a perfect plan.

Judith and Ben McDonald—They've served the Maynards for years.

Jack Maynard—His reputation as the "No-Budge Judge" cost his family dearly.

Steven Craighead—Bodyguard or betrayer?

Cynthia DeBecque—Why does the murdered prostitute's name keep popping up?

For the Fensoms.
Thank you for always making me feel welcome.
Happy holidays!

And for the IMPROV gang.
You really are making a difference in the lives of young people. You made a difference in mine.

Chapter One

What a hell of a day.

Mitch pushed the door buzzer on the Gothic fortress of a house north of the Plaza and waited. He hated sucking up to the commissioner like this. But when the man in charge of his next promotion called and asked for a personal favor, Mitch was hardly in a position to refuse.

A house check was so routine, he normally would have assigned it to a uniformed patrol. He'd have passed it on to his staff sergeant for *her* to assign it to a uniformed patrol. He'd even offered to send two of his best detectives in his stead. But Commissioner Reed had insisted on privacy.

Mitch pocketed the electronic gate key the commissioner had given him to get onto the estate grounds, and wondered just what kind of fool's errand he'd been sent on. His boss had been closemouthed to the extent that Mitch knew very few details about what he was even checking for. "It's an old family friend," he'd said. "Just see if there's any trouble."

Trouble? Like what? A break-in? Vandalism? A lunatic relative running around naked and embarrassing the family?

Why the hush-hush discretion?

If he was honest with himself, Mitch didn't really mind doing such a favor. He missed having regular contact with the people who really needed the police's help, instead of spending most of his hours talking to the press or running the administrative end of Kansas City's Fourth Precinct.

But not this kind of house. Not these kind of people.

The commissioner didn't know what he was asking of him.

Mitch checked his watch and then smoothed his leather gloves back into place. It was 6:00 p.m. Surely no one went to bed this early anymore. Maybe the gray November air had driven the residents to the far wing of the house, where they nestled in front of a fireplace, sipping cognac to chase away the chill of the evening.

He punched the doorbell again, laying on the buzzer for an impolite length of time. They could damn well send the servants to answer the door, the tips of his ears were feeling the bite of Missouri's damp winter.

"This has to be a wild-goose chase," he muttered to himself, ready to climb back into his Jeep Grand Cherokee and phone Reed on his private line to report no one at home. This was probably some test of his loyalty before the new assistant commissioner was named in January.

Well, Mitch Taylor didn't play games. If he got the job because he was the best qualified, then fine, he deserved it. But if the selection would be based on politics, he didn't have a prayer.

Schmooze or you lose, the commissioner had once advised him. If that was the case, Mitch was bound to lose.

His annoying second-guessing was cut short by the crackle of static from a hidden intercom panel. "Yes?"

Mitch looked up toward the source of the raspy voice and located the speaker and camera recessed behind the carved walnut paneling lining the front door. He stepped back, reached inside his coat and pulled his badge from his belt. Holding the identification beside his face, he looked up at the camera.

"I'm Captain Mitch Taylor, KCPD. I'd like to ask you a few questions, ma'am, and, if possible, check the premises for you. We got an anonymous call that there was some trouble here."

Following orders, he left out the commissioner's name and treated this like a routine investigation of a reported disturbance. Then, confident that the ID and his authoritative voice would reassure the woman this visit was simply standard procedure, he clipped the badge onto the breast pocket of his coat and waited to be let in.

"There's no trouble here." The woman responded too quickly and too breathlessly for him to believe her.

Ah, hell, if Reed had sent him out on a domestic-violence call without any backup...

Mitch reached inside his coat and unsnapped the holster beneath his blazer. His guard-dog hackles went up at the possibility of facing a cop's most dreaded call, but he forced his voice to remain calm and even pitched.

"Ma'am, if you could just come to the door, I'd like to speak to you face-to-face."

Before the intercom went silent, he heard a flurry of activity. Mitch's initial suspicions flared a notch. He adjusted his tie, never blinking his gaze from the doorknob. Then, through the double blockade of the front door and storm door, he heard the distinctive sound of a solid object crashing to the floor, followed by a stifled yelp.

His hand stilled on the knot of his tie.

"Ma'am?" he called. "Ma'am, are you all right?"

Nothing but dead silence answered him. Rusty warning signals that had kept him alive when he worked on the streets labored into overdrive. A spot at the nape of his neck tingled with awareness whenever he sensed something was wrong. Right now, the skin above his collar tickled like crazy.

He unholstered his Glock 9 mm pistol from beneath his suit jacket.

"Ma'am?"

Nothing.

Damn. This was supposed to be routine. A polite introduction, sorry to disturb you and good-night. Some routine. More like a shot in the dark. He'd wake the commissioner tonight and find out exactly what kind of wild ride he'd been sent on.

But first, he had to protect that woman.

"I'm coming in," he announced.

Mitch flipped his gun around, clutched the barrel and hammered at the glass in the locked storm door. When it shattered, he reached inside and opened it. The wooden door inside was locked, as well. Taking two steps back, he released the safety, aimed his weapon and fired two rounds into the locking mechanism.

The wood splintered around the knob, and the door loosened from its frame. Leaning his shoulder against it, he braced his legs and pushed. The door swung open and he stumbled inside.

The lights in the house immediately flashed on, and a loud, repetitive alarm blared to life. The woman screamed from the back of the house, yelling a warning over the din.

"Routine, hell!" he muttered under his breath.

He rolled to the wall and straightened himself against the ceiling-high paneling. The security lights he'd tripped had a strobe effect on his vision, blinding him more than the utter darkness of the place had.

Mitch relied on his sense of touch to get his bearings. He slid along the paneling until he found a set of double

French doors. Locked. He peered in through the glass and saw shrouded objects each time the lights blinked on. A closed-off wing of the house.

A few steps farther his foot hit an abutment. He lifted his foot and found another level. Stairs. With narrowed eyes, he made out a grand staircase leading up to a second-floor landing.

But the cry had come from the main floor.

Moving around the stairs to the opposite side, Mitch trailed his right hand along the paneling. His fingers curled into a recess in the wall and touched something hard, cold and smooth. When the lights flashed on, he jumped back from the face staring at him.

He slammed his gun between both hands and stepped out to defend himself. The lights flashed on again and he swore.

He'd bumped into some sort of damn shrine filled with trophies, framed medals and photos. With one slow, steadying breath, he regained his equilibrium. The woman's face staring back at him belonged to a framed, glossy photograph. He'd been spooked by a picture of a coltish young redhead waving a bouquet of flowers in one hand and gripping a medal in the other.

Pushing aside his curiosity, Mitch closed his eyes to listen for any telltale movements in the house. Except for the deafening blare of the alarm, the place was quiet. Too quiet.

Holding his gun up in his left hand, he crept farther into the interior of the house.

The next recess he came to was an open doorway. Catching his breath and thinking a prayer for no more false alarms to increase his blood pressure, he cautiously stepped around and peered inside.

The lights flashed on long enough for him to see an

object hurtling through the air toward him. He was plunged into darkness a split second before it whacked him across the face.

His string of curses was brief and to the point. The blow hadn't been hard enough to do serious damage, but his nose and skull throbbed with the impact.

"Police! Put down your weapon!" He recited the line by rote, feeling the rising rush of adrenaline crowding out his more rational thoughts.

Mitch reached out blindly and was rewarded with another blow to his wrist, this time solid enough to knock the gun from his grasp.

"Son of a…"

When the lights flashed off again, Mitch was ready. He glimpsed the grayish afterimage of his attacker and lunged in that direction.

With all the finesse of a linebacker sacking the quarterback, he rammed his assailant, pinned his arms and took him down, landing the perp flat on his back with Mitch on top. A strangled "oof" grunted between them made him hope he'd knocked the wind out of the guy.

But in seconds, his enemy recovered. One leg coiled beneath him. He guessed the intended direction and rolled, flipping the smaller, wiry man onto his stomach. Mitch snatched a flailing elbow and pinned the twisting body to the floor with his knee.

The other elbow connected with his chin, and Mitch's temper kicked in. "There are laws against assaulting a cop."

He clamped down on the dangerous arm and pulled it behind the attacker's back, shifting his knee to the base of his adversary's spine.

The perp screamed, a husky, high-pitched sound of pain.

"Oh, God! Don't hurt me," wheezed the voice.

No.

Mitch froze above his pinned opponent.

The lights flashed on, and he caught a glimpse of a long braid the color of golden cider sprinkled with cinnamon.

The image vanished with the lights.

But the memory didn't.

Mitch moved his knee, suspecting the truth, but needing to see it with his own eyes. He tugged on one of the arms to roll the body over and look at the face. When he reached for the opposite shoulder to anchor his attacker in place in case he was mistaken, Mitch's hand brushed against something pillowy and soft.

A woman's breast.

"Ma'am?"

The lights flashed on again, giving Mitch a glimpse of the woman's pale, terror-stricken face. Wild, smoky gray eyes glared at him with flash-fire intensity.

The impression was fleeting, distracting. Vanishing when the light did. Too late, he realized he'd underestimated her. Something swift and solid with four hard knots slammed into his left temple. Bright spots swam before his eyes in counterpoint to the blinking security lights.

Mitch caught her fist when she swung at him a second time. He swallowed her hand in his grasp and stretched her arm up over her head. The action flattened his body on top of hers, reaffirming his discovery that this was no intruder, but the person he'd been sent to check on.

The girl in the photograph.

Very much a woman now.

"Dammit, lady! I said I'm a cop. I'm not here to hurt you."

She writhed beneath him, her fear or fury so intense that Mitch didn't dare let go. If she harnessed the adrenaline pumping through her, she could knock him out cold.

While the dizziness behind his eyes abated, he protected himself by trapping her beneath him until her energy was spent. Mitch cursed the unprofessional torture to which he'd subjected himself. The woman's firm breasts pushed against his chest, leaving the imprint of graceful curves through the layers of clothing between them.

And her hips—full, wide, womanly—cradled the lower half of his torso. Rocking against him in her struggle. Teasing him. Taunting him with an awareness of needs he had buried long ago.

Damn, he was a sorry, lustful excuse for a man to find his body so tempted by the struggles of a frightened woman he was trying to subdue.

He pinned her for over a minute before her thrashing ceased abruptly. She lay perfectly still for a second, then groaned, deep in her throat. Her face contorted in the next flash of light, and Mitch watched her grit her teeth and squeeze her eyes shut. Darkness returned, hiding her expression, but he felt the muscles in her arms and body clench to the point that she started shaking.

"You're hurting me." Her husky voice caught and rasped into a sob. "Please don't hurt me."

Mitch scrambled off her and rocked back on his heels, berating himself for botching this "routine" visit beyond excuse. "I'm sorry."

His apology fell on deaf ears. She rolled onto her side and curled into a fetal position, hauling in deep gulps of air that racked her body.

He reached for her arm. She tried to pull away from his touch, but her muscles wouldn't respond. Mortified to know he had truly hurt her, Mitch obliged her by letting go. "I was only defending myself. I haven't been in a brawl like this since I made detective. You don't know your own strength."

He thought that might elicit a laugh, break the tension, but she didn't even look at him.

"I didn't call the cops," she whispered between breaths. "Why are you here?"

In the shadows of his jumbled vision, he watched her prop herself up to a sitting position, then scoot away on her bottom until she leaned up against a desk. She dug her fingers into her right thigh and kneaded her leg through her jeans.

Mitch curled his fingers into his palms, squelching the urge to help her. He had inflicted whatever pain she was suffering. He doubted she'd appreciate any attempt to touch her again, no matter how altruistic his intentions.

Instead, he called upon his years of experience. This woman was a victim. Of his own carelessness, if nothing else. She might be frightened or confused. He gave her the space she needed to feel safe again, backing away even farther. He lowered his voice to its gentlest pitch and spoke quietly. "Are you Cassandra Maynard?"

The commissioner had only supplied a name and address.

"I don't remember your name." Her clipped response sounded like an accusation.

He refused the bait and stayed calm. "Mitch Taylor."

Automatically, he reached for his breast pocket. He patted the empty space where the brass shield should be and glanced around quickly. Unable to see well for any distance, he apologized. "I lost my ID in our little tumble."

Her gaze filled with the same intensity she had trained on him earlier. "A badge doesn't prove anything."

Her chest rose with a huge sigh before she sagged back against the sturdy oak desk. Physical distress seemed to finally be conquering her indomitable will. "I'm Casey Maynard."

One Good Man

Flattening one palm against the rug, she pushed herself upright and gingerly adjusted to a more comfortable position. Mitch wondered if the tight white lines bracketing the corners of her mouth were a trick of the illumination or a grimace of pain.

"Do I need to call an ambulance?" he asked.

"No. It'll pass." She breathed in deeply through her nose and released the air gently across the generous curve of her bottom lip.

Hell. What was wrong with him? He was here as a cop, not a blind date, but he seemed to be going out of his way to notice her striking features, from the unusual shade of her French-braided hair to the delicate bone structure of her cheeks and pointed chin. Though *delicate* seemed an odd impression since she had almost bested him in their fight.

"Why did you attack me?" he asked, forcing himself away from unprofessional concerns. "Who did you think I was?"

Casey shook her head. "I get to ask questions first. How the hell did you get up to the house? What do you want?"

The whole evening took on a surreal quality. Lights flashed on and off at regular intervals. An alarm blared in the background. They sat on a patterned Persian rug. The victim questioned the cop.

Mitch needed his world back in order. He stood up and straightened his clothes, taking his time before answering her. "Police Commissioner James Reed called me this evening and asked me to check on your family and the house. He gave me his key to bypass the security gate. He said he was watching the property for a friend. He thought there might be some trouble."

"Uncle Jimmy always was a worrywart."

Uncle Jimmy?

Casey twisted her body, grabbed the top of the desk and hauled herself to her feet. Bracing her weight against the solid oak top, she hobbled around the desk. Her full mouth narrowed into a grim line with each step. Had she dislocated something? Twisted her knee?

In two steps, Mitch was at her side, cupping her elbow and waist and taking her weight into his hands.

She stiffened when he pulled her against his side. "Don't."

He'd never met such a stubborn woman. Mitch tightened his grip, but his voice was gentle. "I'm going to help you, no matter what, so shut up."

She didn't exactly relax, but some of the tension eased from her. She inclined her head toward the swivel chair overturned on its side behind the desk. "I just need to sit down."

Though she continued to favor her right leg, he noticed how she carried her shoulders and chin with grace and determination. Mitch righted the chair and steadied it when she turned to sit. The crown of her hair brushed along his jaw, and the faint scent of vanilla filled his senses.

She might pretend to be one tough cookie, but her ladylike femininity was hard to hide.

"That wasn't so difficult, was it?"

If he expected to be rewarded with a smile or thank-you, he was destined for disappointment. She twisted the chair away from him and pulled out a sliding keyboard tray. The computer monitor on her desk blinked on, and she pulled up a series of screen commands. She selected one with her mouse, then clicked.

The lights in the house flooded on, and stayed on. Just as abruptly, the alarm stopped.

"There's no problem here, Captain."

She raised her head and offered him a fake smile. "I'm

sorry to have wasted your time. I don't know where Uncle Jimmy gets his ideas. But tell him I appreciate his concern.''

Mitch knew a goodbye when he heard one. This had turned into one hell of an evening. His skull throbbed with a headache. He'd ticked off an ungrateful woman who had every right to sue him. And he had a growing list of questions that no one wanted to answer.

It would have required a better man to keep the sarcasm out of his voice. ''It's been real fun getting to know you, too, Ms. Maynard. I'll be sure to pass your regards along to Uncle Jimmy.''

In the clear light, he easily spotted his badge on the carpet. He picked it up and clipped it to his pocket. He retrieved his gun from beneath a side table and snapped it into his holster. As he straightened, something else caught his attention.

A brown stick protruded from beneath the corner of a black leather sofa. Is that what she'd hit him with?

Keeping his back to her, Mitch used his foot to slide the piece of wood into view. A cane?

His preformed image of Cassandra Maynard, pampered society princess whose elite circle of friends included the commissioner of police, shifted a notch. He'd driven into this ritzy Plaza neighborhood expecting to find people living the lifestyle his late wife had struggled so ruthlessly to attain.

After the commissioner's phone call, Mitch had fully expected to find Ms. Maynard preened and poised on her perch high above the mortals like himself who had to work for a living. She'd lie about whatever trouble had prompted the intrusion on private family business, and then politely send him on his way.

She had the lie part down pat, and she sounded eager

to be rid of him. But this wounded woman in the jeans and gray sweatshirt seemed more brittle than icy. And the disdain in her voice didn't match the terror in her eyes.

He glanced at the cane again. Richly polished walnut inlaid with a ring of brass at the handle, the item itself bespoke wealth. But a cane was a cane, a symbol of injury or handicap in one so young and apparently athletic as Ms. Maynard. Maybe she'd had surgery, or injured herself in training.

His lean years growing up in a decaying neighborhood north of downtown Kansas City had taught him to recognize some basic tricks of survival. Attacking before the enemy could identify your weakness was a classic.

Uptown or down, Mitch recognized vulnerability.

"So why would Commissioner Reed think anything was wrong here?" He nudged the cane out of sight with his toe, allowing her the security of hiding the extent of her disability from him.

He turned, catching the startled expression on her face before she quickly replaced it with that stoic mask. "I don't know. I'm surprised he didn't call me himself."

"He probably figured you'd lie and say everything was all right so he wouldn't worry."

She shrugged. "Everything *is* all right. Other than you breaking down the door."

He stepped toward her. "Something scared the hell out of you tonight."

"You did."

"No. Before I showed up, something wasn't right." He advanced farther, and enjoyed the transient satisfaction of seeing her mask slip a little.

Even at the cusp of winter, the mansions in this old-monied neighborhood had an unlived-in perfection about them. Lawns were manicured, homes and fences were decorated for the holidays and welcoming lights blazed from crystal-clear windows and porches.

But not the Maynard estate. The imposing structure was half-hidden behind a high granite wall and black wrought-iron gate. Inside that barrier, ancient oaks lined the driveway, casting shadows across the yard that even twin porch lights couldn't illuminate. One wing of the house was closed off. The interior had been dark. The items he'd stumbled over in the hallway and in this room were arranged in pristine, untouched perfection.

So who kept the princess locked in the tower?

Fairy tales had never topped Mitch's reading list, but he couldn't think of a better analogy. Where was the *family* the commissioner had asked him to check on? He'd bet his next paycheck that she lived alone in this overbuilt monstrosity.

"Are you married, Ms. Maynard? Live with a boyfriend or fiancé?"

He interpreted the sharp, humorless sound that passed as her laugh for a no.

"What about your parents?"

"I'm twenty-eight years old, Mr. Taylor. I don't live with Mommy and Daddy anymore."

Touché. So he wasn't the only one who resorted to sarcasm under pressure.

"Where are they?" He took another step.

"Now that they've retired, they spend their winters in a warmer climate." Not much of an answer, so he switched tactics.

"Why did you attack me?" He reached her desk.

"I thought you were an intruder." She squared her shoulders. "Most visitors ring the buzzer at the gatehouse before I send them on their way."

He ignored the obvious hint. He braced his hands on the desktop and leaned toward her. "I said I was a cop."

She tilted her chin upward. "I don't care if—"

Garbled voices from the front of the house interrupted their standoff. By the time he spun around, two uniformed patrolmen had entered the room, positioning themselves with guns drawn and pointed straight at him.

"Hold it right there," one of the officers commanded.

Mitch calmly raised his hands. He heard a strangled gasp behind him, a soft, barely audible sound of despair. He glanced back at Casey. If possible, her fine porcelain skin had blanched even further.

Guns? Cops? Or men in general?

Something about the blue-suits, something about *him*, terrified her. Not because she thought he was breaking in. Not because she valued her privacy.

Him.

The discovery hit Mitch in the gut with all the force of her cane smacking his face. She was afraid of *him*. And fighting like a regal hellcat to prove she wasn't.

Ungrateful though she might be for his help, the need to protect surged through him. Despite her proud and prickly demeanor, she looked too weak to deal with more unexpected visitors. And rule number one in his self-written code of ethics was to always defend the underdog.

So Mitch took up the banner for her. He pointed to his badge and identified his rank.

"Captain?" The officer who had spoken earlier couldn't hide his embarrassment. Once they'd both holstered their weapons, Mitch dropped his hands and moved toward them. He had no desire to chew their butts for the honest mistake. They'd simply been doing their job. Answering a call with promptness and authority.

"I've got everything under control here. I'm guessing it

was a false alarm." The best way to salvage a man's pride was to give him something worthwhile to do. "It wouldn't hurt to check the grounds, though, see if anybody's been snooping around. And find something to patch the front door with."

"Yes, sir."

With curt nods, they exited the room. Mitch turned around in the doorway and studied Casey. She'd closed her eyes and was breathing deeply. She seemed small and out of place in the huge dimensions of the room. He could see now it was a library, lined on three walls with recessed bookshelves. The row of windows on the fourth wall overlooked a dead garden. Her desk stood like an island in the center of the room, covered with neat stacks of paperwork, a computer system, a fax machine and a telephone.

He wondered if she lived in this lonely sanctuary by choice, or if someone had tucked her away and forgotten her there.

"What are you staring at?" Casey's pointed question intruded on his thoughts. The prickly princess was back in place, and Mitch couldn't help smiling.

"Quite possibly the prettiest waste of an evening I've ever spent."

She arched one eyebrow, and Mitch imagined the temperature in the room dropped by several degrees. "Is that supposed to be a compliment?"

"I'm not sure. Do you take compliments?"

"Don't let me keep you from any real police work, Captain."

Oh, man, she was good. Mitch let the cutting edge of her tongue bounce off his well-worn hide. He'd been made this family's scapegoat for the last time this evening. "Don't worry. Your uncle has already seen to that."

"He's not really my uncle. Just an old family friend."

Mitch's retort about missing the point died on his lips.

She anchored her hands on either arm of her chair and stood, wavering for an instant until she found her balance. She breathed in deeply, turned on her exhale and limped toward the couch. She stepped gingerly on her right foot. The whole leg seemed to buckle each time she put her weight on it. Still, what impressed—and shamed—Mitch was the absolute determination on her face.

She might be every bit the condescending princess of the manor, but she was also a woman in pain, a woman in possible danger. And he'd been butting heads with her instead of remembering his duty.

He rushed to the couch to save her a few steps. He picked up the cane and held it out to her in both hands like a peace offering. ''I'm sorry,'' he said gently. ''The commissioner is expecting a report from me in the morning. What would you like me to say?''

He couldn't tell if the resentment that flared in her eyes was because she needed the cane or because he'd gotten it for her. Her gaze locked on his chest, and he wondered if she was staring at his badge or merely glaring daggers through his heart.

''Tell him to call me himself next time.''

She curved her long, elegant fingers around the polished wood. Mitch tightened his grip. She stumbled half a step and might have fallen if their hands hadn't been locked together around the cane. ''What does it take for me to prove to you I'm one of the good guys?''

She tilted her chin to an arrogant angle and taunted him with her stormy gaze. ''You can't.''

A silent battle of wills heated the air between them, leaving Mitch with no clear answers except the discomforting realization that he wanted to blot that sensuous smirk off her bottom lip. His pulse raced at the challenge of softening those lips with his own, and loosing the tightly controlled fire that cooked inside the proper Ms. Maynard.

Appalled at the pattern of his thoughts, Mitch jerked away from her. He raked his fingers through his short hair, angry at her for making him feel those things, and remorseful at seeing her use the cane to maintain her balance.

Jackie had turned him inside out like that. She claimed to like his rough ways, his guard-dog devotion to her. But in the end, she'd chosen class and money over the love he could give her.

He was a smarter man now. It had taken him years to see through all of his wife's games and learn to let her go. The notion that this cool, haughty princess could conjure up the same desires after only one meeting irritated the hell out of him.

"I'm assuming you can find your own way out, Captain. Since you so easily found your way in."

He fisted his hands to squelch the urge to swat her retreating royal backside. Instead, he used her dismissal to spur him out the door to do some real police work and supervise the two uniformed officers.

What a hell of a day, he thought, thinking up and tossing aside ways to tell the commissioner to stuff this Maynard family lackey job without losing his promotion.

What a hell of a day.

Chapter Two

"Cassandra, dear, you know I have only your best interests at heart."

Casey switched the telephone receiver to her left ear to mask her frustrated sigh, and wondered why Jimmy's reassurance made her feel silly instead of safe. "But, Jimmy, why did you send the police here out of the blue last night? You know how I feel about—" she paused to find a word to emphasize just how frightened she'd been "—strangers."

James Reed made an exasperated sound, and she could envision him checking his watch on the other end of the line. "Mitch isn't just any cop. He's one of the three finalists I'm looking at to name as my assistant next year. He's a good man."

He's a force to be reckoned with, thought Casey.

She rested her forehead in her hand and massaged the tension in her scalp. She hadn't slept well at all, and it wasn't just because of the pain radiating through her right hip and up into her back from the exertion of wrestling with the man. His broad shoulders and stocky chest beneath that tailored wool coat, and his stubborn attitude, made her think of a gladiator in a suit and tie.

A fearsome opponent. A formidable ally. But last night

she hadn't been able to decide whose side of the ring he fought for.

"I don't care if he's Eliot Ness. *Why* did you send him here?"

A double dose of aspirin and a hot pad had dulled the physical ache to a tolerable level. But her mind had raced through to the early hours of the morning trying to pinpoint why Mitch Taylor's unexpected visit had left her feeling so edgy.

Perhaps it was his voice. That deep, masculine sound had held too much challenge, too many taunts. His eyes, maybe. She remembered a gentle brown color like the expensive bourbon her father used to sip at night in front of the fireplace.

But there'd been little gentleness in the way he'd looked at her. As if she were guilty of something more unforgivable than assaulting a police officer.

Hearing Jimmy talk around the answers she sought didn't help.

"Have you seen the paper this morning?" he asked.

Casey wrapped her chenille robe around the high collar of her flannel nightgown. The winter air didn't worry her so much as the chill in Jimmy's voice.

"No. Judith's not in yet. I don't feel like venturing out to the gate myself."

"I didn't want to panic you. It could be nothing."

Her heart beat a quicker tempo at his particular choice of words. "Sending a detective busting through my doorway when you know I'm here by myself is your idea of not panicking me?"

"I just wanted to double-check that you were all right."

"Stop treating me like I'm a little girl. Tell me—"

"You're still my god daughter. I promised Jack and Margaret I'd always take care of you."

"Mom and Dad would have given me a straight answer by now! I've half a mind to call them and ask them to come home." The silence at the other end of the line made her regret her flash of temper. "I'm sorry, Jimmy. I know you mean well..."

"You can't call them," he interrupted her apology.

Casey tried again. "I know they're not due to return from Europe for another three months, but I can track them down."

"No, you can't."

As a child, she'd been reprimanded in that very same voice. But she was no longer a child. "Dammit, Jimmy, you can't dictate—"

"Emmett Raines."

If he wanted to punish her for her outburst, he couldn't have said a crueler thing.

She thought of the framed Olympic silver medal in the hallway, and how she could have had a gold one from four years later beside it. She thought of her parents, once pretending to be dead and hiding away in a place unknown even to her so they could stay alive. She thought of tomorrow's Thanksgiving holiday and how she'd be spending it alone. Again.

Because of Emmett Raines.

"What about him?"

A door off the kitchen slammed, startling her before she slipped deeper into a mind-numbing depression.

"Casey! Casey?" a shrill voice called from the hallway.

The Maynards' housekeeper huffed around the corner into the library. The older woman's watery blue eyes glistened with fear.

"Just a minute, Jimmy," said Casey into the phone. "Judith's here. The boarded-up door must have spooked her. Give me a minute to explain what happened."

She covered the mouthpiece of the receiver and set it down. She needed both hands to stand and try to look composed. Judith McDonald might be a hired servant by contract, but she'd been with the family long enough that Casey considered her a friend.

"Are you all right?" Judith paused long enough to ask the question, but moved before Casey could answer her.

The housekeeper crossed the room, holding out the *Kansas City Star* newspaper in one hand and clutching her ample bosom to steady her breathing in the other.

"He escaped from prison."

The unadorned statement struck Casey like a gunshot. She needed no other explanation to piece together the evasive truth. Suddenly Mitch Taylor's visit made sense. The blood in her head rushed down to her toes. She sank into her chair and cradled her head in her hands. Finally understanding the situation brought her none of the comfort she had hoped for.

Judith spread the paper across the desktop and pointed to a short article on the second page. Casey scanned the words, and like a well-mannered schoolgirl, she picked up the phone.

"Why didn't you tell me Emmett Raines was out of prison?"

Jimmy's deep sigh matched her own. "State troopers are out in force looking for him. He has no family here anymore. Statistics say he'll try to get as far away from Missouri as he can. I didn't want to alarm you unnecessarily."

Statistics? Her devoted Dutch uncle had gambled her safety on statistics? And backed it up with nothing more than an overbearing, overwhelming gladiator sent to check the premises?

A touch of something fiery licked through her veins,

thawing the fear that tried to take root inside her. "I testified against the man in court! The newspaper says he killed a laundry-truck driver and drove away from Jefferson City. How unalarmed do you want me to be?"

Judith reached across the desk and squeezed her hand. Casey squeezed back, tapping into her own strength by sharing it.

"Don't do anything, Cassandra. Stay in the house and lock the doors and windows." For the first time that morning, she appreciated the clipped authority in Jimmy's voice. "I'll have Iris rearrange my schedule and I'll get there as soon as I can. I'll take care of you, dear. I promise."

She hung up the phone and relayed the message to Judith. While Judith left to do a visual check of the entrances to the house, Casey turned on her computer and accessed the security system to verify that it was up and running.

She was glad she rated high enough on Jimmy's list of priorities for him to postpone a meeting. But she felt no relief. Not yet. Maybe not ever.

No one understood Emmett Raines the way she did. No one could unless they'd been his victim, too.

She'd given up trying to explain why she'd secluded herself in the home where she'd grown up. After Emmett's trial, she let the press make up stories to explain her withdrawal from society. Fear of more criminal repercussions. Shame over losing her career. Sorrow over losing her parents.

She couldn't tell them about her unique phobia.

And she couldn't risk more uninvited guests busting their way into her sanctuary.

Casey logged on-line and found the site she was looking for.

No more strangers.
She'd see to that.

"HEY, OLD MAN!"

Mitch grunted his answer to the cheerful greeting and strode through the Fourth Precinct offices, shedding his coat and barking orders along the way.

"Ginny. Dig up a file for me. Cassandra Maynard. Society lady. Age twenty-eight. She may have been recently injured in an accident, so check the traffic reports."

The petite blonde sat back in her chair. "Casey Maynard? Judge Jack's daughter?"

Mitch stopped in his tracks. "You know her?"

"I know *of* her," said Ginny. "A few years back, she was in all the papers. I was in the academy at the time. The story was required reading. Her father, Jack Maynard, sat the bench in criminal court for almost twenty years."

"The 'no-budge judge'?" Mitch mentally kicked himself for not connecting the names sooner.

"Yeah. 'No-slack Jack,' whatever nickname you want to use." Leave it to Ginny to know her history. What his detective lacked in size and intimidation factor, she more than made up for in keen intelligence and impeccable memory. "She got hurt, and then the judge and his wife supposedly died in that horrible car accident. It wasn't revealed until months later that their deaths had been staged so they could go into hiding. I'm pretty sure he never returned to the bench."

Mitch propped his hip on her desk and asked, "What do you mean 'hurt'?"

"It was several years back. But if I remember right, she was assaulted."

"I've heard of her." Mitch's newest detective, Merle Banning, in only his third year of police work, walked up with a mug of coffee and joined the discussion. "I remember my mom goin' on about what a tragedy it was. She was training for her second Olympics. A swimmer, I think.''

Mitch nodded, hiding a cringe of guilt as he remembered how rough he'd been with Casey, and how she'd fought against him with every weapon available to her, including her sarcastic tongue. Her defensive actions made sense if she had once been assaulted.

He put his self-recriminations on hold and searched the vaults of his own experience, looking for facts to answer his questions. He had never testified in Jack Maynard's court, but he could recall a few old friends who had. ''The judge had a reputation for no leniency, long before the three-strikes rule. I definitely want to see her file.''

He stood and clamped his hand over Merle's shoulder, scenting the trail of a case that had yet to be opened, or maybe—if the tingle on his neck was any indication—had never been closed.

''I want to know everything we've got on Jack Maynard.''

''Everything?''

Mitch ignored Banning's query. ''I want to know names and dates of the cases he tried.''

''*All* of them? That's a huge project, Mitch.'' *Stunned* would be a mild description of the bespectacled detective's expression. It provided enough humor to sweeten the tension in Mitch's stomach. He pressed his lips into a thin line to avoid smiling.

''Then you'd better get on it.''

''Yes, sir.'' Merle set down his coffee and logged on to his computer.

Mitch had watched criminals enter their holding cells with more enthusiasm. The father figure in him relented, just a smidge. ''Ginny can help you when she's done.''

Merle and Ginny exchanged supportive glances over their paired-off desks. The rookie detective squared his shoulders and nodded. "I'll get it on your desk ASAP."

"Good enough."

Mitch looped his coat through the crook of his arm and crossed to his lieutenant's desk, confident the work he asked for would get done. "Joe. I put in a call to Commissioner Reed. Give it priority to my office when it comes through."

"Will do."

Joe Hendricks followed Mitch into his office and waited while he shed his jacket and loosened his tie. Mitch shuffled through the messages on his desk before sitting down. He stood up again, feeling too edgy to stay put for any length of time.

"Here's your coffee." Joe handed him a mug of the steaming dark brew.

A deep sigh drifted through Mitch's barrel chest before he accepted the offer. "I'm that obvious?"

The mahogany-skinned detective grinned and made himself at home in one of the chairs across from Mitch's. "Drink before we talk."

"That sounds ominous." Mitch inhaled the intoxicating aroma and took several sips before sitting again and staying put.

"So what fly is buzzin' around your head this morning?"

Mitch cradled the mug in his hands and stared into its depths. The darkness reminded him of the previous night. It wasn't the usual stresses of the job so much as that prickly princess locked away in the tower that made him more of a grizzly than a teddy bear that morning.

She might very well sue him for his honest mistake. But that wasn't what bothered him. He was ninety-nine percent certain she wouldn't sue. In fact, he'd bet she wouldn't have another thing to do with him.

Or anyone from the outside.

Why did he think of her as a prisoner? The leg, probably. Listening to Ginny's and Merle's accounts, she apparently had some kind of permanent handicap. But that wasn't the impression that had stayed with him through the night and played havoc on his normal morning routine.

It was her eyes. Smoky, dark and deep. He'd seen fear there.

Fear of him.

He downed a hasty swallow of coffee and nearly scalded his tongue. Hell, nobody should be afraid of him. Nobody except the bad guys.

What did she have against cops? He'd worked damn hard for his badge and rank. He shouldn't be bothered by implied insults from damsels in distress who didn't want to be rescued.

He shouldn't be bothered by her at all.

He compromised on his response to Joe. "The commissioner's got me playing some cat-and-mouse game I haven't figured out yet."

Joe thumbed over his shoulder toward the squad room behind him. "What does Judge Jack have to do with it?"

"The commish called yesterday and asked me to check Judge Maynard's house. Personally. See if there was any trouble."

"Was there?"

"Not that I could see. That's why I'm trying to make some kind of connection. Reed wasn't eager to share details." Mitch leaned forward, resting his elbows on his desk and splaying his hands in a gesture of frustration. "The only person there was the judge's daughter. And she definitely wasn't thrilled to see me."

Joe laughed and tapped the bridge of his nose, indicating the purplish bruise decorating Mitch's own nose that morning. "Is she another conquest you charmed and left by the wayside?"

Mitch felt his own mouth curling up into a wry smile. Casey Maynard had certainly packed a wallop. He'd never so much as experienced a slap on the face from one of his dates. "Even on my best days, I was never charming."

"Hey, now don't sell yourself short. I just put five bucks on you bringing a hot date to the big awards banquet."

Mitch shook his head, his mood momentarily lightened by his friend's teasing. "Don't I give you enough work to do?"

Joe smiled innocently. "Most of the guys say you're going stag to the big event. Ginny thinks you'll take an old friend."

"Save your cash, Joe. Isn't that fourth baby due pretty soon? I figured you'd have more sense than to waste your money like that."

"Impending daddyhood just makes me all the more romantic. I know you got a pretty lady stashed away somewhere."

He dismissed Joe with a cajoling smile. "Back to work, Lieutenant."

The two men stood, old friends at ease with each other's various moods. Joe feigned hurt feelings. "What about the morning report?"

Mitch shooed him toward the door. "Let me return these calls on my desk. Then you can update me on our priority cases. And Joe...?"

Hendricks turned in the open doorway and waited expectantly.

"Step up patrols in Ms. Maynard's neighborhood. But *nobody* goes into that house unless I give the okay."

Joe touched a finger to one eyebrow and saluted. "Will do."

"You're a good man."

"That's what my wife says."

Mitch smiled and dismissed him with an answering mock salute.

Poor Joe. He could kiss his money goodbye. Mitch had no intention of spoiling that banquet by sharing the evening with a woman who didn't understand what that service award and promotion meant to him. Who *couldn't* understand.

Women wanted attention. They demanded the spotlight. They expected to be spoiled. And if good ol' Mitch Taylor, the Fourth Precinct's resident old man, couldn't give a woman what she thought she deserved, then she'd look elsewhere. Jackie had.

Mitch swallowed hard, sending the bitter taste in his mouth down to his stomach. His work had saved him from hell and given him a chance to be somebody. It had given him an identity. A power and an authority that he'd earned with blood and sweat and a lot of hard work.

But his work was a mighty cold companion when he lay in bed at night. It didn't laugh with him over his mistakes, nor rally him when his faith faltered. It wouldn't grow old with him.

Ignoring the debilitating influence of his own thoughts, Mitch unbuttoned the cuffs on his broadcloth shirt, rolled up the sleeves and sat down to do some of that work. He noticed the full mailbox on his computer screen and brought up the messages.

He scrolled through work-related contacts, but stopped when he came across an all too familiar name.

Captain Taylor

A convict named Emmett Raines escaped from Jefferson City. If you wish to alleviate your guilt from last night, you can tell me what KCPD knows about this.

Casey Maynard

"Guilt?" Mitch berated the computer screen. "She thinks *I* feel guilty?"

He ignored the fact that guilt had plagued him since learning he had used force against a handicapped assault victim, no matter how deadly her right hook might be. But her smoky eyes and proud little mouth had teased his dreams last night. Today Miss High-and-Mighty's note aggravated that awareness into a full-blown distraction. He switched screens and typed in his response. "She's got a hell of a nerve."

The message he left was equally concise.

Look, princess, that kind of information is confidential. The state patrol and area enforcement officers will handle the case. Questions by vicarious thrill-seekers would only interfere. BTW, the number of forms I had to fill out last night more than makes up for any guilt I *might* have felt.

Your ever faithful civil servant,
Mitch Taylor

There. He clicked the send button and enjoyed a buoy of satisfaction that he had reminded her arrogant highness of her place in his life.

After that, Mitch dug into the paperwork on his desk. He worked steadily, ignoring the faint tickle at his nape. It was probably just his hormones working overtime. Casey Maynard had really gotten under his skin. He hadn't quite felt sorry for her, but he'd felt *for* her.

Her grace. The delicate scent of her. That memorable shade of strawberry-gold hair. He might have found all of those things attractive. But she'd been so cold, so haughty.

So scared.

Mitch paused in his work. He leaned back and pressed his fist to his mouth. Is that what this was all about? She had needed him. For a few moments, anyway. When she'd been too weak to struggle. And later, when the blue-suits had walked in.

For a brief time, he'd gotten caught up in her need. He'd deluded himself into thinking she needed *him.*

He slammed his fist down on the desk, stirring papers and sloshing the dregs of his coffee. You'd think he'd learn. Hell. Jackie had *needed* him. She'd wanted someone solid and reliable to get her through those last days after her boyfriend had dumped her. A lot of people *needed* him because of his job. To protect and serve the citizens of the community. He was good at that.

But it could have been any decent guy. It could be any cop.

That's why the princess was such an irritation. Wounded pride. He almost laughed. He hadn't allowed himself to feel that in a long time. It was because of the bad day he'd been having, he rationalized. Casey Maynard had caught him at a weak moment.

Well, it wouldn't happen again.

Mitch pulled out a handful of tissues and blotted at the coffee spots he had splashed across a memo. A blinking light out of the corner of his eye caught his attention. An incoming message on his e-mail.

Great. Just when he'd talked himself out of messing with her.

Mitch,
What kind of forms are you talking about? Police
reports? I think it would be best to draw as little attention to me as possible. Please leave my name out
of anything you file.

                                              Casey

How about that? She'd deigned to move to a first name
basis. He turned to the keyboard and answered her.

Princess,
Of course police reports. I discharged my weapon and
investigated what I thought was a suspicious situation.
It's standard procedure. And your name is already on
the dotted line.

                                              Mitch

He pressed the send button and waited, almost relishing
the anticipation of what she'd say in response. She didn't
disappoint.
"I didn't ask you to come last night."
Several moments passed, and then another message appeared.
"What if I talk to Jimmy for you? Maybe we can forget
the whole thing."
Just what kind of pull did she think she had? Every
officer, no matter what his rank, had to file reports whenever he used his weapon, whether it be against a perp or
a door lock. Why did she think he'd change the rules for
her?

Rules are rules. Talk to "Uncle Jimmy." I think he'll
support me on this.

                                              Mitch.

There was no pause this time.

"No! Don't use my name. He'll find me."

"He'll find you?" Mitch questioned aloud. He sent a brief message. "Who?"

He waited.

"Emmett Raines."

"Who is Emmett Raines to you?" Mitch typed. "Did you think I was him?"

"Please!!!" she answered.

Mitch ran the name through his head and drew a blank. Maybe Emmett was an old boyfriend. She said he'd escaped. Maybe she saw enemies where none existed.

But the itch along his neck had him thinking otherwise. Real or not, her obvious fear dissipated the remnants of his anger. Reminding himself that it wasn't *his* help she was seeking, he typed in a response.

"I'll have one of my men look into it."

He could almost feel her answer leap off the screen, as if he were talking to her in person and could read the expression in her eyes again.

No! Forget it! Just forget it! Don't send anyone else to the house. Don't come here again. And don't call me princess!

What? The message ended abruptly, and he knew she'd signed off. Mitch stared mutely at the screen, wishing his own frustration could be transported across the modem links. He didn't know what irritated him more, the idea that she thought she could dictate his actions and go over his head to his superior, or the discovery that she might be a little human like the rest of the world.

She didn't like the nickname. She had gotten personal.

Their little e-mail interlude had left him as heated as last night's face-to-face encounter. He could picture her eyes darkening along with her emotions. He could imagine that stubborn little chin pointing upward as she vented her fury on him.

He could see the fear in her posture as she stiffened her shoulders and tried not to let it show.

"Joe!" He bellowed for his lieutenant.

"Boss."

"Sorry." Mitch looked up guiltily, finding Joe waiting in the open doorway with his usual forgiving smile. "Emmett Raines. Check the wires. He just walked away from Jeff City. I want to know everything there is to know about him."

"Anything in particular I should look for?" asked Joe.

"A connection to Jack or Casey Maynard. Something isn't right." He glanced at his computer screen. "I need to figure it out."

Joe jotted the name on his notepad. He pointed to Mitch's phone. "The commissioner's on line two. I'll get right on this."

Mitch nodded his dismissal, punched the blinking light and picked up the receiver. "Commissioner Reed."

A smooth, politic voice answered. "Mitch. I'll forgo the pleasantries. We need to talk."

"You're damn right we need to."

"WHO THE HELL does he think he is?" Casey muttered to herself, still stewing over her computer conversation with Mitch Taylor earlier that morning. The words on her monitor blurred together as her eyes glazed over. She removed her gold-rimmed reading glasses and rubbed at her tired eyes.

Normally, she found the content of medical articles an interesting read. But today it was simply a jumble of technical jargon that made little sense. Knowing she was ahead of her deadline, she saved the text she was editing and turned off the screen. Her clients shouldn't be penalized for her inability to concentrate.

She slipped into her shoes and tied them, adjusting the platformed boot on her right heel before shifting onto her feet. Needing the extra support after last night's uncustomary stress, she tightened the Velcro closures of her leg brace and walked over to the row of windows that gave a panoramic view of the backyard.

Judith's husband, Ben, tended the pool house with efficient regularity, just as he had in her training days. But what had once been a symbol of her family's success and personal triumphs now stood like a glass-domed testament to all she had lost.

Her dreams. Her family. Her faith.

She'd worked hard after the attack to get her body into shape. To teach herself how to walk again. Months of physical therapy in her private gym and in that pool had put her body back together as much as the shattered remnants of it would allow.

But no amount of training could restore her trust or heal her wounded heart.

Casey breathed in deeply and exhaled, fogging up the window in front of her. She rubbed the spot clear, acknowledging that her restlessness wasn't entirely Mitch Taylor's fault.

She missed the color that had once been part of her life. She missed the activity. She missed the demands she used to make on herself, the anticipation and reward of setting goals and achieving them.

But it could never be any other way. Especially now. She had to keep a lower profile than ever or *he'd* find her. Though he'd be smarter to run in the opposite direction, she knew Emmett Raines would come looking for her. She'd made a mistake once he wouldn't allow her to make again.

The jangle of the front-gate buzzer made every muscle in her body tense until she looked over at the clock on the mantel—it was 12:10. The McDonalds were still here. She breathed again, consciously forcing herself to relax. Shoulders first. Biceps. Elbows. Wrists and hands.

Almost as soon as Casey was breathing normally again, Judith entered the library and announced, "Mr. James Reed is here to see you."

Casey's dread changed into a cautious smile. "You don't have to be so formal."

"Some habits die hard. Should I fix him lunch?"

The drawn look that had haunted Judith's face eased a little with the arrival of company. For that, Casey was glad, even though she knew Jimmy's visit would include a painful discussion on the subject of Emmett Raines. "I'll ask. Go ahead and let him in through the kitchen."

Minutes later, Police Commissioner James Reed, looking fit and dapper with his silver hair and charcoal suit, entered the library with a broad smile. "Cassandra."

He met her halfway and gave her a stiff hug and a pat on the back. Holding herself on her good leg, Casey kissed his cheek and tightened her arms around his neck. "I'm glad to see you."

He pushed away from her, holding her elbows in his palms. "I can only stay a few minutes. But I didn't want to disappoint my favorite girl."

He made her feel all of ten years old. She tried to match his smile but failed. "I thought you'd be here...sooner."

From across the room, another voice answered in a dark, taunting baritone.

"We shouldn't be here at all."

Casey looked over Jimmy's shoulder to the man filling the doorway. Mitch Taylor was even bigger than she remembered. The room shrank as he strode in. He stood a couple of inches taller than her Dutch uncle's six feet, and she suspected the imposing dimensions of his chest and shoulders could be attributed more to the man than to the tailoring of his suit.

She lifted her chin to ward off the impact of his raw masculinity. Jimmy stepped aside, allowing Mitch's whiskey-brown eyes to peruse her from head to toe. The warmth she experienced under his scrutiny left her feeling much more grown up than her uncle's reassurances had.

Unaccustomed to having any man besides her doctors study her so thoroughly, and even more unfamiliar with the responding tension tingling along the surface of her skin, she angled away from him, automatically shielding the weak side of her body. "Captain."

"How badly did I hurt you?" He spoke in a hushed rumble that shivered along her spine. The unexpected softening of his hard-edged expression did funny things to her pulse rate. She felt her own features relax.

"I'm a little…" *Stiff and sore,* she would have finished. But Jimmy's patience with polite conversation had ended.

"You didn't. She requires her cane or leg brace to walk." His crude explanation shattered the illusion of compassion, and reminded Casey of the real problem at hand. She threw back her shoulders and lifted her chin.

Without making direct eye contact herself, she saw Mitch look at Jimmy, then back at her. His on-the-job mask returned.

"You should be in a safe house. Or at the very least, under around-the-clock police protection."

His back-to-business mode made it easier for her to summon her defenses. "I asked you not to come here."

"No, you *ordered* me not to, princess." He swung his gaze over to Jimmy. "But a higher authority prevailed."

Acknowledging his cue with a nod, Jimmy took Casey by the upper arm and guided her toward the sofa. "We want to talk to you, Cassandra."

Once she was situated, he sat beside her and clasped her left hand between both of his. Not a good sign. "I didn't want you to know about Raines's escape so soon, but now that you do, I want you to know that I'm taking care of everything. I put him away once, and I'll put him away again. He won't get any satisfaction coming after my family." He climbed off his soapbox and gentled his tone. "I promised your father that I'd look after you. And I trust that Mitch is the man to help me do that."

She glanced over at Mitch, who struggled to make himself fit in the brocaded wingback chair across from her. He shook his head as though he already doubted the wisdom of this so-called plan.

Definitely not a good sign. She looked back at Jimmy, only half-joking with her question. "What, you're going to send him over to the house and have him scare me to death every night?"

Jimmy's hands tightened around her own. "No, dear. I'm assigning him to be your bodyguard."

Chapter Three

Casey clicked her stopwatch as the outstretched fingers touched the wall. A dark-haired nymph shot up out of the water and splashed Casey's shoes as she turned and sat on the edge of the pool.

"How was that?" Frankie Reilly asked, her young chest heaving with the exertion of her efforts.

She tossed Ben and Judith's twelve-year-old granddaughter a towel. "Not bad. But I was swimming an extra length in that same time when I was your age."

This afternoon, she found it difficult to concentrate on the observations and advice a trainer should give her pupil. But then she didn't usually have six feet two inches of disgruntled detective nosing around the pool deck and adjoining rooms, either. She glanced at Mitch running his hand along the seams where the exterior glass walls connected to the steel support beams that formed the building's skeleton.

He prowled back and forth, his eyes on a continuous scan of both the building itself and the yard outside. Silhouetted against the waning sunlight like a dark sentinel, he created an ominous presence that should keep stalkers and murderers and madmen at bay.

But despite the heated interior of the pool house, Casey

crossed her arms and hugged herself to contain a shiver of apprehension. She should feel safe having such an imposing protector on the premises. Instead, she felt more vulnerable than when she had learned of Emmett's escape.

She'd felt safe with her bodyguard seven years ago. So safe that she never realized the perfection of Emmett Raines's ability to disguise himself. Until it was too late.

Until she realized her bodyguard *was* Emmett Raines.

"Casey?" Frankie tugged on her arm, startling Casey from her silent study of Mitch. "Do you want me to swim it again?"

Fortunately, the girl had caught her staring instead of the detective. She wasn't ready to explain her need to memorize identifying details about people, especially when the person in question seemed to delight in pointing out anything about her that seemed suspicious.

She apologized for her distraction. "Let's pack it in for now. Building your endurance is important, but so is dinner."

Frankie pulled on her nylon jacket, then leaned over to whisper to Casey. "He's cute, isn't he?"

The conspiratorial note in the budding adolescent's observation about her interest in Mitch caught Casey in open-mouthed surprise.

"For an older guy, I mean," the girl amended.

Casey pressed her lips together and formed an appropriate reply. "*Cute* isn't exactly the word I'd use to describe him."

Intimidating, maybe. *Compelling.*

"Oh, c'mon. I've seen you watching him. Almost as much as he watches you."

"What?"

Frankie shrugged, as if the explanation was simple and Casey was a dingdong for not catching on. "Besides

Grandpa, he's the only guy I've ever seen you hang out with.''

''I am not hanging out with him.'' She tried to defend herself against a twelve-year-old's philosophy.

''That's right.'' Mitch's keen radar picked up that he was the topic of their conversation. His deep voice didn't alarm Casey half so much as being captured in the crosshairs of those ever watchful eyes. He invited himself to join them. ''I'm just the hired help.''

She heard the challenge in his voice and wondered at its cause. He'd certainly made it clear he wasn't interested in being her bodyguard, but it wasn't her choice. Jimmy had dismissed every argument she made. She hadn't been able to convince either man that she'd be safer on her own.

So why did he keep on pushing the point? She'd be just as happy if he did take his big, brooding presence and leave.

''Isn't that right, princess?'' he prodded.

Casey breathed in deeply, curbing her tongue in front of their rapt preteen audience. ''Somehow I don't think you're referring to me as the heroine of a fairy tale.''

He swept his arm out in a broad circle. ''If I told you this Gothic house of horrors would be a nightmare to defend, with its locked-up rooms and see-through walls and blind drives, would you come with me to a safe house?''

''No.''

Frankie chose that moment to add her own observation. ''Did you know there's a hidden stairwell from the upstairs down to the back of the kitchen?''

Mitch made a face that earned a laugh from Frankie. ''Why doesn't that surprise me?''

The girl was on a roll. ''There used to be a tunnel, too, that ran from the main house out to the pool house. But

Grandpa boarded it up since no one lives out here anymore.''

"It just keeps getting better and better." He shifted his gaze up to Casey. "And you feel safe here?"

"I did." Casey emphasized the past tense, letting her expression tell Mitch that *he* was the reason she felt threatened in her own sanctuary.

"What is it with you and cops? The commissioner said I had to be here, so I'm here." He crossed his arms and edged forward, the bulk of his shoulders closing in like the granite walls of her estate. Casey stood as straight as she could, holding her ground against him.

"I have known cops and worked with them my whole life. I am not afraid of them." She tipped her chin to meet the aggressive thrust of his jawline. "And despite what you're implying, I am not some snob who looks down on them because I'm a judge's daughter and you're an officer who serves the court."

"So why don't you want me here?" he demanded, the tip of his nose nearly touching hers.

"Because I'm afraid of…"

Of what? Him? Men? What he reminded her of?

What he made her feel?

That he made her *feel,* period.

"What scares you, princess?" he demanded.

Casey clamped her mouth shut and tried to make sense of the emotions churning inside her.

This close, she could smell the faint spicy scent of his aftershave clinging to the shadowy stubble of his beard. With the fire of verbal battle still hot within her, that slightest of sensations sneaked past her defenses and awoke something that had lain dormant too long for her to immediately recognize it.

Casey zeroed in on the mouth that spoke such a challenge to her. *Sexy*. Firm and flat and as unerringly masculine as the breadth of his shoulders or the timbre of his voice.

An incredibly politically incorrect thought crossed her mind. He liked to argue. He seemed to bring out the worst in her red-haired temperament. Sparring with him made her feel strong. Opinionated.

What if he simply silenced her arguments with a kiss?

She hadn't been kissed for so long.

"So you're not going to answer me?"

Mitch eased back, tilting his head to the ceiling and releasing a deep breath that made her wonder if he'd been as caught up in the moment of fascination as she had.

Casey breathed again, too. The respite allowed her to clear her thoughts. But rational thinking gave way to an almost physical pain. She wanted to laugh at her absurd expectations. What could a man as vibrant and self-assured as Mitch Taylor see in a crippled recluse like herself?

The embarrassment that flooded through her scorched her cheeks and she turned away. Into Frankie's told-you-so smile.

"Uh, excuse me." Frankie pointed to the office. "The phone?"

Casey reprimanded her with a pointed glare and headed for the office, glad for the ringing reprieve from both Frankie's idealistic romantic thoughts and her own self-condemning ones. But Mitch beat her to it. By the time she reached the desk, he already had his hand on the receiver.

"Mitch, it's just—"

"No." He jabbed his finger in the air to silence her. "Until I get surveillance equipment set up, no one answers the phone, door or intercom except me."

In full protector mode, Mitch picked up the receiver and turned his back to her. "Taylor."

Casey swallowed her offer to provide information with a smug smile. Frankie nudged her elbow and giggled.

"I see." Mitch's gruff voice maintained its crisp, professional tone, but the stiffness eased from his shoulders. "I'll let them know."

When he hung up, Frankie was ready with an explanation. "That's Grandma's private line from the house. There's no outside connection here."

Casey's amusement turned into a full-blown smile. She felt Mitch's gaze hone in on the change in her expression. The corners of his stern mouth relaxed, and some of the heat that had consumed her earlier returned. This time, though, a gentler, safer temperature warmed her.

Mitch relayed the message. "Judith says she's got cookies hot from the oven waiting for us with a glass of milk."

"Oatmeal Scotchies?" asked Frankie.

Casey's own taste buds perked up at the prospect. "Yes."

"Cool! C'mon, let's go." Frankie snatched up her coat, bounded through the outside door and zoomed down the path to the main house.

Casey and Mitch followed at a slower pace, shrugging into their coats and locking the pool-house door behind them.

Mitch shortened his stride to match Casey's measured steps. "You know, if you *are* in danger, it'd be nice if you people acted like it."

Casey turned up her wool collar and shrugged at his comment, not knowing where to begin explaining her ordeal with Emmett Raines and how she'd learned to cope with it over the years. She settled for the simple advice

Jimmy had given her so long ago. "I find a lot of comfort in the predictability of my lifestyle."

He shook his head. "It makes you complacent. A variable routine makes it harder for anyone stalking you to catch you off guard."

She couldn't stem the sarcasm that slipped into her voice. "I'm very much on guard, Captain. I think your presence here has taken care of that."

They had reached the garage, which opened into the kitchen and provided the rear entrance to the house. Casey grasped the knob, but Mitch stretched his arm across the doorway, blocking her path.

"You don't have to like me, princess. Or even respect what I do. But know this. I'm good at my job. And I'm going to do it with or without your help. 'With' just makes it easier. For both of us."

He snared her in the dark light of his eyes, and Casey read the clear warning etched there.

She retreated a step to put some much needed distance between them. "What kind of help do you want from me? I won't leave here. I know every tree and corner like the back of my hand, and the people even better."

"You could answer a few questions."

He shoved his hands into his pockets, making him appear less of a threat. But Casey's guard went on full alert. "Like what?"

"Tell me what makes Raines so different that you and the commissioner won't handle his escape through standard procedure. You weren't the only witness to testify at that trial. What makes him such a threat to you? I'd rather hear it from you instead of a police report."

She huddled inside her coat, shaking with the aftershocks of fear as her false bravado shrank inside her.

"Try not to look like you've been damned, Ms. Maynard. I'm on your side. I'll let you eat your oatmeal cookies first.''

He opened the door for her and followed her inside. He even helped her with her coat. But Casey wasn't fooled by his gallantry for an instant. The detective wanted answers from her that she'd never fully shared with anyone besides Jimmy.

He might be nice to her now, she thought. He might charm the socks off Frankie, Ben and Judith as he joined them at the kitchen table. But Casey inhaled the sweet smells from the kitchen as though she were facing her last supper.

Because once the McDonalds left for the Thanksgiving holiday, she'd be alone in the house with Mitch Taylor.

And then—she tried to swallow a bite of delectable cookie past the lump of dread in her throat—let the inquisition begin.

''YOU'RE SURE you won't change your mind and come to the house for the weekend?'' Ben McDonald loosened his bear-hug grip on Casey and stood back. Fatherly concern creased his well-worn features.

Casey patted his arm and smiled. ''I'm sure. You'll be jam-packed with relatives and you won't need me and my problems to put a damper on the celebration.''

''Honey, we raised you as much as your folks did. You know you'd be welcome.''

''I know.'' Ben and Judith had been the ones who stayed with her at the hospital after the attack, when her parents had been whisked away for their own safety and couldn't come.

Casey hated being the cause of any more worry for them. Back then she'd been in too much pain, she'd been too lost and confused to argue when they said they'd stay on with her at the house, even though both had earned their early retirement. But now she was as healthy as she would ever be. She was a responsible adult. And she owed them much more than a generous salary.

"I'll be fine." It might be a lie, but she said it with all the serenity she could muster to put their worries to rest.

Ben nodded. He clearly didn't believe her as much as he wanted to, but he accepted her decision. He zipped his coat shut and turned to Mitch, who waited at the doorway to the library while Casey and the McDonalds traded goodbyes. "I put that new door on like you requested, and switched the entry codes so that the key alone can't get you in here."

"I appreciate it," said Mitch.

"Let me show you what I worked out with the front gate."

"I'll walk you out and make sure everything's locked up tight behind you." Mitch might prefer giving orders, but as they exited down the hall, he listened to Ben's instructions and chatted with the older man as though they were equal partners on the case.

She was grateful for the way he used his authority and mutual respect to lessen Ben's and Judith's concerns. Not for the first time, she wondered why she didn't rate the same kind of attention from him. Did he resent Jimmy's orders so much? Was she the symbol of a task he considered beneath his rank? Or was the antagonism between the two of them something more personal?

Judith's hand on her shoulder stopped her musings. "You're sure you don't want me to come by tomorrow and fix you something to eat?"

"I could swim Friday instead of Monday if you want some company." Frankie's eager offer caught her from the other side.

Casey laughed and shook aside both propositions. "Have a happy Thanksgiving, both of you."

She hugged each one in turn. "You prepared enough food to feed a whole clan. I think I can manage. Now go home and enjoy your family."

"You'll let us know if there's anything we can do?" asked Judith.

"Of course I will." Casey guided them toward the door.

Frankie gave another vote of confidence for her favorite detective. "Mitch is cool, you know. He'll take care of you."

"I'm sure he will." Casey's response lacked the girl's enthusiasm. She didn't doubt that Mitch would do his job. She only wished doing his job didn't bear such a high emotional price for her.

Judith and Frankie left in another flurry of hugs and good wishes, leaving Casey to face the ominous silence of the house alone.

She'd been alone before. Since her attack, she'd become quite good at being alone. Weekends, holidays. With her parents gone on a well-deserved trip abroad and Jimmy occupied with the prized social functions required by his political career, she'd had little choice but to learn how to handle so much time to herself.

It was all a matter of outlook. She normally focused on the security and quiet of being on her own, the self-sufficiency it required of her.

And if she could just stay busy enough, she'd never see what might be missing from her life of solitude.

Broad-shouldered bodyguard aside, she expected this four-day holiday to be no different from all the others she'd learned to endure on her own. Now if she could just get Mitch to forgo the torturous questions he wanted to ask…

Cursing the distracting pattern of her thoughts, Casey sat at her desk, pulled out her stationery box and immersed herself in her work.

A stack of invitations lay at the bottom of her in-basket. They were mostly from old family friends, wishing her well or inviting her to join them for the holidays. She appreciated the effort and would thank them, but she would decline each one.

The only thing lonelier than spending a family holiday by herself was spending it as an outsider in someone else's home.

Besides, by staying here she endangered no one else. Jimmy had taught her the wisdom of that. After failing so miserably at Emmett Raines's trial, she took comfort in knowing she could do that one small thing to protect others.

She'd failed to identify him once. But no one else would pay the price for her mistake again.

Casey pulled the next envelope from her correspondence file and slit it open. She'd saved this one for last because of the impersonal printing on the envelope. She recognized the look of a bulk mailing after years of assisting her mother with charity functions, and suspected it was an invitation to some sort of seasonal fund-raiser. She'd decline attending it, as well, but she could do so with a simple check instead of writing out a "kind of you to think of me but sorry" letter.

She pulled out the gold-embossed notecard, which read The First Cattlemen's Bank Of Kansas City, and opened it to see how much money they wanted. A folded-up piece of plain white paper fell out. "A personal note?"

It wasn't her bank, so she wondered who would take the time to write. Curious, Casey set the card aside and unfolded the paper.

She read the single line printed there.

"The house that Jack built will come tumbling down."

CASEY THREW THE NOTE onto the desk, snatching her fingers away as though a rattlesnake had come to life in her hands. She shoved the blotter, sending an avalanche of books, papers and the telephone across the floor on the opposite side.

Gasping for a breath that refused to come, Casey scrambled out of her chair and hobbled around the desk, ripping at the Velcroed anchor patches on her brace. She pushed the cumbersome support unit off her leg and collapsed to her knees. Righting the phone, she picked up the receiver and speed-dialed Jimmy's number.

"Commissioner Reed's office."

"Iris?" Thank God it was someone she knew.

"Cassandra? Is that you? How are you?"

Casey sat back against the desk and tucked her left leg into her chest, curling her arms around it and pressing the phone to her ear. She ignored the polite greeting from Jimmy's assistant. "Is Jimmy still there? I need to speak with him right away."

"He's at a dinner meeting right now. I shouldn't interrupt him unless there's an emergency."

"It is. I just got a message from…" Casey stopped and swallowed, forcing the panic out of her voice. "It says, 'The house that Jack built…'"

"Casey? I'm back." Mitch's call from the kitchen pierced the fog of incoherent fear that prevented Casey from thinking clearly.

"'The house that Jack built…'" Her words trailed off altogether as she listened to them out loud herself. She sounded so juvenile, so silly for a twenty-eight-year-old woman.

"That's a nursery rhyme, isn't it?" prompted Iris when the silence continued.

She heard the back door close and Mitch's footsteps in the hallway.

Or so she thought.

A deeper wave of alarm swept through her, clouding her mind with memories. Mixing up the present with the past.

"Yes," she answered automatically, dismissing Iris and bringing her focus back to the house. Back to the library.

Back to the footsteps closing in on her.

Casey hung up and scanned the room for something with which to defend herself. But there was nothing close at hand, and she wasn't in a position to move quickly. So she simply leaned back and braced herself.

She'd be smarter this time.

She'd have to be smarter.

"You okay?"

The dark-haired gladiator appeared in the doorway. He halted there, taking in the scattered mess and her sitting in the middle of it. An invisible suit of armor slipped over his shoulders and he stepped inside, cutting the breathing space between them and blocking her only avenue of escape. "I told you not to answer the..."

Her strangled gasp echoed in the room. She flattened her back against the desk. The man who looked like Mitch froze midstride, towering above her.

"Casey?" Her name crackled in the air.

She looked hard into his eyes, seeking something familiar, fighting through the fog of panic that threatened to shut down her ability to think.

The tension in the room vibrated through Casey. Her breath deepened in short, punctuated gasps. A golden light flared in his eyes, a predator sensing danger.

But was she the prey? Or the protected mate?

She inched her way up the desk, carefully balancing herself so she wouldn't crumple to the floor. She couldn't tear her gaze from his. To look away would mean giving him an advantage she wouldn't surrender. Better that he be distracted first. "Would you hand me my cane? It's in the stand by the door there."

He hesitated an instant, then turned away, his movements slow and controlled, as if he expected her to bolt. He held out her cane, keeping as much distance between them as possible. When she wrapped her fingers around the handle, he held on, connecting an electric current between them.

"You want to tell me what's going on?" His voice, low and commanding, skittered along her nerve endings.

Casey looked harder. She saw warmth in his eyes and something that comforted her more than any other emotion could have. Suspicion.

Emboldened by the inexplicable reassurance, she reached up and cupped the left side of his face. He jerked at the unexpected touch, then held himself still beneath her hand. She felt the rasp of beard stubble in her palm, the forceful jut of his jaw. She dragged her fingertips over his skin, then held them to her own face, identifying the spicy scent of him and noting the absence of any makeup.

"Mitch?" Her fear seeped out in one long breath. "It's you. It's really you."

Without questioning her need to do it, Casey reached out with her left arm and slipped it around Mitch's waist beneath his open coat. She didn't care whether he responded out of duty or real concern; she only recognized a sense of profound relief when his sheltering arms folded around her and pulled her close.

"You want to tell me what's going on?"

She shook her head at the gentle question. She grabbed

a fistful of his jacket in her hand and burrowed even closer. Even the omnipresent bulk of the gun and holster beneath his arm reassured her. His hand spanned her back between her shoulder blades, rubbing light, consoling circles there.

"You have to talk to me, princess."

"Not yet," she murmured. "Just hold me so I know that it's you."

"I am holding you."

Casey shook her head.

"More," she begged on the barest breath of a whisper.

His arms tightened imperceptibly, and she felt his chin settle against the crown of her hair. His chest filled with a sigh beneath her cheek, and she allowed herself to relax along with him. She had never doubted Mitch's strength and determination. Now, surrounded by his warmth and gentleness, she reveled in the full experience of being held and protected by this man.

For the first time in days, in years perhaps, she felt truly safe.

And as she drew her own strength from the respite he offered, she became aware of other things. Other sensations.

The dampness of the evening air clung to his clothes, bringing out the comforting smell of fine wool and the inviting scent of the man underneath. The nubby texture of his tweed jacket brushed her cheek in a rough caress. And she could hear the steady staccato of his heartbeat beneath her ear.

Gradually, she became aware of her own body's reaction to the embrace. Her cheek, breasts, arm and thighs tingled wherever they touched him. Her own heartbeat jumped in a quicker rhythm.

Suddenly, Mitch wasn't comforting to her. He wasn't

her bodyguard or even a kind officer doing his duty. He was a man. And she was a woman. She was…

She wasn't ready for this.

Casey pushed away. The abrupt motion stirred the papers at her feet and reminded her with merciless speed of the reason she had sought safety in Mitch's arms.

"Who was on the phone? I called from the back door. Did you think I was him?"

His quick return to the questioning detective gave her an odd feeling of normalcy. It was less complicated to think of him in this role than as a man who made her want and feel things she had no right to. If he could dismiss the heat that had sizzled between them so easily, then she could, too. If he wanted to be the cop, then she would be his cool and proper princess.

She answered the easiest question first.

"I tried to call Jimmy. But all I got was his assistant." With the tip of her cane, she pushed aside the papers on the floor and pointed to the cruelly skewed nursery rhyme. "That came in the mail this afternoon."

He knelt down in front of her, studying the creased white paper and its computer-generated type without touching it. "From Raines?"

"I think. It was in with a card from a local bank."

Mitch read the phrase to himself. He pulled a plastic bag from his pocket and placed the letter inside before standing. "That's not how the rhyme goes, is it?"

"No. But my father's name is Jack." She looked at the paper herself again, and wondered if he could see the same stain of hatred on it she did. "Don't you think that could be a threat?"

"Anything's possible. I'll run it through the crime lab. See if they can pick up any prints. Do you still have the envelope it came in?"

"Yes."

When he finished cataloging the evidence, he surprised her by kneeling down again to pick up the fallen items and return them to her desk. Casey lowered herself beside him, put a hand on his arm and took the telephone from his grasp.

"You don't have to clean up my mess."

"It's my job to clean up the city, ma'am." After a silent moment to analyze the lighter pitch in his usually deep voice, Casey laughed at the boyish tilt to his smile. The rush of air in and out of her lungs and the healthy beat of her heart chased away the shadows of paranoia and lightened the dread she'd felt at spending the extended weekend in Mitch's company.

He compromised by handing her the blotter, basket and papers and letting her put them back on the desk.

In that one brief moment of shared smiles, a seed of trust planted itself in Casey's heart. It didn't blossom or even send up tiny shoots to battle for life in the sun. She recognized the seed and allowed it to remain, dormant for now.

But nurtured by longing and the protected haven she'd discovered in Mitch's arms, she knew that seed could very easily take root and grow.

HE PICKED UP the wire-framed glasses that had fallen to the living-room floor early in the silent, futile struggle, and put them on his own face. He pulled the Wharton school tie from around the man's neck and began tying it beneath his own collar. He found a mirror in the bathroom and adjusted the glasses on his nose.

He didn't realize how much he'd enjoy being back in charge once more. The thrill of success quickened his movements, but, as always, he drew on his patience. No need to rush a masterpiece.

He opened his tackle box of stage makeup and pulled out two foundations. Something light, with a tad of yellow. The man in the other room had worked inside most of his life, a tricky pallor to match. But not impossible.

He mixed the colors on his hand and dabbed the cream on his face, sliding it back across his cheeks in long, smooth strokes. The pampering caress fortified him inside and out. While he continued to blend his canvas, he experimented with several different expressions until he found that uniquely friendly but subtly superior half grin he'd seen on the young executive's face when he'd applied for a savings account two days ago. The man had been too busy stuffing envelopes to even give him the attention he deserved.

Such an idiot. It had been so simple to slip his own message into an envelope.

And then the fool made the mistake of turning him down.

No one would tell him what he could and could not do anymore.

He'd make a fine bank officer. Probably a more promising prospect than that fool lying dead on the living-room floor.

When finished, he took the knowledge that he could pass for the man's twin as a sign of prophetic good fortune. Turning that rehearsed smile into one of his own, he went to the kitchen and rummaged through the doors and cupboards. At last he found what he was searching for.

Looking inside the recessed bread box, he laughed aloud. This guy was so predictable. More than likely considered himself a gourmand. He'd spent hundreds of dollars on this set of chef's knives, and probably didn't know how to use half of them.

But he did.

He selected two of his favorites, then returned to the living room.

Chapter Four

Mitch punched down the pillow he'd hauled from the linen closet and threw it on top of the blanket spread over the leather couch. He'd slept in more uncomfortable places before—behind the wheel of his Jeep on a stakeout, in a double bed with two of his cousins growing up in the apartment over his uncle's store—but he'd never before felt so out of place.

It wasn't the upscale decor of this mansion that rekindled his young man's desire to fit in with the right people in the right places; it was a certain haughty-chinned redhead with smoky eyes so full of fear and hurt that he couldn't help but take her in his arms and try to protect her from all the pain life had inflicted on her.

Holding her had felt so right.

Yet it couldn't be right.

Casey was cut from the same mold his wife had been. Privileged. Pampered. Proud.

So unlike him, the son of a cop who walked a beat, raised by an extended family who could barely afford to feed their own.

And he wanted her all the same. Even though his timing was lousy and the situation stunk.

He pulled his holster off his shoulders, folded it and set

it on the mantel. The fire in the hearth had cooled to glowing embers, but he still felt hot in this room where Casey seemed to spend most of her time. He shrugged out of his shirt and sat down to remove his shoes.

Fitting his big frame on this little couch seemed to be the least of his troubles.

He'd been so determined not to like her. He'd assumed Casey would be as stuffy and condescending as Commissioner Reed. And, on the surface, she was. But that upper-crust facade had slipped more than once to reveal a bona fide temper. He'd seen glimpses of a caring, intelligent woman when she worked with Frankie and said goodbye to the McDonalds.

And when she walked into his embrace and clung to him like a lifeline to her own sanity, he'd even forgotten why he was there in the first place. As a cop.

Correction. As the commissioner's handpicked errand boy.

He hadn't wanted to offer her the protection of his gun and badge and twenty years of experience on the force. He'd wanted to bury his nose in the sweet vanilla scent of her hair. He'd wanted to tip that proud chin and see if her lips tasted just as sweet. He'd wanted to shield her the way a wolf protected its lair, the way a street kid protected his turf, the way a man protected his woman.

Thank God for the late hour and the sure-to-distract reading material Merle Banning had dropped off. The case file on Emmett Raines. If neither honest fatigue nor harsh, cold facts couldn't stop him thinking about Casey Maynard sleeping across the hallway from him, then remembering the disaster his marriage had been should be enough to steer his thoughts away from society beauties.

Maybe the sharp snap of her tongue would remind him of his place and permanently erase these errant musings that had his almost-forty body heated like a randy teen-ager's.

The duffel bag he kept in the Jeep held a change of clothes and a toothbrush. So he stripped down to his underwear and pulled on the battered pair of jeans he kept in the bag.

A low, guttural laugh tickled his throat as he draped his jacket and slacks over the back of a chair. He could just imagine the high-minded lecture Casey would give him if she found a naked man sipping coffee in her kitchen Thanksgiving morning.

If he could keep that self-righteous image of Casey foremost in his mind, he might just forget those tender feelings that disturbed his equilibrium, along with the need to measure up that he thought he'd outgrown long ago.

"Mitch?"

The laughter died in his throat, along with the delusion that he could turn off his fascination with Casey. He hardened his smile into a professional mask before turning around. If only he could control his emotions so easily.

Casey stood in the doorway with her glorious hair tumbling down around her shoulders. She leaned on her cane as if too weary to stand with her usual elegant posture, but her clear eyes looked straight at his…bare chest.

Mitch breathed in deeply, quelling the burst of heat that sparked in his traitorous body under her curious stare. Her eyes danced at the unintended display.

"I hope I'm not disturbing you." Her soft voice trembled.

"Is everything all right?" Mitch heard a husky twitch in his own voice. No woman should look at a man like that unless she wanted…

"Yes, fine. I just wanted to make sure that you were all

right down here. Would you prefer one of the guest rooms upstairs?''

He shook his head. This was something more than a simple good-night, but he let her lead the conversation instead of pressing her. ''There's no sense opening up one of those rooms. This is fine.''

''I wanted to explain what happened earlier.''

She cleared her throat and averted her gaze, giving him the cue that his state of undress embarrassed her.

He felt the snub like a splash of cold water. He reached for his shirt and shoved his arms into it, buttoning a couple of buttons to cover himself. Lord, he was messed up, thinking his battered old body looked good to her. He was more out of practice than he thought, wishfully misinterpreting the flush of her cheeks as a sign of interest instead of offense. Whatever lustful attraction he'd felt for the princess clearly wasn't shared. She'd come to talk to the cop, not the man. He might as well oblige her and do what he did best.

''I was just settling down to do some reading.'' He softened his clipped words. The only one he should be angry with was himself. ''It can wait. Sit down. You've had a long day.''

She smiled shyly, almost gratefully, as she worked her way to the empty wingback chair and sat. Mitch settled on the sofa across from her, a legitimate curiosity kicking in when she hesitated before speaking.

''I'm sorry. I didn't really think you were him, you know.'' She started by way of apology. She fidgeted with her hands, and Mitch wondered exactly what she was apologizing for. Then he made a sobering connection.

''You thought I was Emmett Raines when I came in from the garage, didn't you?''

She looked him in the eye. She created a stark combination of self-assurance and vulnerability with her shaky tone and tilted chin. ''As you've probably pieced together, I have flashbacks sometimes. I get confused as to where I am and who I'm with.''

Mitch nodded. ''That's not unusual with victims of violent crimes. Especially knowing the perp's on the loose again.''

''But it's more than that for me.'' He waited while she searched for the right words. ''Emmett is a master of disguise. He can make himself up and alter his voice and mannerisms to imitate a person so perfectly that you can't tell the difference between him and the real thing.''

''You couldn't identify him?'' The wheels turned inside his head, trying to piece together the unrelated facts he knew about the case.

''Not at the trial. I got confused with him sitting there, staring at me. He looked so different, I…'' Casey breathed deeply and then her words tumbled out in a rush. ''Sometime during the twenty-four hours before my attack, Emmett killed my bodyguard—a police officer named Steven Craighead. He took his place. And I didn't even see the change until he pulled the knife and…''

She squeezed her eyes shut as if blocking a memory. Mitch curled his hands into fists to keep from reaching out to offer comfort and accidentally startling her.

Her eyes shot open, revealing a panic so intense, he gripped the seat cushion to keep from going to her. ''I kissed him good-night. That last night before I locked myself in my room.'' She rubbed her arms, erasing a chill Mitch could only imagine. ''But did I kiss Steve? Or Emmett Raines?''

Mitch waited for his angry compassion to abate to a controllable level. ''I imagine the defense attorney made a big issue out of that.''

"Mom and Dad and I each had bodyguards assigned to us. It wasn't the first time one of his trials warranted it. Steve and I were old friends. He knew my training schedule and didn't mind the odd hours." Her knuckles whitened around the grip of her cane. "I asked for him to be assigned to me. We'd dated a couple of times. But that morning, I didn't see the subtle changes until it was too late. He was a bit taller than Steven, so he slouched. He had darker hair, right at the roots. I think I would recognize Emmett Raines if I saw him now, but..."

"But you don't trust your own judgment." Mitch finally understood her confusion. He stood and crossed to the fireplace, needing a physical outlet to channel his sympathy for Casey's plight into a constructive train of thought. He paced, wishing he had the facts of the case in his head instead of in the unopened file on the sofa.

But one fact about this tragedy of errors remained clear. He knelt in front of her, hating the way she flinched in the chair, but refusing to back off. She needed to understand this. "You can't be afraid of me, Casey. I can't protect you if you avoid me or doubt I have your safety as my top priority."

He caught her gaze and admired the determination blossoming there.

"I know. Tonight..." She smiled, and Mitch suspected the joke would be on him. "Your voice is distinctive, and you wear a real chip on your shoulder, but I still had a moment when I wasn't sure it was you."

The subliminal awareness that the two of them could share much more than an attitude refused to stay buried. He smiled in answer to the warmth of the princess with all her walls down. "What are we going to do about that?"

She reached into the pocket of her chenille robe and pulled out a small velvet box. "I want to give you something to wear. Something that's one of a kind, so I can recognize it—and you—without any doubts, even if I have a flashback.''

''Sounds like a good idea.'' His simple praise seemed to strengthen her. ''What is it?''

''This belonged to my father.'' She opened the box and held up a small silver lapel pin. ''I had it specially made for his fiftieth birthday. It's a miniature copy of my Olympic medal.''

She laid the pin in his open palm. Sterling silver, he'd bet. A work of art. And most importantly, a memento of her father. ''I can't take this.''

She curled his fingers over the pin and pressed his hand between both of hers. ''Please. I have to put my faith in you to protect me, right? I think my father would approve.''

Of the gift? Or him?

The winter wind whistled past the windows, securing them from the cold of the night. The light from the dying fire and a single lamp swathed them in a glowing sanctuary that kept the shadows of past terrors and current dangers at bay.

Casey looked properly chaste in that high-collared nightgown she wore. But the fuzzy blue robe she covered herself with made her seem younger, and cuddly. Approachable.

The years of being second-rate, second choice, lessened their sting. Casey's simple gift, this huge leap of faith for her, narrowed his world down to the cherishing sensation of his big hand held in hopeful trust by both of hers.

His gaze fixed on the unadorned lushness of her lips. He drifted closer. One kiss. Just one sample...

''Mitch?''

He blinked away his foolish thoughts, clenched his

hands into a fist and pulled away. He berated himself silently and resumed his pacing.

The voice she had described as *distinctive* was now purposely devoid of any kind of inflection. "Thank you. Next time you see me, I'll have this on."

"I...okay. I'd better go."

He watched her limp away, shoulders back and chin held high. He heard the admission of pain in the hiss of air through gritted teeth each time her right leg took her weight. But Mitch riveted his feet to the floor and made no move to help her. He didn't trust himself to get that close right now, not when he was torn up inside with anger and compassion and desire. He didn't think she needed the help anyway—she was a lot stronger than the commissioner or her staff or even she suspected.

At the door, she stopped and turned. "Thank you for listening. And taking me seriously."

The odd addendum stirred him from his thoughts. "Any reason why I shouldn't?"

"No. Good night, Mitch."

"Good night, princess."

Only when he heard her door click safely shut behind her, did he realize he had used the nickname he'd dubbed her with. And this time, he admitted to himself that his reasons for using it had changed. Casey Maynard possessed every bit of class the name implied.

Sure, she came from a different world than he did. She belonged to the wealthy social class his wife had always wanted for her own. But Casey's class went beyond dollar signs. It was evident in the way she carried herself, despite her pain. It was evident in the way she treated the folks around her like real people.

Even him.

"Thank you," she'd said. How many times had anyone

bothered to thank him? And he hadn't even done anything yet.

Mitch set the pin on the mantel beside his gun. He slit open the Raines file and sat down to start reading.

The scarcity of facts on file made the back of his neck tingle. He read Casey's grim account of events with forced detachment. Beyond that, he found nothing to confirm Emmett Raines as the clever monster Casey had described. The arresting officer's report had been sealed in a separate file. He'd put in a call to his staff to track it down in the morning.

He'd cross-referenced the file to get information on Darlene Raines, Emmett's twin, who'd been on trial for extortion and manslaughter at the time of Casey's attack. The single sheet of information on her proved equally vague and brief.

Mitch sat back and fingered the thin manila envelope. He couldn't shake the feeling that something vitally important was missing from Raines's file. Was it sloppy bookkeeping? Or was the gap in information something decidedly more sinister?

He set the envelope aside and shed his shirt. He turned off the lamp and waited for sleep to come.

He'd have to fill in the holes himself.

The bank would be closed tomorrow, but he'd pay a visit there on Friday to check any leads on the nursery rhyme from Raines. So far, there were no signs that it had come from Emmett. The commissioner himself didn't believe that Raines would come after Casey. He'd assigned Mitch more as a test of his loyalty than as a real precaution. Plus, if she couldn't identify Raines as her attacker at the trial, then why should the man come after her now?

Thank you for taking me seriously.

Casey believed Emmett Raines would come after her.

She'd turned to Mitch for help.

Because she'd asked, Mitch couldn't say no.

And because she believed, so did Mitch.

CASEY TRIED TO MOVE, but the heavy weight inside her head shifted, slamming into her right temple. She held herself perfectly still, hearing her own tortured breathing as uneven groans of pain.

She lifted her hands and tried to brace herself so she could sit up. But they wouldn't function. Her muscles didn't obey when she tried to separate her arms onto either side of her. A sharp flash fire of pain seared her wrists, and she blinked her eyes open.

Tape. He'd strapped her hands together with gray reinforced duct tape. And the pain in her head. He'd choked her. With those plastic handcuffs. They'd chafed and cut into her skin until the burning pressure in her throat exploded. And then blessed nothingness.

Until now.

"Steve?" she muttered. A blue uniform spun through her vision, and she tried to remember. "What happened?"

"That's it, champ. You come back to me."

Casey squinted the world into focus and concentrated on the man hovering over her. The first things she saw were his eyes. Nearly colorless chips of blue glacial ice. A relatively attractive face, she thought abstractly. Such a sweet guy. Steve could be so sweet.

Not Steve.

She fought through the cotton clogging her mind and caught a glimpse of something sinister. A long, shiny knife glinted in the afternoon sun where it bled through the curtains, and the blade reflected the light directly into her eyes. She closed her eyes against the brightness that seared through her brain.

"No, no," he reprimanded. "Stay with me, champ. We need to talk about Daddy."

Casey tried to concentrate. Panic set in, further scrambling the fog in her brain. She was so confused. Who was this man? What happened to Steve? Had the man told her what he wanted from her? Or had she just forgotten?

Something cold touched the base of her throat. A gasp of fear rocketed through her, clearing her mind into frightening awareness. "I don't know what you want!" she rasped, her throat burning like drops of acid eating through metal.

Then he smiled, and Casey thought it was the cruelest mockery she had ever seen. She shivered violently as he drew the tip of his blade down across her chest. She lay on the floor in nothing more than her swimsuit, bound at the wrists, pinned by his knee on her hip, powerless to do nothing except force herself not to retch at his touch.

He stroked the knife over her belly and touched her thigh, but in a moment of detached awareness, she knew this man wasn't going to rape her. There was nothing sexual about this. In fact, it had nothing to do with her at all.

The awareness must have shown on her face because in an instant, his smile vanished into a cruel sneer. He flipped her onto her stomach and grabbed her ankle. "Listen good, champ. Here's what I want you to tell Daddy...."

The knife pierced the skin over her Achilles tendon.

HER OWN SCREAMS WOKE HER.

Casey lurched up in bed. The darkness of the night and the twisted covers pinning her legs and hips left her feeling trapped, unable to escape the horrible images from her dreams.

"Casey!"

The deep voice bellowed through the darkness.

"Help me!" She thrashed at the covers, struggling to free herself from her bonds. "Help me!"

The door to her room flew open, and a massive figure emerged from the hallway. The overhead light snapped on, and a dark blur of motion swept into the room. Casey scrambled backward until she cowered against the headboard. Soundlessly, the figure slipped into her room, up to her bed. Her throat burned with terror, and when she opened her mouth to scream, no sound came out at all.

The lamp on her bedside table flicked on, flooding his face with blessed light, bringing the shadowy intruder into sharp focus. She stared in mute shock at the man, his dark hair tousled with sleep, his impossibly broad shoulders and torso bared down to where a pair of unsnapped jeans clung to his hips. In his left hand, he gripped a lethal-looking gun. And in his right, he clasped a tiny silver pin between two fingers.

"Mitch."

She barely spoke his name, but in that instant, a fire lit in his eyes. She was on her knees and crawling toward him when he lifted her in his arms and crushed her to his chest.

"Dammit, Casey! Are you all right?" His voice broke in the middle of his question, choked with some overwhelming emotion. He gripped her with an urgency matching her own, one hand cradling the back of her head while the other spanned her rib cage so tightly she could scarcely breathe.

But Casey held on to him for all she was worth, her arms squeezing his neck, her face buried in the hollow beneath his chin. "Mitch. Mitch."

She breathed his name over and over like a sob, though there were no tears, only the racking sensation of terror working its way out of her system.

"Shh, babe. It's okay now. A bad dream. It wasn't real."

But Mitch was real. She didn't know how long she held on to him like that, clinging to his strength and comfort. Gradually, the pressure around her middle eased, and she felt the warm, callused stroke of his hand brushing up and down her spine. Beneath the calming sound of his whispered reassurances, she also loosened her desperate grip.

"I'm sorry. I didn't mean to panic you like that. I was so scared." She relaxed against him, brushing her lips along the salty tang of his neck as she spoke.

A sound rumbled heavily in his throat, a release of some sort. He curved his arm beneath her bottom and lifted her, changing places so that he now sat on the edge of the bed with her in his lap. He released his hold on her only long enough to set the safety on his weapon and lay it on the bedside table beside her father's pin.

Then he cupped her head and pulled it back against his chest. He tunneled his long fingers into her tresses and massaged the tension near the base of her skull, all the while whispering reassurances in that incredibly deep voice of his. His sheltering touch and soothing words lulled her into a state of sweet contentment.

"You scared me, princess. I was just getting used to that lumpy old sofa and started to relax when you cried out." He didn't share whatever else he'd been feeling, but only hugged her tighter. Casey didn't care; she just knew she felt safe.

She sighed in relief, forgetting any misgivings she'd had earlier about her reactions to Mitch. "You're good at this."

"Scaring off the bad guys?" His voice echoed beneath her ear, along with the quickening beat of his heart.

"No. Holding me. I haven't been held in such a long time. You…"

Casey flattened her palms against the nutmeg-brown mat of curls that formed a V across his chest. The crisp softness tickled her palms, just as she had imagined it would when she saw him in the library earlier. She'd nearly forgotten the purpose for her late-night visit then.

She'd nearly forgotten why he was here with her now. She pushed ever so slightly, and he loosened his hold, allowing her to lean back and look up into his face. "You seem to be getting a lot of practice. Sorry to be so much trouble."

"I don't mind." The banked fire in his sinfully rich voice simmered along her nerve endings, igniting a long-extinguished flame of feminine awareness deep inside her. She reached up and laid her hand gently over his cheek, tracing the prominent bone with her fingertips and allowing her thumb to settle at the corner of his lips.

The muscles alongside his mouth relaxed a moment before she realized his intent. She tipped her head back, waiting for his kiss. Welcoming it.

His arms stiffened around her. And instead of touching his lips to hers, he pressed them to her forehead, holding her still beneath the platonic gesture of comfort. The stubble of his beard caught a few strands of her hair as he withdrew. A mask of steel replaced the dark fire in his eyes.

Her mouth felt cold, strangely deprived of something she hadn't known she wanted. Her ego didn't fare much better.

They'd been caught up in a moment of shared fear. He was her protector, fulfilling his duty with the embrace. She'd needed his warmth and strength. He had both in abundant supply. She'd be foolish to think he'd want anything like that from her.

She could feel his withdrawal in the bunching of his muscles beneath her hands, and knew that the cop was asserting himself once more. Before he could set her aside, Casey crawled from his lap back to the center of the bed.

"I'm sorry I woke you. You were up late. You need your sleep."

He stood and tucked his gun into the back of his jeans and pocketed the pin. "Don't sweat it. It's all part of the job." She missed the teasing inflection in his voice as much as she missed the chance to share his kiss.

"Tell me about the nightmare."

Startled by the order, Casey looked up at him. But he was already striding across the room to make sure the windows of her bedroom were secure. He tilted his head to listen as he moved about the room.

"I remembered when he attacked me. Thinking it was Steve at first. I felt so betrayed. And then I knew it wasn't him and..." She squeezed her eyes shut against the memory of the flashing knife. "I guess talking about it made it all seem real again."

"I bet a lot of things have triggered your memories lately."

Casey opened her eyes and watched Mitch work. Dressed like this, if she could call it that, in jeans worn soft and threadbare by years of wear, he looked more like her imagined version of a henchman or undercover cop. His preferred suit and tie was just window dressing to hide the real Mitch. This raw, unpolished man would never be Jimmy's first choice for deputy commissioner.

But she couldn't think of anyone she'd rather have as her champion in a fight. Or as her lover in the shadows of the night.

Casey cringed inwardly and drew her flannel gown down over her legs until it covered everything except her toes. God, what was she thinking? She'd known the man for less than a week, had never even kissed him, and already she was fantasizing about what it might be like for him to bare his emotions and other assets and make love to her.

Except, of course, that he'd never do that. Fantasies, nightmares and paranoia weren't much to offer a man. What could Mitch possibly see in her beyond the initial challenge of breaking down her emotional barriers? Was it really only his job that had led to those loving embraces? Were crushing hugs and tender words the way he protected all his charges?

He obviously possessed a protective nature. It was probably one of the traits that made him a good cop. He took charge of everything he came in contact with. How much of what drew her to Mitch was the security he offered, and how much of it was the man? And was she so desperate for loving attention that she wouldn't be smart enough to tell the difference?

"I'm sorry." Mitch's voice startled her from her reverie. He stood at the door again, less of a threat in the light, though no less powerful.

"Sorry?" she asked.

"Sorry about what almost happened. You said Steve kissed you the night before the attack. I didn't mean to remind you of that."

He was apologizing for *not* kissing her? "But…"

A weariness weighted his shoulders. "The house is secure, so try to get some sleep if you can."

Casey sat motionless, clutching her good knee to her chest and staring at him, trying to understand why he felt compelled to apologize. At opposite ends of the room, they seemed suspended in time and space.

"Ah, hell," he muttered.

"What's wrong?"

"You're not going back to sleep, are you?"

"I'll try."

"No, you won't. You're scared to death the nightmare will come back." He strode toward the bed. "I don't blame you. Scoot over."

"What are you doing?"

He set his gun on the table and reached for the covers at the foot of the bed. "Move your sweet little keister— I'm coming in."

"You can't do that!"

He ignored her protest, and Casey slid over to the far side of the bed to avoid being pinned beneath him. Mitch rolled onto his side and straightened the sheets and blankets, pulling them up and tucking them under her chin. She squirmed and worked her hands free to wedge between them and push him away.

"Mitch, you don't have to do this. I'll be fine."

Somehow her protest softened into a breathy plea. Instead of pushing, her fingers had curled into the roped strength of his shoulders. She felt a sting of unshed tears in her eyes, felt a hollowed-out place in her heart spill open to expose seven years of fear and neglect and hiding her true spirit.

Mitch never let her hide. From her fears. From her past. From her feelings.

This man cared that she hurt. In his own gruff, take-no-prisoners way, he cared.

He smoothed the covers and laid down on top of them, gathering her into his arms, blankets and all, and pulling her close. He seared her with his heat and hardness and strength, even though layers of wool and cotton and flannel separated them.

"Why are you doing this?" The newly awakened soul of her womanhood sent up a silent prayer that this was Mitch the man attending her with such tenderness, and not the dutiful cop.

"You feel safe when I hold you, right? I won't get any sleep, either, waiting for the next time you cry out." He'd left the light on beside the bed, and she could see the sparks of checked emotion dancing in his eyes. "You need someone to hold you right now, and it looks like I'm the only one around to do it. I promise I'll behave myself."

He caught her chin and held her gaze when a flood of disappointment made her look away. "I want to do it."

If he had kissed her then, her joy would have been complete. But Casey knew to ask for small favors, to appreciate the gift she'd been given and not risk losing this moment by asking for more.

She finally relaxed, letting his broad hand cradle her head against the pillow of his shoulder.

"Don't worry, Casey. No evil villain is going to plague your dreams tonight."

Casey yawned unexpectedly, feeling drowsy in her secure haven, allowing his physical warmth and the fire of his convictions to seep into her. Her questions about his motives didn't seem to matter right then.

But as she drifted off toward peaceful slumber, a different set of troubling images floated through her mind. The expression of the hurt young boy she'd seen in his eyes when she gave him her father's pin. The look of a child who didn't believe he deserved a simple gift.

"Mitch?"

"Hmm?"

"Who holds you when you get scared?"

The laughter rumbling in his chest sounded forced, unnatural. "Go to sleep, princess. I'm the protector here."

That was no answer. Despite her exhaustion, she roused herself to demand a satisfactory response. "I'm serious. I don't even know if you have a wife or a girlfriend. Is there someone who looks after you while you're busy taking care of everyone else?"

He lay so still for so long, that she thought he might not answer.

"My wife died of cancer five years ago. There's no one special."

Casey settled against him once more, weighing the import of his response with the toneless voice that spoke it. "Your wife was a very lucky woman to have you around to take care of her."

"She found her comfort elsewhere."

The muscles in his arms bunched an infinitesimal fraction, as though he wanted to draw her closer, yet was afraid she might not appreciate the gesture. "But I vowed to stick by her for better or worse. I'll do the same for you. As long as you need me."

His gruff answer told her a lot.

He was a man of his word. A fierce protector. Loyal to a cause or person because he had given his word.

And lonely. Maybe as lonely as she had ever been.

Chapter Five

Casey sighed and stretched in her cozy haven. How utterly decadent, she thought. Neither Coach Mills nor her parents ever allowed her to sleep this late, unless it was a holiday.

The first rays of awareness peeked into her brain. She pushed the heavy fall of hair back from her face and squeezed her eyelids tight against the morning light. It *was* a holiday. Thanksgiving. No coach. Her parents were away. No training today.

She snuggled deeper into the inviting warmth of the feather ticking that covered her mattress. Judith must have sneaked in this morning and placed an extra comforter over her. She felt so incredibly, deliciously warm.

Judith didn't work on holidays.

Casey awakened to the next level of consciousness. She had the house to herself this weekend. She wasn't in training anymore. Her parents weren't due to return until...

"Not a morning person, huh?"

The deep, drowsy voice stirred the crown of her hair.

With a rapid bing, bing, bing, Casey jolted into full, wary alertness. Her palms sizzled where she flattened them to push herself upright. She was only inches away from the whiskey-dark eyes of the man lying beneath her.

Casey shook her head, pinpointing the sensations of

warmth surrounding her. The sensation of Mitch surrounding her. Held in his arms, sprawled on his chest.

His wide, lazy smile magnified the tension zinging through her. He didn't seem to mind that she'd made herself at home with his big, rangy body. In fact, he seemed amused. How long had he lain awake watching her sleep. How long had she…?

Her hands and forearms rested on his chest. Her stomach draped across his torso with only the soft worn flannel of her favorite nightgown to separate her from the searing fire of his skin. She clutched at her neckline.

His smile straightened.

Thankfully, the buttons were in place at her throat. But a shock wave replaced her short-lived relief as she zeroed in on the most vulnerable part of her.

The hem of her nightgown was hiked up to her thigh, and her crippled, wounded leg was wedged very tightly, very intimately between his legs.

Her humiliation was instantaneous. Protective anger followed in the next breath.

"What are you doing in my bed?"

A steel mask eclipsed the indulgent humor in his eyes. Casey pushed away, tugging at the hem of her gown, hiding her leg and escaping off the side of the bed, dragging blankets and the sheet with her.

"I mean, get out of my bed!"

Mitch's rugged face clouded over. With a slow deliberation that mocked her own frantic efforts, he rolled off the opposite side of the bed. Casey clutched a pillow to hide herself from his all-seeing eyes, which raked her from head to toe.

He tucked his gun in the back of his jeans.

She watched him pick up her father's pin between his thumb and forefinger. He held it up to study, and her attention flew to the pin, too. Then he looked beyond the pin and captured her gaze in the dark void of his eyes. The implied message wasn't lost on her.

She'd given him that pin as a gesture of trust.

And her actions this morning had shattered that tenuous bond.

"You're welcome, princess."

His cold, cold sarcasm grated across her like the winter wind whipping across the window pane.

She'd accepted his comfort. Had asked for it. Had succumbed to the generous promise of shelter in his arms.

She'd even tried to offer some fraction of comfort in return. But she could never... He would never...

What a man thought he wanted in the sleep-softened edges of the night might not measure up in the bright light of day.

She needed to explain. But couldn't he see? She was little more than scars and pain and therapists' coping strategies. Did she have to shame herself all over again, and still face the rejection—or even the revulsion—she'd find in his eyes?

She crushed the pillow in her grasp and summoned her mother's ability to put on a good face and soften the blow of any travesty.

"Thank you for your help last night. But I'd like you to leave now."

"Yes, ma'am."

Casey stood tall and weathered the brunt of Mitch's cutting tone. When the door closed behind him, she whirled around and slung the pillow at his exiting backside. She picked up a second pillow and turned to fire, but ended up wrapping her arms around it and sliding down onto the bed. She hugged the pillow tightly, cursing her leg, her luck and, most of all, Emmett Raines.

One Good Man

Without that man's violent influence in her life, she'd be a whole woman. She could hide her imperfections from the rest of the world. But for how long could she hide them from Mitch?

MITCH SWITCHED the channel back to the Chiefs-Lions football game and idly wondered if the temperature in Detroit was any colder than the chill here in Casey's library.

He felt like a kid at his first junior-high dance, slyly sneaking looks at Casey working at her computer, then looking away when she glanced at him watching television. Judith McDonald had fixed the tastiest Thanksgiving meal he'd ever eaten, even reheated in a microwave oven. But the tender turkey breast and dressing and potatoes sat like a rock in his stomach. He didn't have the heart to sentence the pumpkin-cheesecake pie sitting in the refrigerator to a similar fate.

This holiday had turned out to be like most others for him. He usually worked so that more of his officers could spend the day with their families. The fact that he could sit and watch football wearing jeans and a sweatshirt didn't change the knowledge that he was on the job today.

Casey had made herself very clear. He worked for her. He had overstepped the bounds of their professional relationship when he lingered in bed with her this morning. Holding her when she was afraid was fine.

Enjoying himself while he did it was not.

Downtown boys and society ladies did not mix company. He'd tried it before. Growing up, in school, with Jackie.

But with Casey, he had forgotten the unwritten rules. They could sit down at a table together and share a meal, but they didn't have to talk. They could be in the same room, warmed by the same fire on a cold winter day, but they couldn't pursue the same interests. And they could wake up in bed together, totally at ease with each other, intimately entwined—but they would deny the connection that drew them together time and again like a parched man to water.

Lying in bed this morning, he'd actually looked forward to spending the day with Casey. Last night, she'd snuggled up to him like a lover. She'd entrusted him with a family heirloom. But in the cold light of day, she'd relegated him to the status of hired help.

She left the library with her coffee mug in hand to refill. Hell, he couldn't even ask her about Emmett Raines.

Where would he start? He didn't need an account of the actual attack. About the only thing recorded in copious detail in the Raines file was the extent of the injuries he'd inflicted on her. Strangulation. Contusions and lacerations around her face and throat. A latticework of knife wounds up and down her right leg, severing a tendon, detaching nerves, spelling out a hideous word that brought bile to his throat just thinking about it.

Payback.

And they couldn't keep that bastard behind bars? Mitch rested his elbows on his knees and buried his face in his hands. Crap like that made him want to give up being a cop, and it had made him want to be that cop in the first place.

Accessory-after-the-fact to extortion. Breaking and entering. Making threats.

Simple convictions, to Mitch's way of thinking, considering what Raines had gotten away with. He wanted to nail him for Officer Craighead's murder and Casey's assault. But until he could find the key to his crimes and a possible cover-up seven years old, Mitch had little chance of doing either.

"Truce?"

A slice of pumpkin-cheesecake pie passed beneath his nose. The tangy scent combined with the softly spoken question made him hungry for something to fill his soul rather than his stomach.

He sat back and gazed up into troubled gray eyes. Could the day's forced silence be taking its toll on Casey, too?

"For homemade pie? I'd agree to almost anything."

His puerile attempt at humor brought a shy smile to Casey's full mouth. The resentment in his gut eased a little. She handed him the plate and fork, and sat beside him at the far end of the sofa. He demolished his slice in a few short minutes while she nibbled at her piece. She asked about the game, and they chatted about impersonal matters until she finished and set her plate on the coffee table. This was the day he'd hoped to have with her.

There must be a catch.

It came with her next question. "Isn't there someplace you'd rather be spending Thanksgiving?" she tucked her left leg beneath her, and Mitch got the impression she would have curled into a ball and retreated into the corner of the sofa if the brace on her right leg would let her.

Though she'd made a friendly overture, he tried not to be offended by the distance she seemed determined to put between them. "You're not getting rid of me, so don't ask."

"I didn't mean that." Her gaze traveled the room, then settled on him, clear and direct. "I'm sorry about this morning. To say you caught me off guard would be an understatement. I was rude and ungrateful and I'm…sorry. I just wondered if you had any family who'd be missing you today."

Mitch wondered where dear old Dutch uncle Jimmy was today. There hadn't been so much as a phone call. He reminded himself that the movers and shakers of the world sometimes put more emphasis on appearance than on actual feelings. But the sorrowful ring in her apology had him thinking of ways to cheer her up.

"I was invited to watch the game and share dessert with Joe Hendricks's family. He's my lieutenant. But they've got a baby due, so I imagine their house is already overrun with grandparents and aunts and uncles. At least here I'm sure there's enough pie to go around."

The soft laugh in her throat gave him more pleasure than a commendation for meritorious service to the community. The sound of her laughing, sweet and strong and free from fear, made him reckless. It made him feel like challenging the differences that had separated them all day long.

"Have you ever seen the Plaza lights turn on?" he asked, checking his watch. The big event was less than thirty minutes away.

Casey shrugged at the unexpected shift in their conversation. "Are you kidding? I grew up here. It's just two blocks away."

Mitch leaned back and gauged the suspicious gleam in her eyes. "I thought all you rich folks cleared out on Thanksgiving to avoid the tourists and suburbanites and downtown boys like me who invaded your turf for the big event."

"My turf?"

"It's a long hike down here from where I grew up." The shame and envy he once felt was a thing of the past, but she frowned at him as if the injustice he'd felt as a child still shaded his voice. "But I hitched a ride and came down whenever I could. It was the closest thing we ever had to Christmas lights."

"Christmas wasn't a big event at your house?"

He laughed at her innocent question, and was surprised

to hear nostalgia in the sound. "When I was really young, yeah."

"Why not later?" she asked.

"When I moved in with my aunt and uncle, it just didn't seem important anymore. We never had anything fancy. Some years, we couldn't even afford a tree. But I always had a present. A deck of baseball cards or pack of gum. Uncle Sid made sure of that."

"That sounds like a lot of love."

The tightness around his heart softened a little as he shared the memories. "Yeah. He tried. But he had six kids of his own, you know. I was always number seven."

"What happened to your parents?"

The image of a sticky summer night and the uniformed officer sitting across from him tripped into his vision. He blinked and made it disappear just as quickly. "My dad was a cop, too. He and Ma went to a movie one night. On the way home, they stopped for a drink. There was a hold-up. He tried to stop it and..."

"Both of them?" Casey leaned forward and reached across the sofa. Her fingers hovered within inches of his own, but she stopped just short of touching him.

He imagined he could feel the heat radiating out of the tips of her fingers and caressing him. He could easily turn his hand and capture hers, taking the same gentle comfort she had offered last night, but today, for some reason, refused. Maybe she didn't want to lower herself to his level again, and her kind attention was an outpouring of pity rather than genuine interest.

But the internal battle he saw behind the shimmer of tears in her eyes made him rethink his silent accusation. Although curious, he decided to respect whatever caution had made her stop the impulse. He didn't mind pushing and prodding a response out of her, but he didn't want to take. If she didn't offer it willingly, he wouldn't force her to care.

Instead, he stood and carried their plates into the kitchen. He'd long ago come to grips with his parents' deaths. But the loss of what might have been always saddened him at times like this. The lost holiday celebrations. Career milestones unnoticed and unappreciated. The people who touched his life whom his parents would never know.

Standing at the sink, Mitch looked out the back window at the glass-domed pool house surrounded by a barren yard and another granite wall.

A prison, he thought again.

She had probably endured holidays and milestones all alone, too. A woman with all the fire and intelligence Casey possessed shouldn't willingly lock herself behind these walls. An idea formed as Mitch realized the tragic bond he shared with Casey.

He met her in the hallway, en route to the kitchen with their coffee mugs in hand. "Can you see the Plaza from your house?"

"From upstairs." He grabbed the mugs and set them on the trophy shelf beside them. She tilted her head in wary suspicion. "Why?"

Her question made him smile, and smiling felt good. Smiling with *her* felt even better.

He hurried out to the main foyer and stopped at the bottom of the staircase. Casey's curiosity didn't disappoint. She followed moments behind him. "What are you up to?"

"Can you go upstairs?" he asked.

She looked up the carpeted steps. "The doors are closed off and the furniture's covered. But nothing's locked."

He looked down at her, wanting her to tingle with the same anticipation he did, "No, I mean…"

He touched her elbow and she tilted her chin up, her eyes questioning him. "I don't know how else to ask." He tightened his fingers imperceptibly, in case he overstepped the boundaries of their truce and she pulled away. "Can *you* walk up the stairs?"

Her silvery gaze left his. "Oh."

The mute rejection of his idea triggered the edge of his temper. Like a perp fighting against a pair of handcuffs, she tensed. Her eyes flashed fire, and the walls of distrust slammed firmly back into place. But Mitch hadn't survived twenty years on the force by giving up easily.

"We ought to do something to celebrate today, even if we are housebound. Have you ever seen the lighting ceremony?"

Her shoulders rose and fell in a huff of air. "Contrary to what you 'downtown boys' think, some of us rich folks like to celebrate the holidays, too. I've seen it lots of times."

"Watch it with me tonight," he dared her.

"It'll take me until Christmas to get all the way up there."

She was scared. Her brief rebellion was nothing but fear talking. Mitch's temper dissipated in an instant. Overriding her protest, he tucked her hand through the crook of his left elbow and guided her toward the railing. "What a coincidence." He smiled in encouragement. "I'm free until Christmas."

He couldn't tell if she smiled at that or not. All he could see was the top of her head, and feel the tension in her body, as she faced off against the twenty or so steps.

"I don't want you to miss it." She balked once more.

"I won't." He squeezed her hand beneath his. "You won't, either."

He watched with admiration as she squared her shoulders and lifted her chin a fraction. Then he felt her weight on his arm as she raised her leg to the first step. Surprisingly light, the burden felt good. He felt useful again, knowing at that moment, he was the only one who could help her with this. She breathed deeply, then moved to the second step.

Her slow but resolute gait triggered a pang of sympathy in Mitch. He took a simple action like going up the stairs for granted. But Casey had to think about each movement beforehand, where to place her foot, testing her balance before putting her weight on her damaged leg. Mitch kept a slow pace beside her. He briefly considered swinging her up into his arms and carrying her the rest of the way. While he might enjoy the close contact, the rigid determination in her posture prevented him from doing so.

He slowed along with her as she tired near the top step. By then, pride had pushed aside any sympathy. She leaned on him a little more heavily now, but Mitch did nothing more to take this accomplishment away from her.

But when they cleared the landing, he couldn't resist picking her up and swinging her around in his arms. "Yes!" he shouted. "I knew you could do it."

He was as out of breath as Casey when he finally set her down. She fell against him, clutching handfuls of his shirt to steady herself, pressing into him from her thighs to her breasts. He held her like that for a moment, his gaze on her parted lips, their breaths coming in synchronized gasps.

He had to kiss her. If he didn't kiss her soon and get this obsession out of his system, he just might explode.

But then she unwound her fists and pushed some distance between them. How could she not…? Didn't she feel it, too?

Mitch released her and pulled himself up straight, granting her the space she'd requested. He tamped down his desire and buried the hurt the perceived injustice sparked in him. Covering his feelings for her was a remarkably easy habit to fall into.

Jackie had done that to him a lot before her cancer struck. She'd get him hot and achy, needy for a woman's touch. And then she'd pull away from him with some convenient, superficial excuse.

He was too dirty and sweaty after working overnight on a case and he couldn't muss her clothes. He'd been gone so long on an undercover assignment that she needed time to readjust to his schedule. Or she plain old wasn't in the mood.

Mitch knew all the excuses. And he knew how to pretend he wasn't hurt by them. Casey might not be playing him for a fool the way Jackie had. But it seemed obvious, even to an over-the-hill, out-of-practice hired gun like himself that she didn't want him the way he wanted her. Not right now.

Maybe not ever.

She pointed to the far side of the landing. "We have a picture window overlooking the Plaza. Mom used to make us cocoa, and we'd sit up here and watch the lighting ceremony every Thanksgiving." Her sentimental voice was barely a whisper. "You don't want to miss it."

Miss what? He stood in place, a churning mass of raw nerve endings and frustrated desire, watching her follow the balustrade around to a sitting area in front of a group of windows. Even from here, he could see the shadowy skyline of the Plaza buildings, entrepreneur J. C. Nichols's vision of the world's first shopping center, a 1920s mecca of Mediterranean architecture, fountains and high-class stores.

Casey pulled a sheet off a high-backed chair and reached to uncover its mate. In midstretch, she stumbled, grabbed the back of the chair and clutched at her side. Her sharp intake of breath muffled her yelp of pain.

"Casey!" He forgot his own petty needs and dashed to her side. He moved behind her, wrapping his arm around her waist to steady her. "Are you hurt?"

She shook with her pain, breathing hard and unable to speak. He followed her nonverbal cues and discovered her kneading her right fist into the juncture of her right hip and waist. He pushed her hand aside and reached beneath the hem of her sweater. He pressed with his fingertips until he felt a rock-hard knot of muscle near the top of her hip.

"Here?" he asked. "Is this where it hurts?"

She nodded mutely. Mitch dug in with his fingers and massaged the cramp through her black wool slacks. She gasped once and clawed at his hand.

"It's all right, Case. Let me do this."

She nodded again, her own fingers digging into his arm at her waist. She clung to him as though she might not be able to stand on her own. And still Mitch kept working, kneading at the cramp until he felt the knot release and the muscles relax.

Casey sagged against him. He tightened his arm around her and brushed his cheek against her hair, drinking in the delicate fragrance of her. Though his hand had stilled, he left it on her hip, a protective gesture, ready to ward off the pain should it strike her again.

He felt like a beast, so consumed by his own reckless needs that he'd neglected to fully appreciate her struggle. He was so used to defending himself from anyone who might look down on him that he hadn't considered any other reason for her hesitancy in coming up here. He'd discounted her as a snob, or at the very least a woman who was immune to his sorry charms. He'd selfishly thought only of himself when he should have been thinking of her.

He owed Casey his apology for subjecting her to this agony. She'd already earned his respect. Now he hoped he could earn her forgiveness.

"I'm sorry," he breathed into her hair. "I didn't mean to hurt you. I shouldn't have pushed you so hard."

She shook her head. "It's my fault. When I get tired, the muscles in my leg don't work right. I compensate and then I feel it in my hips and back."

Mitch felt rotten. Her pain was his fault. If he hadn't dared her. Hadn't goaded her. Hadn't wanted her so much.

"Mitch, look!" The breathiness in her voice had nothing to do with pain this time. He felt the excitement energizing her body. He looked over the crown of her head and saw the million or more green, red and white lights lining every rooftop up and down the streets of the Plaza. The Christmas lights blazed brightly enough to transform the canopy of dampness in the air into an ethereal fog. "It's like a fairy tale. Thank you."

Mitch watched the transformation in Casey's profile. The lines of pain bracketing her mouth relaxed, and her eyes sparkled with a childlike wonder. In all the years he'd seen the lights go on, he'd never felt this connection. He'd never felt the spirit of the holidays so profoundly as he did at this moment, seeing the spectacle not with his own eyes, but through hers.

It was worth it. The guilt was worth it. He'd trade all his holidays to be here at this moment with this woman, and share the joy that shone so clearly in her expression.

"Happy Thanksgiving," he murmured against her ear.

Then, unable to help himself, he pressed his lips against her neck, nuzzling the warm hollow beneath her ear.

The shudder he felt could have been hers, could have been his own. Her fingers tightened on his arm, drawing his attention to the exquisite weight of her breasts resting there. He nipped at her earlobe, teasing the soft skin beside a pearl button earring. "I want to kiss you, princess."

She twisted her head, angling away from his lips. "Why…why do you call me that?" She stuttered, as though his touch distracted her from forming coherent words.

She wriggled her bottom against him, adjusting her body to the assault of his lips on her neck. Mitch's own thoughts scattered. With his hand on her hip, he pulled her back and held her still, enjoying the rush of heat coursing through him.

"This *is* a fairy tale," he whispered raggedly against the softness of her collar, "and you're the princess."

He could scarcely remember the high-and-mighty impression he first had of her, and now the nickname seemed to fit for entirely different reasons. His answer seemed to please her, adding to the enchantment of the moment. She stretched like a cat, allowing him to dip his head and trace his tongue along her delicate collarbone.

A contented sound, much like purring, rolled deeply in her throat. Mitch splayed his fingers along her rib cage, catching the curve of her breast with his thumb. He felt her breath catch along with his.

"I want to kiss you," he repeated, loving the satiny feel of her skin against his lips, but wanting—no, begging—to taste all of her.

With the briefest nod of consent, she turned her head and lifted her mouth. Still holding her body flush with his, he captured her chin and guided her lips to him.

His tenderest intentions rocketed into oblivion when they finally touched. He pulled her onto her toes and crushed her mouth beneath his. He took advantage of her startled reaction and plunged his tongue inside, devouring her mouth with a hunger too long denied.

Tangy sweet, like the sugar and spice from their dessert. Soft, like floating in the clouds of a dream. And so damn hot he thought he might burst into flames himself.

"Mitch?" His name on her husky voice revealed a combination of panic and frustration.

He turned her in his arms, his hands tunneling into the silken weight of her hair. He gentled his kiss, suckling at the decadent fullness of her lower lip. "I'm sorry," he spoke against her mouth. "I didn't mean to hurt you."

"You didn't." Her eyes opened wide, sparkling as brightly as the lights below them. "I'm just a little out of practice."

He smiled down at her, liking the clash of shy words and bold heat in her eyes. "No way, princess. There's not a damn thing that's not working right on you."

She rewarded him by winding her arms around his waist and stepping closer. She nipped at his lips, tasted him with her tongue. Then she surprised him yet again when she rose up on tiptoe and kissed him full on the mouth.

"Happy Thanksgiving, Mitch. I'm thankful you're here with me."

She dropped back onto her heels and leaned into him, tucking her head beneath his chin. The gesture was more explosive than that kiss, more healing than her words; Mitch loved holding her. Casey burrowed into him as though this was the one place in the world she most wanted to be.

He adjusted his arms around her back to hold her more securely. The frustrated heat in his loins cooled in proportion to the warmth swelling around his heart. This was the one place *he* wanted to be. Standing with her in his arms for as long as she'd let him hold her.

"You're a perfect fit," he whispered, rubbing his chin against the silken weight of her hair. "Perfect."

She shifted and wedged a barely perceptible distance between them. Her shoulders arched back, and he could almost see the cloak of pride settling around her.

"What's wrong?" he asked. She pushed and he released her, severing the last connection between them.

She hugged herself, and he wondered if she felt the same sudden drop in temperature he did. "I really should be turning in. We were up late last night."

Mitch couldn't shut off his emotions so easily. Her ability to do so must come with the uptown chill factor. He raked his fingers through his hair and shook his head. "You blow hot and cold faster than any woman I've known."

Her chin shot up, and he itched to kiss her again and bring her highness back down to the lustful level of mere mortals she'd succumbed to only moments ago. That same beautiful chin quivered, and for a fleeting instant, Mitch considered something more than remembering whom she was with had made her pull away so suddenly.

"Are you all right?" Maybe she was hiding the real extent of her pain.

"I'm just tired. Do you want me to set out the pillows and blankets for you?"

Somewhere between resentment and concern, his detective's curiosity kicked in. Why the sudden brush-off? "I'll get them later. I think I want to watch the lights for a while. You go ahead, though. Unless you need my help?"

"If I can get up the stairs, I can get down them."

Mitch quelled the urge to shake the touch-me-not posture that lifted her regal shoulders. "Good night, then."

"Good night."

Once the tread of her uneven footsteps faded, and the downstairs bedroom door closed behind her, Mitch crossed to the window. He leaned a hand on the frame and looked out at the thousands of people milling around the Plaza, gazing at storefront displays, listening to wandering carolers, celebrating the beginning of the joyous holiday season together.

Together.

Mitch stood above them all and watched. Alone.

With his blood still boiling from Casey's kisses, he rested his forehead against the cold windowpane. How far would she have gone to make her apology for this morning? To console him after hearing about his family?

To the top of the stairs? To the depths of passion?

Passion like hers couldn't be faked. Her temper. That fiery kiss. Those clingy hugs that made him feel stronger, more potent and more necessary than any almost-forty-year-old should. Casey couldn't fake that, could she?

He was a fool. A lonesome, middle-aged, lustful fool.

"Mitch!"

Casey's scream turned the blood in his veins to ice.

"Mitch!"

He ran, taking the stairs four at a time, checking the identifying medallion pinned at his collar, cursing the distance between him and his gun on the mantel. "Casey!"

He slammed into her in the hallway, running to him as he ran to her. He grabbed her by the shoulders, righting her when she swayed back. He literally leaned her against the wall and bent his knees to put himself at eye level with her.

"What is it, sweetheart? What happened?"

The endearment slipped out without evaluation or notice. The wild storm in her eyes and the deathly pallor of her skin frightened him more than he cared to admit. But her expression was clear; she was with him in the present. She wasn't flashing back to the attack. He cupped her cheek in his hand and forced her to focus on him. "Talk to me, Casey."

"In there." She pointed to her room. "In my dresser. I was getting ready for bed."

Before she'd finished, he ran through her door. The windows were sealed in both her bedroom and the adjoining bath. When he came back, she'd joined him at the foot of her bed. The second drawer of her dresser stood ajar. Her nightgown hung over the front edge. And on the floor was a brown envelope whose contents had been scattered.

Fearing the horror that he'd seen etched in Casey's pale face, Mitch knelt down and examined the papers littered there.

"My God. How the hell did he get in here?" The string of curses that followed was as much for his own carelessness in watching over her as for the bastard whose message came through loud and clear from the depths of Casey's lingerie drawer.

Pasted to the plain white paper like the mismatched pieces of a jigsaw puzzle was a newspaper clipping of Casey. Judging by the faint yellow tinge of the newsprint, he figured the photo to be about ten years old. He could make out her Kansas Jayhawks jacket over a dark swimsuit. She waved to an audience and held up a medal that was draped around her neck. The body in the picture showed a young, lean, vibrant Casey.

But her face had been sliced to ribbons.

And beneath the photo, in plain Courier type, was another skewed line of the nursery rhyme.

"This is the maid, all forlorn, who died in the house that Jack built."

Chapter Six

Casey huddled in her chair, staring at the unread journal in front of her. Mitch's lieutenant, Joe Hendricks, stood across the desk from her, charming his way through a difficult phone call. She controlled the restless urge to crawl right out of her skin through the ceaseless, silent tapping of her left foot on the carpet.

"I know it's the holiday, Elliot. But from what you told me about your wife's cooking, you shouldn't mind running down those files for me."

Casey concentrated on the page number in the top right corner, trying not to see two more detectives walk past the library door.

Joe laughed at something. "Yeah. I'd rather check out your morgue than mine."

Morgue? The voice of paranoia inched its way into the back of her mind, stretching her fragile patience to the limit. She'd cooperated with every request made of her so far that evening. She'd been ordered to stay inside. *Inside* the home Emmett had invaded. She'd been sent from one room to the other, always in the company of one of the detectives, always out of the path of Mitch's investigation. He wanted to piece together Emmett's trail, retrace her own activities throughout the day and find out exactly when and how Emmett had gotten in.

The forced inactivity reminded her of the month of training she'd had to miss in college because of a torn shoulder muscle. She'd hated watching her teammates improving their times, building their endurance, sharpening their form, while she sat on the bench throwing out towels. She knew it was for her own good, but doing nothing meant accomplishing nothing.

And oh, how she itched to do something, anything, right now to help put an end to this terror, this not knowing. In college, the team doctor had assured her she'd heal and she could return to swimming, given enough time. But with Emmett Raines, she didn't know if she could live long enough to get past his impact on her life.

The front door closed with a solid thud, startling her.

She didn't realize how loudly her foot had hit the chair leg until she saw Joe cover the mouthpiece of the receiver. "Whoa. Hold on there."

"Hold on to what? I'm not doing anything!" She slapped the journal down on top of her desk. Joe's unblinking glance alerted her to just how strident she must have sounded. She reined in her fear and frustration and sank back into the chair. "Sorry. I didn't meant to interrupt your call."

"Not a problem."

She could see the hesitancy in his posture. She waved aside his concern and forced a smile. "Reporters, I take it?"

"An old friend." Joe accepted the diversion, though his watchful gaze never left her. "He's someone I trust. I've handed him a few scoops over the years in exchange for his discretion during investigations."

Casey didn't remember any reporters whom she'd describe as discreet. In her experience, they all wanted a new angle on a tired old story, and would pump her and plague her until they'd stolen one of the few crumbs left of her privacy.

"If you say so," she answered under her breath, not really believing him, but unwilling to argue the point.

"Miss Maynard?" Joe was nothing if not diligent in his watch over her. "You want me to call Mitch?"

"No!" Of all the things teetering her routine world out of balance that night, Mitch topped the list. He'd bludgeoned his way through her defenses, granting her the memory of an enchanted evening, reducing her pain with the strength of his hands and kissing her with a hungry abandon that short-circuited her own doubts and self-control.

He made her feel again. And feeling hurt. All those unused nerve pathways she'd closed off to shield herself from the loneliness of her existence had sprung to life again under his touch, his kiss, his desire. Her efforts to recover her defenses left her feeling out of order as he breathed life into parts of her that she'd purposefully turned off long ago.

Nearly two hours had passed since she'd opened that envelope, and she'd given up all hope of her life returning to normal. The impotent rage and crippling vulnerability she'd felt at that moment had receded to a manageable level. But the memory of Mitch's words—"I want to kiss you"—the heat of his touch, the addictive strength of his embrace, still parked along her frayed nerves like electrical relays overwhelmed by a lightning strike.

"No, I don't need Mitch." But she *did* need to do something. This waiting was intolerable. Mitch's team had taken over her home, searching it inside and out, pushing her safely to one side—out of harm's way, out from underfoot and out of contention for being in charge of her own life.

"Would you like some coffee?" It wasn't much, but at least she could keep her hands busy and make some contribution toward organizing the chaos. She rolled her chair and stood. "I have a feeling tonight is going to last longer than anyone planned."

Joe smiled, relaxing his vigilance over her at last. "Hey, if you're offering, I'm a taker."

"I warn you, I make it pretty strong."

"We're cops," Joe chuckled. "You can't make it too strong for us."

Casey appreciated his gentle humor. She felt a pang of guilt that she'd taken him away from his family on Thanksgiving. But she discovered she was equally grateful to have his steady, good-natured presence around this evening. It was like having a friend, she thought. She could use more friends like Joe.

And fewer undermining distractions like Mitch.

Feeling more in control now that she'd made up her mind to do something, she saluted him. "Mississippi-mud coffee coming right up."

Joe shook his finger at her as she walked past. "Plenty of sugar, too. I don't mind if it burns out my stomach, but I want to have a good time doing it."

"You got it." Her face relaxed into a genuine smile.

Joe returned to his conversation with the reporter. He was trying to track down the source of the newspaper clipping from Emmett. Casey had given him a general timeline for when the photograph in question was taken. But she'd have to refer to her own scrapbooks to find the exact source, and most of her swimming memorabilia had been locked away in the unused wing of the house to gather dust and be forgotten. Joe's connection at the *Kansas City Star* offered a quicker way to find some answers.

Though the kitchen wasn't her usual territory, at least the solitude allowed her a moment to drop the veneer of civility she'd put on to deal with the three detectives who had descended on her home within thirty minutes of Mitch's phone call. While she stood at the sink, rinsing her hands, she watched three beams of light work their way through the back toward the pool house. The interior lights reflecting off the kitchen window prevented her from seeing the bodies attached to those flashlights, adding an eerie specter to the search. When two of the lights turned toward the house, she ducked away, unable to shake the sensation of being stalked again.

Goose bumps prickled along her skin at the unstoppable memory of red-and-blue lights blinking around her while paramedics rolled the gurney she'd been strapped onto inside the emergency room of St. Luke's Hospital. Numbed by painkillers and struggling for consciousness, she'd been blinded by the glaring spotlights of the press snapping gruesome photos of the judge's mutilated daughter.

Casey's stomach heaved. She grabbed the counter to anchor herself in this world and closed her eyes to forcefully block out the waking nightmare. "Stay in the moment," she chided herself, repeating her trauma counselor's mantra.

She peered through slit lashes and focused on the coffeemaker, brewing and bubbling. The normal little sounds of the water percolating through the filter pattered over her eardrums in a quieting massage. "Stay in the moment." Gradually, she loosened her grip and shifted her focus to the knife she'd used to cut the pie earlier. Without looking up to the window again, she slid over to the sink and washed the knife under the hot water. Soon, she recognized her ability to breathe again. "Stay in the moment."

The back door to the garage opened and closed. She heard stomping feet and the murmur of voices checking off a list of instructions. "After Merle gets the tunnel boarded up, post a guard."

"Yes, sir."

When the detectives entered the kitchen, the conversation stopped. Casey turned off the water and reached for a dish towel.

"Where's Joe?"

Mitch's low voice sliced through the air behind her. Her hand jerked and the knife clattered into the sink.

"In the moment," she whispered to herself, breathing in through her nose and out through her mouth. "On the phone in the library."

There. Her voice sounded fairly normal. She reached for the knife.

"He's not supposed to leave you alone." His growly pitch skidded through her. She fisted her hand around the knife handle and turned on him.

"What difference does it make?" Her pitch sounded strident even to her own ears. "*You* were here with me all day long, and he *still* got to me."

"Casey…"

Her fists shook with the avalanche of pent-up fears and fury crashing through her. "You're here to protect me, but you didn't. Steven didn't. You didn't."

"You don't know how sorry I am about that."

"Sorry!"

His head inclined the slightest fraction, and the compact female detective with him left the room. "I screwed up today. I admit it. But I'm taking steps to correct that."

"Correct it? He was in my room." She punctuated each

angry, tearful word with the punch of her hand in the air. Mitch's narrow gaze darkened but she didn't heed the warning. "We were in the house, and he was in my room."

The distance between them closed in a rush. She felt the pinch at her wrist before recognizing the clamp of Mitch's hand. He twisted her arm. Her fingers snapped open, and he shook the knife free from her grasp.

A jolt of pain echoed in her wrist moments after Mitch released her, moments long enough to clear her mind and understand that she had advanced on him with a knife in her hand. The similarity to Emmett's favorite style of attack sickened her.

"I didn't mean to threaten you." Her toneless apology hung in the silence of the room.

"I know." Mitch picked up the knife and returned it safely to the cutting block behind him. "I have to tell you that that's a lot healthier reaction than the ice princess you've been showing us this evening. My butt deserves to be royally chewed. But you've been so sweet and polite that I was worried about you. Now that the fire's back, I feel a lot better."

She recognized his attempt to divert her attention but she couldn't work up the will to rise to his challenge. She turned to the sink, shocked at her actions, raw with emotion. "I'm sorry."

"Don't you dare apologize for that bastard. You have every right to feel the way you feel. Every right to take it out on me."

She sensed when he moved to her side. She smelled the winter on his coat. Those broad shoulders she had instinctively run to earlier blocked her peripheral vision. She wanted to deny his assertion, to seek the shelter of his arms once more. But an emotional wariness kept her on edge.

He *had* failed her. As safe as he could make her feel, as alive as he could make her feel, he still had failed her. "He was in my house. In my room. In my things."

She spoke of Emmett's violation as if it explained everything inside her. But it was an explanation Mitch seemed to understand. "I'm sorry I let Raines get to you. I don't like the idea of you being afraid."

"Can't help it. A madman's on the loose." Her shaky laugh bordered on tears.

A moment of shared silence passed before he reached for her hand. He pressed it between his long blunt fingers, rubbing the soreness from her wrist and kneading in warmth by brushing his thumbs along the backs of her knuckles. She reached with her left hand to stop the hypnotic comfort, but he captured that hand, too. "Your skin's like ice."

Casey watched him work, soothed by the contrast of callused fingers and a gentle touch. "So Emmett got in through the pool-house tunnel?" She needed to know. Knowing might help her understand and move on.

Mitch never paused in his healing ministrations. He answered with a cop's blunt finesse. "Some of the boards Ben put up had been pried off. He followed the sealed-off hallway beneath those stairs Frankie told us about. Came in through the closet of your room. I don't think he was ever in the main part of the house."

"What sealed-off hallway?" She pulled her hands away and stepped back, ignoring his tacked-on reassurance.

"I thought you knew all the crooks and crannies of this old house."

"The stairs hidden behind the kitchen wall go up to the second floor. There's nothing running along the first floor." She scanned the remodeled kitchen, wondering in what other warrens Emmett could be hiding.

Her suspicions were reflected in Mitch's voice. "Merle and I retraced the path from your closet."

Casey hugged her arms together, feeling the chill Mitch's hands had dispelled sink back into her bones. "I want out of here. I don't want to be in this death trap anymore."

"I'll get you out of here tonight, I promise." His big hands closed over her shoulders. "As soon as the area is secured, we're out of here. I'll leave Joe in charge to supervise the crime-scene team."

She dug her fingers into the front of his coat, tugging at him, pleading with him to see that she couldn't take another moment in this haven turned hell. "Why can't you take me now? Why can't we just drive away from this place and lose ourselves in the countryside? Why can't we find a hotel?"

His grip tightened, shaking aside her flare of panic. "We're not leaving here until I have someplace safe to take you. I have friends working on that now."

"What am I supposed to do in the meantime? Just wait for you and your friends? I've waited for seven years to feel safe! I don't..."

"Princess." That gravelly deep voice silenced her. The sound drew her attention to his mouth. Firm. Male. A devilish distraction almost more inviting than the promise of safety. "I'll keep you safe. But I need you to believe in me."

When she realized his intention, she should have pulled away. Common sense and self-preservation should have made her push against him and stop this.

Instead, she curled her fingers into the lapels of his coat and held on as his mouth closed over hers. His lips brushed hers, and when she didn't resist, he rewarded her with the soft stroke of his tongue. As fierce and needy as that kiss upstairs had been, this one was gentle and giving, offering comfort and peace, making a tender request for her trust. She clutched his coat and tried to give him that faith he needed.

"Taylor! What the hell are you doing to my girl!"

She jerked away. Mitch stiffened and angled himself between her and the source of the intrusive voice that had shattered the sweet reverie they'd shared.

"Jimmy?" She recognized the voice, though his appearance seemed out of context with the rest of her wild night.

"I can report later, sir. Casey has a lot to deal with right now."

His answer was more right than he could possibly know. Her emotional roller-coaster ride tonight had as much to do with him as it did with Emmett's graphic note.

And she had no one to blame but herself for allowing that pointless attraction to get out of hand. She scooted past the defensive wall of his shoulders and hurried across the kitchen.

"It's good to see you." She wrapped her arms around Jimmy's waist and pressed her face into the pleated front of his tuxedo. "I'm glad you're here."

"Cassandra." He wrapped an arm around her shoulders and patted her back. "I understand there's been some trouble."

"Emmett was here. He found the old tunnel and snuck into my room while we were upstairs."

The material in his fine-cut wool coat smelled of cognac and expensive cigars. She wanted to bury herself in his paternal embrace and drive longings for Mitch's brand of comfort out of her head, but he pulled her around to his side and tucked her beneath his arm. "This is how you protect her?"

She followed his dark gaze across the room and met the formidable fortress of Mitch. He stood with his fingers splayed at his hips, coat pulled back, holster and badge reflecting the fluorescent glow of the kitchen light. She felt her uncle shift his stance to match the challenge in Mitch's posture.

What was going on? she wondered. Weren't they both cops on the same force? Weren't they both on the same side? Her side?

She squeezed Jimmy's waist where she clung to him. "I think things are under control for now."

"I assigned you to do a job, Taylor," Jimmy went on as if she hadn't spoken. "Not to botch it. You are aware that your performance is being monitored with regards to the January promotion?"

Mitch ignored the taunt. He also ignored her attempt to intervene. "Do you know what day this is, Commissioner?" he asked.

"It's the day you nearly got written up for insubordination."

"Jimmy!" Casey unwound her arms and stepped away, only now aware of the spectators gathering in the doorway behind them. Mitch's detectives, Joe Hendricks, Ginny Rafferty, Merle Banning and...

"Iris."

Her uncle's assistant wore a mink coat that made her look more like a date than Jimmy's office manager. A frown marred the perfection of the fiftyish blonde's smooth complexion. "James was worried about you when he received the message at the governor's reception. He excused himself almost immediately. Are you all right?"

Casey nodded. "It was just a note. Emmett's toying with us. He doesn't want to be seen just yet."

A spark of realization played through her head, but with

the tension in the room, she couldn't quite put her finger on the significance of that newly discovered knowledge.

"Is that where you've been this evening, Commissioner?" Mitch's low-pitched question brought her attention back to the kitchen. "Instead of spending the holiday with your family? Or even calling to see if she's all right? Casey seems easy for you to forget."

"I'm working today, Taylor. Lobbying for funds, if it's any of your business," answered Jimmy.

"James, the governor is waiting."

Casey watched Iris's gloved hand slip between them to rest on Jimmy's arm.

"Detective Banning, did you let the commissioner and Ms. Webster in at the front gate?" asked Mitch, his eyes never leaving Jimmy.

"No, sir."

Mitch moved forward, punctuating every other word with a defiant step. "Then how did you get up to the house, sir?"

"I have a key card to the estate. How else could I check on Cassandra's welfare?"

Mitch stopped just a few feet away, matching her uncle's stance like opposing linemen with Casey caught in the middle.

Caught in the middle, but unnoticed.

"Mitch," she warned, feeling the surge in temper from both sides.

"How many of those cards do you have?" he asked. "I thought you gave me yours to check here on Tuesday."

"What are you implying?" Jimmy's clenched jaw barely moved.

Iris spoke, her bright voice a jarring intrusion. "We keep a spare in the safe at work, for emergencies just like this."

"You were expecting something like this?" probed Mitch. "And you didn't see fit to tell me?"

"If you did your job properly, there wouldn't be any need to explain whereabouts of keys to the estate." He leaned toward Mitch, forcing Casey to step aside. "I gave you a chance to prove yourself with this assignment, and you screwed up. I shouldn't have to back you up...."

"Enough!" Casey yelled. She pulled up to her full five feet seven inches and jabbed a finger at Jimmy. "Your concern for my welfare is touching." Sarcasm drizzled off her tongue in the succinctly implied accusation. "Go back to your party. Since you're not here to see me, I don't need anybody else around to worry about."

Jimmy's jaw dropped open, and for once, the would-be politician was speechless. Mitch relaxed his stance and nodded toward the hallway. "You heard the lady. She doesn't want you here."

Casey spun around, furious to wipe that cocky self-assurance from Mitch. "And you..." She poked him in the chest. He actually retreated a step, his eyes wide with surprise. "This petty little standoff isn't even about me. Don't you ever speak for me again! I have a mind of my own. I'm a prisoner of my body and nothing more. I'm perfectly capable of fighting my own battles."

She sucked in a reviving breath and let it out in a rush, spent yet energized by finally giving vent to her anger. In a much calmer, saner voice, and fully aware that she had the attention of everyone in the room, she excused herself. "You two can duke it out if you want, but I've had enough of being coddled and set aside for one night."

"I didn't mean..."

"Cassandra..."

She ignored both men, shoving her way between them into the hallway. Once she was alone, she slowed her pace and breathed easier. She swiped a hand back through her hair and imagined her mother's voice, admonishing her for losing her temper. But then she smiled as she imagined her father giving a secret wink to congratulate her for standing her ground. With that rare pleasant thought to sustain her, she headed for the library.

She ended up at the windows, looking out over the desolate yard lit by security lanterns that had failed to live up to their name. She rubbed her arms, feeling a chill from within and without, despite the sweater she wore.

How could she have come so far and still be so dishonest with herself? She acknowledged her fears of the world but avoided dealing with them by hiding behind walls of iron and stone. Ranking so far down the list of Jimmy's priorities hurt, but she made excuses for him because he was the only family she had left.

And she'd sworn she would never drop her guard with a man and seek out his kisses as though he could really care. But she'd lost her perspective with Mitch tonight, set herself up for humiliation. Her life might be spinning beyond her control, but she could answer for her heart. She had no business desiring to be kissed and held or anything more. The painful reality of a man waking up one morning and finding he'd been cheated by caring for her was one pain she could avoid.

No man need ever learn the truth of all her disfiguring shortcomings. She might be forced to give up control of her life to Mitch—for the time being.

But she could never give him control of her heart.

"Is it safe to come in?" She steeled her resolve against the seductive timbre of Mitch's voice.

When she faced him, she saw the swagger in his earlier posture had been replaced with the slumping shoulders of fatigue. She tamped down the swell of compassion for the toll his long hours had taken on him. She didn't have to make his job more difficult; she just had to keep herself from caring. "Did Jimmy and Iris leave?"

"A few minutes ago. I sent Merle to lock up behind them."

Joe stuck his head in the doorway. "Everything's set to go when you are, old man."

"Thanks, Joe." The lieutenant bustled on to his destination, and Mitch stepped farther into the room, encouraged if not welcomed by Casey's cool avoidance of his question. "I asked Ginny to pack a few things in a bag for you."

"Pack? Am I finally going somewhere?"

"A safe house. Like I should have insisted on from day one."

"Set up by your friends?" He absorbed the barb from her tongue as if he deserved the punishment.

"Friends who aren't cops. So maybe you'll trust them."

The weary lines etched beside his handsome mouth made her regret her taunt. "I want to trust you."

"But you don't," he stated flatly. "Your choice. But I'm still gonna do my job." He breathed deeply and offered up a smile devoid of humor. "We're doing things my way now. I'm tired of playing the commissioner's game."

"My life is not a game."

"Exactly."

Casey debated the stark agreement he'd made. She wanted to avoid getting hurt by Mitch. But she also wanted to stay alive. "Where will you take me?"

"My turf." He swept his dark gaze around the room, and she recalled his derisive comments about anything *uptown*. "I'm asking you to give up the perks and frills of this mausoleum and come home with me."

"You'd endanger your family."

"The people I call my family are a lot tougher and more street-smart than you or 'Uncle Jimmy' ever will be. Uncle Sid runs a butcher shop, and he smells like his work when he comes home." The flash of gold in his eyes warned her he still had some fight left in him—and dared her to find some fault with an honest man making an honest living. "But he damn sure remembers where I am on the holidays. And he doesn't send somebody else to look after his own when they're in trouble."

His words hurt. The implication that she would turn her nose up at his adoptive family's working-class roots hurt. Did he really think she was such a heartless ice princess? But Casey lifted her chin, moving beyond his groundless intimation without defending herself. Maybe if Mitch believed she belonged to the same snobbish class as his late wife, he'd be less inclined to offer her his most personal protection. But still, his home?

"I don't know," she said hesitantly. "I don't want to stay here, but…"

"I'm not giving you a choice."

So she hadn't really put him in his place, not completely. His authoritative tone rankled. But then she remembered her advice to herself. He could barge in and take over her life. But not her heart, not if she didn't let him.

Maybe her fate was in her own hands after all.

"I'll go help Ginny pack."

MITCH ADJUSTED his navy paisley tie and leaned back in his chair to scan his surroundings. The First Cattlemen's Bank of downtown Kansas City was a pricey affair. The leather upholstery and brass appointments spoke of old money and tradition. The building itself towered several stories higher than his own outlet bank, and he suspected clients had to be second-or third-generation customers before even being considered for a loan.

Not the kind of place to welcome a working-class kid making his own way in the world. His badge had gotten him in the door, and his rank in the department had gotten him a meeting without an appointment. But Mitch sensed he would have been treated as a tourist, a lost soul to be hurried out with a polite smile if he had come in as a client instead of a crime investigator.

The Cattlemen's Bank was the sort of place he expected Commissioner Reed to keep an account. Casey would feel right at home here. She had more class in the tilt of her chin than all of these pin-striped suits combined. He'd bet next month's paycheck that the bank officers on the floor would be falling over themselves to wait on her if she walked through the door.

So why did the idea of all those men showering attention on Casey make his gut tighten into a knot? He'd left her sleeping in his condo—in his bed—long before the sun was up that morning. With Merle Banning and his oldest cousin, Brett Taylor, standing watch over her, it had been easier to leave and get some serious investigating done instead of pretending he could sleep on the sofa in the living room.

The size of the makeshift bed wasn't the problem this time. Everything in the rambling warehouse his family's money and hands had renovated to help save their neighborhood from decay was built to fit Mitch's proportions. But the soft snoring of Casey's exhausted sleep had kept him awake in the dark hours of the moonless night, remembering the jolt of pure predatory longing that had engulfed him when she paraded out in one of his flannel shirts asking if Ginny had packed her robe.

Unaware of the effect her long, lithe body had on him, she'd worn the shirt buttoned up to the neck, and the tails hung down past her thighs. The soft cotton swallowed her up, adding to the air of vulnerability reflected in her translucent skin and shimmering halo of flame-gold hair. He wanted to swallow her up in the same way. Carry her to his bed. Find the curves hinted at beneath the shirt with his own hands.

He must have said something or changed his expression because suddenly she blushed. He thought it was prudish embarrassment at first. But then he realized she'd turned to hide her braced leg from him. His initial anger toward the unspoken standards of this world that made her assume she had to hide her handicap from him became a sadness that overwhelmed him. Sadness that she didn't trust him. Not with her life, not with her body, not with the inevitable fire burning between them.

He liked the idea of her at his place. Sleeping in his shirt. Trading words and kisses with him. He didn't like knowing it was a temporary illusion. She would never fit into his world, nor he into hers.

"Downtown boys and Plaza princesses just don't mix." He muttered the cruel reminder Jackie had once used on him when he'd confronted her on her affair. By the end of the day, she had moved out of the suburban home he'd bought for her and into the trendy brownstone she shared with her lover.

Despite his own best advice, he wanted Casey. Not just to snuggle beside him. But under him, skin to skin. Around him. Holding him. Loving him.

"Detective Taylor?" a bank officer said, interrupting Mitch's thoughts.

He breathed a silent curse at the intrusion and immersed himself into the thing he did best. The one thing Casey distrusted more than any other.

Being a cop.

Chapter Seven

Schooling his opinion of the bank and its penchant for making him wait, Mitch rose to meet the assistant loan officer.

"It's Captain Taylor," he corrected, shaking the man's callused but manicured hand. *Odd,* he thought. Either this guy was as new to the Cattlemen's spit-and-polish world as he was, or the guy had some distinctly unbankerlike hobbies.

"My apologies. I'm David Zimmer. My secretary said you wanted to ask a few questions?" He swept out his arm in a friendly gesture, inviting Mitch to retake his seat.

Mitch unbuttoned his suit coat and sat. Mr. Zimmer was a man of indiscriminate age. With his eyes obscured by thick wire-framed glasses, he might have been thirty or he might have been fifty. His neat blond hair and fit, wiry frame revealed no further clues about the man.

Mitch allowed his impressions to sink in without evaluating them. "I understand you were in charge of the bank's Christmas charity mailing this year?"

"Yes. I drew up the list. Approved the copy of the letter that went out. Coordinated the staff. I even stuffed a few envelopes myself this year. The flu has been going around this month, and we've been shorthanded from time to time.''

Mitch pulled out a notepad and jotted a few bits of information. ''Did you have the flu?''

''I was out a few days ago,'' answered Zimmer. ''The mailing went out while I was gone.''

''When you were stuffing envelopes, did you have contact with anyone else? A customer, perhaps?''

Zimmer reached for his calendar and studied the dates. Mitch crossed his right foot over his left knee and studied Zimmer. The guy might be new to this position at the bank, but he certainly wasn't new to the covert skill of smiling and appearing helpful on the surface, while keeping answers to himself. Like a seasoned politician, Zimmer already knew the ins and outs of telling a cop what he wanted to hear without revealing anything more than he had to.

''Let's see.'' Zimmer tapped the calendar with his index finger. ''Monday I did have an odd man come in. He applied for a loan, but I had to turn him down. He didn't give us enough background to run a credit check on him.''

''Is this related to the mailing?''

The banker shrugged. ''Well, I was working on it at my desk when he came in. He was polite enough on the surface, but very sarcastic. I considered calling security, but he wasn't really a threat to anyone. I did leave my desk for a few minutes to consult with Ron.''

Mitch reviewed his notes. ''Ron Cambridge, the chief loan officer?''

Zimmer set the calendar down and corrected him. ''He's in charge of personal loans.''

''Do you have the applicant's name?''

Zimmer thumbed through his appointment book and stopped when he found the information. ''John Darling.''

Mitch remembered Casey's description of Raines's *modus operandi*. John Darling might not have been John Darling at all, but Raines in disguise. He copied down the name, intending to put Ginny on a search of the missing-persons list to see if any link turned up. He sensed the limited flow of information here had reached its end. But he had to ask. "Could I see your records on Darling?"

"You'd have to request that information through official channels, I'm afraid."

Afraid of covering your butt, thought Mitch. Out loud, he asked, "Do you think he might have tampered with any of those envelopes while you were away from your desk?"

Zimmer gave it some thought. "I suppose he could. Though I don't know that he did. Those envelopes weren't sealed until they reached the post office. There were any number of opportunities for someone to tamper with the mailing, as you say."

Mitch nodded a perfunctory agreement. Zimmer was right. He might be chasing loose ends here, but somehow Raines had gotten a hold of that request for money from Casey and added a much more sinister message of his own. Was it cold calculation or dumb luck that had allowed Raines to make that connection with her?

Somehow Mitch didn't believe it was the latter. He wasn't through investigating the Cattlemen's Bank, but he'd had enough of Junior Pinhead. Mitch rose from his chair, pocketed his notebook and pen and reached for his overcoat. He pulled a business card from his jacket and handed it to Zimmer.

"If you think of anything else suspicious from the past week, give me a call. In the meantime, I'll send a sketch artist over for you to give a description of Mr. Darling."

Zimmer stood, as well. "I hope you'll convey our regards to Miss Maynard. I feel partly responsible for any discomfort she might have experienced.''

Discomfort? Terrified beyond rational thought and too damn proud to admit it was a more apt description of Casey's reaction to the two messages she'd received.

Out loud he gave the perfunctory policeman's answer. ''Ms. Maynard is holding up fine.''

Zimmer smiled a polite polished grin, and extended his hand across the desk. ''Glad to hear it. I'll do what I can to help.''

Mitch kept his opinion of Zimmer's helpfulness to himself, shook the man's hand and headed toward the elevator doors. Once inside the solitude of the descending car, Mitch gave voice to his sarcastic thoughts. Rule number six in his private code book was that a smart cop didn't trust anyone with a line as smooth as Zimmer's.

''And, Junior, I don't trust you.''

He was on to something here. The prickle at the base of his neck warned him that something was wrong at the Cattlemen's Bank. It was just too soon to tell what. Mitch was a patient man. He could wait until the answers came to him.

He just prayed Casey had enough time to wait.

THE ARCHITECTURAL SHOWPIECES of Kansas City's skyline gave way to vacant lots and abandoned buildings riddled with gang graffiti, vandalism and neglect. Mitch turned his Jeep north two blocks and drove into the promise of the future. Local residents and generous benefactors were slowly but steadily reclaiming some of the oldest parts of the city by reopening marketplaces, turning old homes into historical sites or selling bricks from razed buildings to lay a safe walkway through a new park. Ethnic neighborhoods laid to waste by crime and poverty were being transformed back into the safe streets his parents had walked as children. A garish casino docked on the Missouri River a few blocks to the north worried Mitch with its massive influx of money and tourists, but for now he was content to help rebuild one block at a time his own little corner of the city he loved.

He drove into the parking garage beneath his condo, braking a moment to make eye contact with the uniformed officer crossing the sidewalk behind him. The youngest of his male cousins, Joshua Taylor nodded and continued on his beat. It had required a bit of string-pulling to get Josh reassigned to the old neighborhood, but knowing his allies gave Mitch a small assurance of Casey's safety that he hadn't been able to give her down on the Plaza.

He punched the garage door shut behind him and killed the engine, rubbing his hand down his weary face. He needed a shave, a hot shower and about ten hours of uninterrupted sleep. He probably looked too scruffy to present himself to the classy lady upstairs.

One of his youngest memories as a child was of his mother greeting his father with a kiss and a hug every time he came home from work, always thankful he'd arrived safely, never minding the sweat and dirt, or sometimes even the blood, on his clothes. During the first few months of his own marriage, Jackie had greeted him that way. Then one night he came through the door, reached for her and was treated to a stiff-armed rebuff and the command to shower and change before he could touch her. When his uniform had changed to a suit and tie, the edict remained the same.

Not good enough to be welcomed in his own home.

By the end of the second year, she wasn't home at all for him to even try to pass muster and earn her kiss.

"Hell." Mitch cursed on a soul-weary sigh and picked

up the briefcase on the seat beside him. He'd gotten along fine without a woman to welcome him for nearly five years. Casey might have resigned herself to staying at his place, but only a fool would waste time wishing a woman like her would open her arms to a man like him.

On the elevator ride up to the second floor, Mitch put on his captain's face. He had plenty of things to worry about besides his own needs, like the fact he'd spent the entire day working on the Raines case at the expense of every other project at the Fourth Precinct. He checked his watch—9:30 p.m. He'd put in one hell of a long day, filled with facts and hunches, without one solitary sensible motive to tie any of them together.

Mitch turned the key in the lock and pushed the door open to the peal of laughter. Loud, colorful, off-key laughter. He hesitated at the unexpected sound, and the door was swept out of his grasp.

"About time you showed up, cousin." A man built like Mitch, just as broad but a few inches taller, ushered him in and locked the door behind him. Brett Taylor might not be a cop, but he put the needs of his family first. A call from Mitch was all it took to earn Brett's allegiance to Casey. Brett slapped his hand on Mitch's shoulder. "She's cleaning us out. There's got to be something illegal in what she's doing."

"You mean Casey?" He deposited his coat and bag in the hall closet.

"Is there another woman here?" Brett grinned at Mitch's consternation. "Hold on to your wallet, and don't believe a thing she says when she bats those innocent eyes at you."

He followed Brett into the dining room. Just like those times he entered the staff break room unannounced, everything went abruptly quiet. Mitch glanced at Casey, but saw nothing innocent in the stormy smoke of her eyes. Her cheeks were flushed with laughter, and the expression she wore revealed an openness, a reckless abandon that hit him in the gut and heated his body with a matching recklessness he hadn't felt since his teenage years. It was the same look she'd had when she watched the Plaza lights. The same look that turned his hard-edged resolve into dust.

But in a single blink she changed, and he recognized the cautious guard she erected between them to put him at a distance and keep him in his place. Staving off the answering irritation, he turned his attention to a pile of pennies, dimes and quarters in the middle of the table.

"Taking up gambling, Joe?" He directed his question to the man sitting next to Casey.

Joe threw his five cards facedown on top of the money and pushed his chair back. "Giving it up." He winked at Casey. "Said she hadn't played since college. Don't believe her. She's a ringer."

Casey smiled back, a broad, beautiful smile that Mitch had never seen directed at him. "It's just penny-ante poker. Would you feel better if I promised to donate my winnings to charity?"

"Only if you make me your charity."

Laughter erupted again. The sting of exclusion unraveled the frayed edges of Mitch's patience. He picked up the stack of discards and slung them into the pot. "Am I the only one here who remembers what's at stake—Casey's life?"

The deafening pall that followed hurt even his own ears.

"Lighten up," Brett warned him. "Nobody's forgotten anything. The neighborhood watch is on full alert, and she's had one of us with her all day."

"Relax, old man." Joe stood and crossed around the

table and pointed to his watch. "The rest of us kicked off work about six. I expected you sooner to relieve me."

"I got hung up going through some reports. I read three different versions of Raines's description from eyewitness testimony. I found out the laundry worker he killed in Jeff City had two kids. And the gate at Casey's estate showed no signs of tampering. Raines is no electronics expert, so he had to have a key and codes to get in. Every key's accounted for except for one. And getting a judge to sign a search warrant for the commissioner's office safe is about as easy as securing enough funding to run the precinct. If you want a break, you'll have to get in line." He sounded like a gruff tyrant, but Joe knew him better than that.

"Not a problem. My in-laws are still in town, so I don't mind putting in the extra hours. You look worn-out." He thumbed over his shoulder. "She's holding up just fine. It seems you're the one who needs a break. You eat anything today?"

A chair scraped across the wooden floor, diverting his focus to Casey. His outburst was directly responsible for the pallor that turned her rosy cheeks to alabaster. Guilt had a funny way of cooling his temper.

"You think Jimmy is involved in some kind of cover-up?"

He'd already revealed more than he should have in front of her. Voicing his doubts now couldn't make her opinion of him any worse. "I think this case stinks. From square one, the commissioner put me on a wild-goose chase. Hell, Casey, you're not even in my jurisdiction, and he called *me* to check on you."

"Maybe he trusted you." Her soft statement cut through him with the precision of the knife she'd unconsciously threatened him with last night.

"I don't know if he's up to anything," he answered, his

frustration spent, his regret kicking in. "But I know that too many things don't add up. There's not even a logical reason for Raines to come after you in the first place."

"But he did."

Mitch had lost his parents at the age of eight. He'd survived a tough neighborhood, a broken marriage and the loss of the woman he'd once loved to cancer. But he'd never felt more helpless, more inadequate than he did at this moment, looking into the bleak reflection in Casey's eyes. "I know. We're going to find out why and we're going to catch him."

"So you've said." She picked up her cane and limped toward the kitchen, shoulders back, chin held high. "If it's okay for me to be alone now for a few minutes, I'd rather not be in here. I'll heat up that stew your Aunt Martha sent over. None of us have eaten much today."

When the connecting door swung shut behind her, Joe spoke. "Sit."

"Is this lecture going to hurt much?" Mitch sat, loosening his tie and unbuttoning his collar. Joe and Brett took the two chairs opposite him. While he relaxed on the outside, inside he braced himself for the inquisition he knew would follow.

"You got it bad, don't you?" Brett looked like a big, affable teddy bear with his dark hair curling down to his shoulders. Mitch had always appreciated his cousin's ability to laugh easily and see the humor in most situations. But he could pick the damnedest times to not mince words.

His blue eyes reminded Mitch of his father. Mitch Taylor, Sr., and Sid Taylor had been brothers. Brett's eyes pierced with the same intensity. "I can see why," Brett continued. "She's got a hell of a lot of spirit. She'd have to, to put up with you."

Mitch resisted the urge to lean across the table and throttle him for being so damn perceptive. Instead, he leaned back and feigned a relaxed pose. "I'm just doing my job."

"Bull…"

"Brett." Joe silenced him with a look. He turned the same stern look on Mitch. "We're just worried about you letting your emotions cloud your judgment. You don't normally recruit half the precinct and the entire neighborhood to keep watch on your place."

Mitch gave up his attempt to deny his feelings for Casey. But he forced himself to be brutally honest about the dead-end possibilities of those feelings. "She's a lot like Jackie. We're way out of her league."

"She's nothing like Jackie." Brett's bold statement held a challenge. "Is that your opinion or hers?"

"Does it matter?" The three men sat in silence. But with the miraculous recuperative powers of close-knit friends at hand, the tension eased. "The sooner we find Raines and get him back in prison, the sooner Casey can go back to her life, and I can go back to mine."

Mitch shrugged out of his jacket. Judge Maynard's pin, which Casey relied on to identify him, hit the back of the chair, knocking loose the anchor piece. The pin slipped free of the lapel and clunked to the floor. He stooped to retrieve the pieces while Joe and Brett cleared the table, returning the atmosphere of the dining room to business-as-usual.

"At least we know why he escaped." Mitch clipped the anchor back onto the pin and set it on the table. He clued the other men in with the information he'd gleaned from the warden at the state penitentiary. "Raines's twin sister, Darlene, was serving time in Potosi for the murder of a prostitute. She was up for parole next week. Guards found her with a fork shoved up under her ribs in the shower room last Tuesday."

"My God." Joe carried the cards and coins to a side table. "Was it a hit?"

"Yeah. They don't know who ordered it yet. But apparently that provided the incentive for him to escape. To seek his own vengeance."

"What would Casey have to do with that?" asked Brett.

"Kill someone he loves. He kills someone you love." An eye for an eye was a standard means of justice in the criminal world. "If he blames the judge for putting Darlene there, Casey would be the logical target for retribution."

"Emmett's sister is dead?" Casey stood in the doorway, her face twisted in a perplexed frown. The three men stilled, looking guilty, feeling worse for allowing her to overhear their conversation. She carried a steaming bowl of stew to the table and set it on a placemat. "My father sentenced her. Her trial was Emmett's excuse for attacking me."

When she slid into a chair, he sat beside her, the cop in him eager to make a discovery on the case, the man in him proud to see the constructive wheels turning in her eyes. "I thought your father stepped down from the bench because you'd been hurt."

"My father refused to give in to his demands. If I'd been conscious of all that was going on at the time, I would have agreed with him." Mitch reached for her hand and squeezed, forgetting the argument he'd made a moment ago, and instinctively reaching out to give her the strength to keep talking. "The day after my attack, Dad sentenced Darlene Raines to twelve to twenty years. On the courthouse steps immediately afterward, he announced his retirement to the press."

"And on their way home, your mother and father died in that car crash." He felt the tremor that shuddered through her. He wanted to snatch her into his arms and give her the shelter she had once taken such comfort in. But her eyes widened, not with grief, but with apology.

"My parents aren't dead."

The only sound in the room was Mitch's long-winded sigh.

Brett sat in the chair on the opposite side and laid his hand on her arm. "It was in all the papers. The mayor declared an official day of mourning. I remember Dad closing his shop."

Her weak smile failed to reassure anyone. "It was faked. Their deaths were staged so they could be relocated under new identities. Before he was arrested, Emmett's threats against everyone in my family were excruciatingly clear. Uncle Jimmy arranged for their protection through one of his contacts."

"Why didn't they hide you, too?" Brett asked Mitch's immediate question.

She spared him a rueful glance, but looked to Mitch to give her answer. "I was in and out of consciousness at the hospital. I had thirty-two surgeries ahead of me, months of physical therapy."

Mitch understood. Intellectually. A part of him would never understand abandoning someone he loved. "It would be practically impossible to keep you hidden with those kind of medical records."

Joe put his hands on Mitch's and Casey's chairs and leaned forward. "But if everyone thinks Judge Maynard is dead, why is Raines stalking you?"

"She can identify him, no matter what disguise he wears," suggested Brett.

Casey frowned. "I didn't do a very good job of that in court when it counted." Mitch saw her eyes go to the pin on the table. ''If he's in disguise now, I probably wouldn't recognize him at all.''

An unpleasant idea planted itself near the base of Mitch's neck. ''How many people know the truth about your parents?''

''Me. Jimmy. Iris. We never publicized the truth. The man who arranged for the accident and new identities knows, of course.'' Casey shrugged her shoulders. ''Ben and Judith. They've worked for us for years and stay with me whenever Mom and Dad travel. They're gone a lot now. I think they feel betrayed by Kansas City's legal system. And I know Dad feels guilty about what happened to me.''

She steadied herself with a long breath. ''Maybe it's easier for them to stay away.''

Mitch's idea sprouted tentacles and grew. ''The only reason that makes sense for Raines to toy with you now instead of killing you outright is because he's using you as leverage to flush out your father.''

''Or the person who ordered his sister's murder,'' suggested Joe.

It didn't take a cop to figure out the obvious. ''That means Raines knows the truth about your dad,'' said Brett.

Mitch might be close to identifying a motive, but the key to Raines's ultimate plan still eluded him. However, he suspected that connection would be made if he could uncover just one more answer. ''So how did he find out?''

EARLY SATURDAY MORNING Casey still pondered the implications of all that had been discussed around the dining-room table the night before. She sipped her coffee and read through the morning paper, seeing the words with her eyes, but processing very little of their meaning inside her head.

Everywhere she looked, she was surrounded by the essence of Mitch. High ceilings and spare wood floors, polished and covered with dark green area rugs, fit his height and breadth—as did the king-size bed he insisted she sleep in. A few designer-style knickknacks and paintings adorned the walls and shelves, but they were window dressing for the real beauty of the place. Wrought-iron trim and rustic wood paneling surrounded hardwood furniture occasionally softened by a linen fabric with a forest-green print. The condo reminded her of Mitch, spit and polish on the surface masking old-fashioned values and a solid strength that endured.

Even the oversize flannel shirt and black sweats she wore belonged to Mitch. She hadn't been able to bring herself to sleep in anything from her dresser. Emmett had been there, had touched her clothes. No amount of washing or sterilization would make her want to put on the nightgowns and undergarments that might have been in Emmett's hands. And though she cautioned herself against the thought, she found comfort in being surrounded by Mitch's things. It filled her with a strength almost as empowering as Mitch holding her hand or shielding her in his arms.

She needed to be strong, maybe now more than ever before.

She had to survive. She had to help catch Emmett Raines. And she had to keep herself from falling in love with Mitch.

She could get used to this place, with its big spaces and warm decor. She could get used to the bustle of activity the Taylor family provided.

She could get used to Mitch.

But dropping her guard would mean losing control. And losing control meant losing her heart.

And what was the point of losing her heart to a man

who deserved so much more than a fractured shell of a woman like her?

Even the simple fact that he was sleeping in this morning made her heart do a silly little flip-flop. He needed someone to take care of him. Someone whose care he'd appreciate. He worked such long hours. He took care of so many people. The signs of strain had deepened the creases beside his eyes. And even though he'd accepted the stew she set before him last night while he and Joe discussed suspects and strategies, she noticed that he'd eaten very little when Brett carried the plates back to the kitchen.

He hadn't asked to watch over her, and yet he did, offering his home and protection. He threatened his health to protect her. He called in favors to guard her every move. He gave up his normal routine to serve her needs. But why?

Her answer showed up on page 3C. Area Cop Earns Service Award. Below the headline was a lengthy article and picture of Mitch, looking distinguished in his dress blue uniform.

On the shortlist of nominees to the upcoming assistant commissioner position, Detective Captain Mitch Taylor…

Duty. He protected her because he was a man of honor and duty. Like her father. Like the Taylor family. Like Joe Hendricks. Like Jimmy?

Mitch had been angry at Jimmy for forgetting her on Thanksgiving. Angry for her. Angry when she should have been angry for herself.

Her father would have her hide for the way she'd been acting toward Mitch. Taking all he dutifully offered her—his interest, his hospitality, his protection—and, because she was too scared of being hurt herself, giving back nothing in return.

Except her smart mouth. And her pride. And her lack of trust.

"Morning." Mitch grumbled a greeting and stalked past her to the coffeepot.

He looked big and imposing, even in the spacious dining area. Caught off guard by his sudden appearance, she didn't have time to raise her defensive barriers before noticing the tight lines of strain that knotted his neck and back. He moved with a jerky stiffness that indicated a good deal of stress rested on those broad shoulders.

Guilt ate away at her. She was probably the major cause of his discomfort.

"Good morning."

He ignored her quiet response. He rubbed at his neck, his blunt fingers digging into the muscles at his nape as if he couldn't find relief from the tension. Barefoot and wearing only a pair of faded, well-worn jeans that clung softly to his backside, he poured himself a mug of coffee, and downed two big swallows of the hot liquid.

"Thank God, it's strong." He sighed and leaned heavily on the counter. Though he was resolute with corded strength, his weariness was evident.

She assumed his fatigue was related to her case. Maybe he'd appreciate a change of topic to get his mind on something more positive. "You made the paper this morning."

A bleary redness rimmed his eyes when he sat down. A dusky beard growth shadowed his jaw and neck. A myriad of emotions worked across his face before he hid his expression with another long drink. He stared into the depths of his mug and shrugged his shoulders before replying. "They say nice things about me?"

His relaxed posture and light tone seemed forced, giving

her the impression that it was all he could do to be civil, much less appear interested in anything she had to say at 8:00 a.m.

"Twenty years on the force is a real accomplishment. No wonder Jimmy and the city council want to promote you."

"Yeah." She couldn't tell whether his surly response was a reaction to mentioning her uncle's name or if her praise made him uncomfortable. He didn't strike her as a man who would be modest about his work. Maybe Mitch simply wasn't a morning person.

He stood abruptly and systematically circled the kitchen, opening the cupboards and slamming them closed after looking inside each one. "What did you find for breakfast?"

Casey hesitated an instant before pushing to her feet, glad she'd put on her brace so she could move with more coordination than her cane allowed. While he stared at the contents of the fridge, she crossed to the oven and pulled out a plate of toasted bagels. She could help, after all. This was one small thing she could do to help. "Sit down, grumpy. I was keeping these warm in case you decided to join me. There's cream cheese on the table."

The refrigerator door closed behind him, and he followed her out to the dining area. "What did you call me?"

"And you said I wasn't a morning person." She risked an amused smile since he couldn't see her face.

"With eight hours of sleep, I might be. I don't usually have company who expects me to be pleasant."

"I wonder why." She set the bagels on a hot pad and went back for a knife and plate.

He met her at the doorway and took the place setting from her. "You don't have to wait on me."

"It's no big thing," Casey insisted, wishing he'd let her

do even more to ease some of the concern she caused him. ''I know you stayed up talking to Joe and Brett after I went to bed. I may keep you from sleeping, but you won't do me any good if you pass out from lack of nourishment, too.''

She almost ran into his back when he stopped abruptly and turned. ''You really think I'm doing you any good?''

She looked up into his dark, glaring eyes and resisted the urge to run from his accusatory sarcasm. ''All right, then. Next topic. Why don't you want to talk about your award?''

''Uh-uh. Smooth move, princess, but we're dealing with your problems, not mine.''

''Being rewarded for doing your job well is a problem?''

''Depends on who you ask.''

''I'm asking *you*.''

He breathed in deeply, the angles and planes of his chest rising and falling from her line of sight where her pointed gaze met whiskey-dark fire. ''Drop it, princess.''

His seductively soft warning hushed her. And piqued her curiosity even more. He pulled out his chair and plopped into the seat. Something was terribly wrong here. What drove Mitch to deny the accolades he deserved?

She bought them both some time to regroup by taking her own cup and refilling it. She used the relative safety of hiding behind him to venture back to the forbidden topic. ''I know you need a college degree to be a detective. If you're only thirty-nine now, you must have gone to school while you were already on the force. That's a lot of hard work.''

''I'm not afraid of hard work,'' he mumbled while he chewed.

That much was obvious. ''Judging by the commendations and promotions listed in that article, a lot of people recognize what you've accomplished.''

His shoulders rose slowly, then sank as he released an almost savage breath. ''It's just a job.''

Just a job? Mitch's work seemed to be as much a part of him as swimming had once been a part of her life. She drew on that unexpected empathy and moved closer, leaving her cup behind. ''How can you say that? Modesty is an admirable trait, but you talk like this award is some kind of punishment.''

''More of a consolation prize.'' Bitterness rose and enveloped him, ringing heavily in his voice.

Reaching out before she could think of all the reasons not to, Casey touched her fingers to the sides of Mitch's neck, kneading her thumbs into the top vertebrae of his spine. At the first contact, he went still. His skin was warm, but she could feel the rigid knots in the muscles beneath.

''What are you doing?''

''It's an old trick my physical therapist taught me. Pressure points.'' Maybe he didn't appreciate even this small comfort from her. ''Do you want me to stop?''

His skin burned beneath her hands. ''It's your choice.''

His cold voice provided little encouragement, but with a wary caution he might use if he thought she had a weapon of some kind, he leaned back and let her work. Casey resumed her massage, moving out across his shoulders and back until she felt the tension in him gradually ease. It was the least she could do for him.

She owed him so much more.

Though her curiosity about Mitch's award remained, she decided to change the subject. ''If you won't talk about your career, maybe you'll talk about my case. What did you and Joe decide last night?''

He rolled his shoulders, shaking off the benefits of her

well-meaning touch. "That we have to solve the crimes of seven years ago if we want to figure out Raines now."

Casey curled her tired fingers into her palms and tried to pull in her raw, confused feelings, as well. Maybe she wasn't Emmett's target. Maybe, just like seven years ago, he was using her as a pawn in a sick game of extortion and vengeance. Maybe she didn't really matter at all.

She didn't realize she had spoken her thoughts aloud until Mitch's inky voice branded her with a fiercely simple statement. "You matter."

He snaked his hand out and pulled her around into his lap. His beautiful dark eyes burned with the same savage intensity.

"You matter to me."

Chapter Eight

"Mitch, I don't think..." He pinned her against his legs when she struggled to get up.

"My opinion may mean nothing to you, but this has to mean something." He tunneled his fingers into the hair at her nape and tilted her mouth up to meet his. Without fanfare or finesse, he ground his mouth over hers, plunging his tongue inside and stealing a taste of her soul before she could even protest.

With his rock-solid thighs imprinting her bottom and his hard, healing lips branding her own, Casey found it difficult to think, much less push him away.

She twisted in his lap, torn between the instinct to free herself and the desire to respond to his reckless need. Why was he so angry? What had triggered this desperation in him? She moaned in sorrow, her desire to help him stifled by the unforgiving assault.

And then, as if the sound had reached him as clearly as a voice, he gentled his hold. He pressed tiny kisses to her bruised lips in tender apology. "I'm sorry, princess," he murmured against her. "I shouldn't have done that. I'm sorry."

Pulling back gave Casey the freedom she needed to respond. She cupped the side of his jaw in her hand and tried to will the wildness out of his eyes. "I'm the one who's sorry. I shouldn't have pushed about the award."

He jerked his face away, his beard rasping her palm with a million pinpricks of sensation. "I ruffle too many feathers. Tonight's festivities are a way to appease me because the powers that be known I'm not gonna move up any further."

She shook her head. "That's not true. You have Uncle Jimmy's endorsement."

"Do I?"

His pointed glare reminded her of Jimmy's warning on Thanksgiving. Rumpled and rugged and needing a shave, the man holding her might set her hormones in motion, but he was the essence of everything Jimmy Reed looked down on. Mitch Taylor was a real working-class hero compared to Jimmy's cultured preening and polish. Jimmy wielded power as if by birthright, while men like Mitch wheedled and scratched, and studied and worked to earn the respect and rewards due them.

"Jimmy's a snob, isn't he?" As she said it, she sagged inside, knowing Mitch saw her no differently. She came from the same background as Jimmy. An intact family. Money. Opportunity. She'd grown up with all the things Mitch had been denied.

And yet Mitch was the one who met life head-on, while she cowered behind the walls of the old family fortress. She became aware of Mitch's heat surrounding her, and she wondered why she ever thought she had anything to offer this honest, vital man.

"Stay." His hands tightened on her hip and shoulder when she tried to pull away.

"I thought I could help. But I'm just making things worse."

Mitch caught her chin between his thumb and forefinger

and forced her to meet his gaze. A fire simmered in his whiskey-dark eyes, banked only by the gentleness of his deep husky voice. "Don't hide who you are, princess. Don't run from what you feel. I'm—" his gaze dropped to her lips "—I'm touched that you...appreciate how long I've stuck with this job." His smile twisted into a frown. "I know you don't think much of cops...."

"I was wrong." She pressed two fingers against his lips to silence his apology. The need to protect him swelled inside her and became greater than her own need to protect herself. "I'm proud of you."

His hands settled on her hips as she arched toward him. She kissed his closed eyelids, kissed the sculpted rise and hollow of his cheek. She nipped at the lobe of his ear and rubbed her cheek against his, tormented by the tender abrasion of his skin on hers.

He muttered something low and male as she touched the corner of his mouth. And then he claimed her again. This time with a loving skill that returned all she tried to give him and more. Her fingers strayed into the soft, short hair at his nape, and she lifted herself into his kiss.

His hands pulled at her, pinning her against his rising need. Her breasts throbbed with an unsatisfied ache where his chest brushed at the tips. Heat curled in her belly and spiraled downward. She gloried at the tactile differences she felt in him, and enjoyed the gift he gave by allowing her to explore those varying sensations. He felt feverishly supple to her fingertips, tasted of dark coffee and tart sweetness, smelled of faint spice and musky need each time she inhaled.

How had she lived without this? How could she have existed without knowing the tender, demanding thrill of this man wanting her, needing her?

Like a survivor struggling for life in the desert, she

drank of his generous mouth. She feasted on the sensations he aroused in her. He moved his hand beneath her shirt, and the callused heat scraped along her bare skin. His hand climbed higher, first brushing against, then cradling the weight of her breast. When he flicked his thumb across the distended nipple, she gasped at the bolt of heat that shot straight to the juncture of her thighs.

"Easy," he soothed her in his dark-as-night voice, breathing hotly along the shell of her ear. Cool air skittered across her torso when he lifted the hem of her shirt and bared her breasts to the morning light. The unexpected drop in temperature and the hungry heat in his eyes threatened to send her world careening totally out of control.

"Mitch?" The intimacy he asked for frightened her. He had taken her beyond an exchange of comfort. He could take her far beyond her ability to give him all he demanded of her.

He hushed her with a gruff voice at her ear, a hot graze of his lips along her neck. "Relax, princess. Let me."

But how could she deny herself the promise of his husky words? She felt a fan of warm air an instant before he closed his mouth over the burgeoning swell of her breast and she started to tremble, overwhelmed with the rush of honey-warm rapture zinging down to that secret feminine spot. The exquisite torture deepened when he touched his tongue to the heated tip.

"Put your hands on me," he muttered hoarsely, shifting his attention to her other breast. "Hold me."

And she did. She ran her hands across his shoulders then up the column of his neck, burying her fingers in his hair and clutching him to her. She gasped into a rumpled ruffle of hair at his crown as she reached for that reward he promised.

"You're so sweet," he praised her, "so sweet and generous I may not..."

A harsh ringing jangled in her ears. Mitch swore a colorful phrase he had to have learned on the street. His wicked mouth stilled and she fell from the edge of paradise.

He covered her with his shirt and tucked her in his arms, holding her close, whispering gentle reassurances to combat the jolting intrusion. An eternity passed before Mitch stood. He picked her up from his lap and deposited her in the chair. Then he raked his fingers through his hair and strode to the telephone.

The whole box nearly came off the wall when he jerked the receiver to his ear. "Taylor."

The chill in his tone betrayed more of his irritation than bellowing over the line would. He listened quietly a few moments, glancing over at her, then turned his back to her and continued the conversation.

Casey wound her arms in front of her and huddled in the hard-backed chair, feeling the warmth dissipating around and within her. His shoulders stiffened and she withered inside. That wasn't a good sign. After a few minutes, he hung up and faced her again, his tight expression more grim than she expected.

"What is it?" she asked, more alarmed than she cared to admit, even to herself.

"I'm sorry, princess." He reached for her hands and pulled her to her feet. "You can call me every name in the book. I was just so damn angry. And you were there for me. Giving and..."

He swallowed hard. She dipped her head to see the expression on his downcast face. When she caught his gaze, she offered a reassuring smile. "I know how it is. Sometimes you get so angry, you don't know how to let it out. I've been there, Mitch. I understand.''

He squeezed her fingers gently and straightened. "I'll bet you do. You've put up with a lot, princess. You shouldn't have to put up with me and my moods.''

He brushed the backs of his fingers across her cheek. "I didn't mean to hurt you.''

Hurt? He'd blessed her by treating her as a woman, using her in a man's most basic way to express his emotions, to alleviate feelings that were too intense to bear. He'd needed someone, for a reason she didn't yet understand, and he'd chosen her. Insecure, combative, damaged—he'd chosen her.

"You didn't.''

His rugged face softened into a sad smile. "You amaze me." He surprised her then by hugging her close. "Everything's unsettled right now. Crazy, on the edge." He rubbed circles on her back, pressing her nearer and nearer with each comforting stroke. "But I feel grounded when I hold you. Whether it's right or not, I don't know. But at this moment, there's no place I'd rather be.''

Tears burned in her eyes at the admission. She wound her arms around his waist and burrowed even closer, seeking the same solace for herself. But as quickly as the hopeful glow suffused her, she snuffed it out. Even as Mitch's words touched her heart, she heard the underlying message there.

For now. He wanted her now, maybe even needed her. But there was nothing permanent between two people who came from such disparate worlds. There could never be any lasting bond between a man strong enough to endure all that life threw in his path and a woman too weak to even stand straight on her own two feet.

She buried her sorrow at that realization beneath a well-trained mask of polite indifference. She pulled back and moved a safe, though not insulting distance away. "So what was the phone call? Police business, I presume?"

Mitch regarded her with unspoken questions. Then he seemed to shake off the speculation. He splayed his fingers at his hips and drew in a businesslike breath. "The banker I interviewed turned up dead last night."

"Oh, no." She clenched the back of the chair with both hands, needing the support. "Emmett's back at work."

Mitch's silence lasted long enough to capture her full attention. "It's worse than that. The body shows evidence that he's been dead for several days."

Casey felt light-headed as the implication hit her. "Then the man you interviewed was…"

"…Raines in disguise."

"DO YOU WANT to put out the APB, or should I?" Merle closed his notepad and looked at Mitch.

"You do it. I'm not sure what description to give, but at least let everyone know he's in the area. I want to have another look around. See if I can get a feel for Raines." He squeezed the younger man's shoulder. "You gonna be okay?"

Merle nodded, but the expression in his eyes still reflected doubt. "I've never seen a body mutilated that way before."

The banker's strangled body had been cut up and packaged as neatly as the meat in his uncle's butcher shop. He couldn't help but compare the work to the pictures he'd seen in Casey's file.

The M.O. was similar. Strangle the victim and then cut him. An in-your-face kind of killer. The type who liked to watch his victims die.

Only Casey wasn't dead. She hadn't even been unconscious when he started cutting into her. Every vital tendon, ligament and muscle in her right leg had been slashed or severed. God, how she must have suffered! And that didn't even count the injuries on her neck and arms where she struggled with the bastard.

"Captain?"

Mitch surfaced through the bile of his anger and stared at the rookie detective.

"Sorry." He unclenched his fist from Merle's shoulder. It was his job to be a steady influence, not the other way around. He was way too damn close to this case. "Don't be too hard on yourself. Some things you never get used to."

"I guess not." Merle hovered in the doorway, still concerned about him. "Need anything else, Captain?"

Mitch dredged up a smile and shook his head. "Just make sure the coroner's report is faxed to me as soon as it's done."

"Yes, sir."

Standing alone in David Zimmer's prefab house, Mitch breathed in deeply. Bachelor bare but respectable, the place *looked* lived-in. He walked through the rooms again. A few dirty dishes sat in the drainer. A pile of towels, waiting to be folded, sat on top of the neatly made bed. Even the john, with an uncapped tube of toothpaste on the sink, looked as if it had been used just that morning.

But the smells weren't right. Breakfast scents should have clung to the tablecloth in the kitchen. A musty combination of soap and dampness should have drifted from the bathroom. On the surface, it looked as if Emmett had been there just that morning impersonating Zimmer.

But it didn't *feel* lived-in.

It felt more like window dressing. The place gave Mitch the feeling that every object had been precisely placed—slightly dirty, slightly askew—to give the appearance of being lived-in.

After recovering Zimmer's body that morning, Mitch believed Emmett Raines was capable of any kind of deception. Mangled beyond recognition, Zimmer's body had to be positively IDed by dental records.

The banker Mitch interviewed Friday morning had had the same silver filling visible on his lower left incisor. Until that moment, he hadn't fully believed Casey's assertion that Raines could kill a man and take his place without being detected.

Now he believed.

And with that knowledge came the sinking certainty that since the body had been discovered, Raines would have to move on to impersonate someone else. Of course, Mitch had no hard evidence to prove Emmett had murdered the banker, only motive and Casey's assertion that he had the ability to pull it off.

Mitch moved to the center of the living room and surveyed his surroundings yet again. He rubbed the back of his neck, responding to the niggling sensation that this place was wrong.

Then he remembered Casey's fingers on his neck. On his face and in his hair. Damn, she was bewitching.

She *had* managed to release the tension that plagued him that morning. But it wasn't pressure points he remembered. It was the silky-soft steel in her fingers touching him. Digging into him. Pulling at him as if she couldn't get close enough. It was the fragile trust she gave by allowing him to touch her.

Casey had every reason to be afraid. Every reason not to trust a man. The cold, perfectly calculated perfection of this house testified to that.

If only he could find something to prove Raines had murdered Zimmer. If only he could figure out where he might strike next. But how could he second-guess a bastard who killed as easily as breathing? How could he predict the next move of a man who became his victims, masking the fact that a murder had even taken place?

And why had Casey's life been spared?

Mitch pieced together what little he knew so far. Emmett was smart; he didn't make impulsive mistakes. He got close to his victims before he attacked. He blamed Jack Maynard, Casey's father, for his twin sister's death. And he was eager to use Casey to draw the judge out of hiding.

Mitch locked the house and headed for his Jeep.

Wouldn't the cop who'd arrested him be an equally tempting target? What about the prosecuting attorney? Other witnesses?

Mitch switched on the ignition and waited several minutes for heat to fill the car.

Why had Darlene Raines killed a prostitute in the first place all those years ago? Was Raines an accessory to that crime?

Mitch checked over his shoulder and pulled into traffic.

Maybe he was looking into the wrong case. If this one wouldn't fall into place, perhaps he should check into one that had already been solved to find some answers.

Mitch punched a number on his cell phone and listened to it ring. A softly musical voice answered. "Fourth Precinct. Detective Rafferty speaking."

"Ginny. Captain Taylor," he identified himself.

"I'm on my way to your place to relieve Joe now."

"Good. I want you to do me a favor. Before you leave, get a file off my desk. I want to know everything we've got on Darlene Raines."

"Did you know the commissioner arrested Darlene Raines?" asked Mitch, not liking the way Casey hovered near the window watching the snow fall.

"He wasn't the commissioner then." The tight clutch of her arms in front of her waist reflected in the window. Her defensive stance angered Mitch. He thought he might have breached the wall of distrust between them this morning, but this afternoon she locked up her feelings tighter than a jail cell, giving him little more than cursory answers to his questions. Maybe blood *was* thicker than water. He wouldn't hesitate to defend Sid or Martha Taylor or one of his cousins if suspicion pointed their way. But then, none of their names ever popped up so often as James Reed's in the closed file of a murder case, either.

"No," Ginny answered, skimming over a report. "He was running for the office. Apparently, he generated a lot of publicity, getting out from behind his desk to do some real police work. Shot his popularity with voters through the roof."

If Ginny Rafferty hadn't been in the room with them, Mitch's veneer of patience would be nonexistent. He wanted nothing more than to shake the pride out of those regal shoulders of Casey's and demand some straight answers. Or maybe he'd try kissing her again, anything to rattle that icy composure and bring back the flesh-and-blood woman who had opened up to him.

"I don't remember too much about the politics." He didn't miss that she directed her answer toward Ginny. "I remember my dad thinking it a little odd that Jimmy chose to handle that case. Prostitution is usually taken care of by vice or a uniformed detail."

"But not Cynthia DeBecque's murder?" asked Ginny.

"No. Jimmy pulled some strings to get the case tried in Dad's court. They were a popular team, the cop and the judge. Both were tough on crime."

"And that's when Emmett attacked you, Casey? To persuade your father to dismiss the case?"

Ginny was asking the right questions regarding the case, thought Mitch. The notion that Casey felt more comfortable conversing with the other woman hurt. He thought they'd connected earlier. With her guard down, Casey was loving and giving and...

And he had no business begrudging the loss of a personal relationship with her. His primary focus should be her safety. And to ensure that, he needed answers. If Ginny was the only one she'd open up and talk to, he would live with that. As long as Casey was safe, he could live with anything.

Including hurt feelings, a bruised ego and a wounded heart.

Needing a few minutes to drop the false smile he knew he'd be wearing the rest of the evening, Mitch slipped from the room to add the cummerbund and bow tie to the monkey suit he'd rented for tonight's banquet. Jackie had always pushed him to buy his own tuxedo for the formal events she loved to attend. But on a young cop's salary, it didn't seem practical, and later, when he could afford it, he'd avoided the purchase as a minor protest against the high society that had shunned him unless they needed to call 911.

Mitch tied his tie twice, cursing silk and big fingers and achievement awards that did more to promote the department than honor an individual's devotion to his work. Finally, he surrendered the battle, shrugged into his jacket and headed back to the living room. Sid and Martha planned to attend the gala to support him. He'd recruit his aunt to help make him presentable.

"How does a call girl wind up living in a penthouse?" asked Ginny.

Oblivious to Mitch's reappearance, the two women sat together on the sofa, heads bent as if they were solving the problems of the world. "Somebody had to be keeping her."

"According to the reports, DeBecque walked in on Darlene Raines burglarizing her apartment. The two women struggled. DeBecque died from a blow to the head."

"If you'd said stab wounds, I'd think Emmett was involved in that death, too. But slicing and dicing seem to be his specialty, not blunt objects." The two women laughed like old friends, but it saddened Mitch to hear Casey picking up on the gallows humor cops often used to defuse a tense situation.

"What was missing?" he asked, turning off his emotions to match the champ herself when he saw Casey's shoulders stiffen at his reappearance.

Ginny hesitated a moment. But if she picked up on the heated undercurrents stirring between Casey and her boss, she wisely made no comment. Instead, she thumbed through the file and pulled out a sheet to hand across the back of the sofa to Mitch.

"A fur coat and some jewelry," he read out loud, noting that Darlene and her accomplice had left other big-ticket items behind. A TV. A state-of-the-art sound system. A diamond-and-emerald cocktail ring. Curious. Intriguing. Yet all the drawers had been searched. Turned upside down. Emptied out.

"Okay, Rafferty," he quizzed, hoping another bright mind would make the same connection he had. "What are you looking for when you rifle through eight small drawers of a twelve-by-six-inch jewelry case and leave behind ten thousand dollars worth of diamonds?"

"Papers," she speculated. "Computer disks."

"Smaller," he challenged.

"Negatives."

Casey turned and looked up at him, reaching the same conclusion. "Blackmail photographs."

Ginny returned the stolen property list to the file. "But who blackmails a prostitute? She already has a bad rep."

"It could have been the other way round," offered Casey. "Maybe Cynthia was blackmailing Darlene Raines."

"With what?" Mitch circled the sofa and sat down on the old trunk he used for a coffee table. "Was Darlene a co-worker?"

"Maybe Cynthia was blackmailing someone else. Whoever that was might have hired Darlene to retrieve the negatives."

"That's a lot of conjecture, Mitch." Ginny's calm voice of reason echoed his own thoughts.

"But it's worth checking out. Get on the horn to Merle. He's down at HQ filling out reports. Let's do a little more digging." He purposefully avoided Casey's intent focus. "Get a copy of James Reed's arrest report. If blackmail was involved that might explain why he had an interest in the case. Maybe he was doing a favor for a friend."

"Right."

Mitch used the cover of Ginny's exit to put some distance between himself and Casey. Looking at the reflection in the window, he struggled with his tie one more time. He knew she wouldn't appreciate his suspicions, would probably defend her Dutch uncle over him and his ideas, despite the gut-deep instinct that told him the commissioner's interest in Casey now—maybe always—was due to a case instead of familial ties. Maybe he kept tabs on her, kept her hidden away all these years to cover up…what? Just what did James Reed have to hide?

"Here. Let me." The softest of touches on his arm followed the command.

Steeling himself against his disproportionate reaction to the impersonal offer, he dutifully turned and let Casey work with his tie. He concentrated on the icy crystals of snow collecting on the ledge outside the window. She tugged and straightened and manipulated the silk with unerring accuracy. Even this mockery of intimacy between a loving couple provided enough fuel to make the room feel hotter. He wondered how many other ties she'd straightened. Her father's? Jimmy's? A lover's?

Mitch squeezed his eyes shut to savor the experience of Casey performing this task for him. He might even learn to like dressing up if it meant she'd be willing to put her hands on him.

"Do you think my uncle's involved in a cover-up?"

As if the window opened, a chill swept through the room, staunching Mitch's errant fantasies. He opened his eyes and shared the least offensive speculation on his list. "He might be protecting someone."

Casey's hands curled into fists between them. "He's all I have, Mitch."

He captured her hands against his chest and trapped her there. "No, he's not. You don't have to rely on him to feel loved. What about the McDonalds and Frankie? They dote on you like family."

What about me?

"They have their own lives. And there's not much left of mine anymore."

She pushed, but he held on, unwilling to let her escape without clueing her in at least to some degree the extent of his growing feelings and respect for her. "It doesn't have to be that way."

She'd taken the first step in reaching for him twice that day, reaching beyond her protective shell that secluded the real princess from the rest of the world. But not from him.

He didn't want her to withdraw from him anymore. With him as her bodyguard, she couldn't afford it. And as a man rediscovering parts of his heart that he thought had died, he couldn't afford it, either.

He released her hands and grasped her shoulders, rubbing warmth into them through her cream-colored sweater, pulling her closer. "The only thing that stands between you and being loved is your pride. I've seen how warm and giving you can be. Jimmy doesn't see that. *I* see it. And Frankie does. And Judith and Ben…" He lowered his mouth, intent on claiming her upturned lips, but she turned her head and he contented himself with grazing along her finely boned jaw.

"I'm trying to keep from getting hurt, Mitch. Maybe I'm taking the coward's way out, but I'm not strong like you."

"Bull…" His lips froze near the tempting warmth of the soft hollow beneath her ear. He pulled back to look down into the pale doubts in her dove-gray eyes. "Do you really believe that? Look how much you've overcome. Look at what you have to deal with every day of your life. And you've done it almost all on your own. I know a lot of people who would have surrendered under that kind of pressure."

Her fingers grazed the tiny silver pin she'd given to ID him. She touched it again, as though reaffirming her trust. Then she grasped the lapels of his jacket. "But you put your life on the line every day. You command the respect of so many people. You don't allow yourself to be afraid. You get angry instead. Or you ignore it."

Mitch shook his head. "I'm not that different from you, Case. I just do what I have to to get by."

He pulled her close again, wrapped her up in the hug that he'd found gave comfort to them both. She softened into him, and the gesture of trust heartened him in ways he didn't dare yet define.

Her lips brushed against his neck. "So the only difference is that when it gets to be too much, you lose your temper and I become the dreaded ice princess."

Mitch smiled into her crown of vanilla-scented hair. "She's not so bad."

Casey shifted and tipped her head back, treating him to the vision of her full-blown smile. "You can't stand her."

He shrugged, joining in the playful mood. "Let's just say I like a challenge."

"You're more gallant than you give yourself credit for, Captain. They're going to love you at the banquet tonight."

Mitch groaned and squeezed her tight. "You had to remind me."

Casey's laughter went a long way to ease his dread of the coming evening. He'd love to share it with someone special. He ached to share it with her.

Grateful for her praise, relieved to learn their truce could be resumed by talking out their fears, he bent his head to capture her unresisting mouth. To thank her. To reassure her. To take the reassurance he needed for himself.

The kiss they shared was too tempting. Too real. Too much of what he wanted to share with her the rest of his life.

Too good to last.

"I got it, old man. Oops..." Ginny walked into the living room, eyes focused on the paper in her hand. Casey's disappointed moan matched his own. She pulled away to a polite distance and hugged her arms across her stomach while Ginny seemed to search the room for a good place to hide. "Sorry."

Mitch ran his hands down his lapels and straightened

his jacket. He could still feel Casey's warmth there and was reluctant to let it go. But he had to. He'd better get used to letting her go.

"Don't sweat it, Gin," he said, slipping into his authoritative mode with a little less ease this time. "You got a hold of Merle?"

The petite blonde's apologetic frown encompassed both Casey and himself. "Yes. He's going to fax the arrest report over. I gave him your number."

The elevator buzzer rang, and Ginny's expression relaxed with relief. "I'll, um, just get that."

Left alone with Casey, he realized the gulf between them had opened up again, but with a subtle difference this time. She might be withdrawing to protect herself, as she claimed, but Casey's chin had settled at an angle a little less proud and distant than what had greeted him before.

"You gonna be okay?" he asked.

She met his gaze and gamely smiled. "I'm gonna try, old man. I'm gonna try."

Before he could reassure her or make a joke or even explain the misnomer of the nickname she'd picked up, Ginny hurried in, taking short, bristly steps, followed by Brett at a much more relaxed pace. "The local Neanderthal has arrived to keep us company."

"Look, sugar, if I'm going to be too much of a distraction for you, I can always call home and tell 'em to send over one of my younger, uglier brothers."

"Brett." Mitch warned off his cousin's lopsided grin. While he trusted Brett to protect Casey, he suspected he'd drive Ginny crazy. When Ginny was on the job, she was all business, while his good-natured cousin rarely passed up the chance to flirt.

Casey giggled, drawing his attention like a magnet. "Go

on,'' she ordered. ''Enjoy your evening. I have a feeling things are going to be pretty entertaining here.''

''Walk me to the door.'' As if it were the most natural thing in the world, he reached out his hand and she took it, wrapping her fingers with gentle strength around his. She fell into step beside him, her limp offset by the graceful carriage of her posture.

At the door, he shrugged into his coat, reluctant to leave her. ''What is it?'' she asked, when the silence between them stretched out long enough to grow uncomfortable.

''I wish you could go with me.''

''If Emmett wasn't out there, maybe I would.''

''If Raines wasn't out there...''

We never would have met. The thought dawned on Mitch and sickened him at the same time. He'd been through more emotions in the past week than he had in the past ten years, thanks to this beautiful, special woman standing before him. It felt good to be alive again. To care.

But he never would have met Casey Maynard if a crazed criminal hadn't been stalking her. If her life weren't in danger, their paths would never have crossed. And when this was over—with Casey safe and in one piece, he swore on his parents' memories—their paths might diverge again and he would lose her.

''Stay safe,'' he answered instead, and pressed a quick, chaste kiss to her lips.

''I will,'' she promised.

He waited for the dead bolt to slide into place behind him before crossing the hall to the utility elevator that took him down to the garage. He couldn't shake the feeling that leaving her tonight was wrong. But whether that warning came from the tickle on his neck or the empty place in his heart, he couldn't tell.

Chapter Nine

Casey leaned back and grinned at the mock intensity Brett used to study his letters on the board game they'd been playing. The man was a tenacious competitor; she had to give him credit for that. But the game wasn't the prize he had in sight. He clearly had an eye for Ginny's pretty, heart-shaped face and feathery blond curls, and had done nothing to hide his appreciation. Yet the detective had dodged every attempt at flirtation, every overture of friendship, every lead-in to a personal conversation.

Now the sparks between her two caretakers had deteriorated into a battle of innate intelligence versus creative thinking, leaving Casey in the middle as a bemused referee. She looked at Ginny, who scanned the room with a wary alertness similar to Mitch's. But Casey recognized the facade masking her irritation in the silent drumming of her fingers on her thigh.

She wondered if Mitch saw her in the same way, a challenge—intentional or not—that any man worth his mettle must try to conquer. Would Brett lose interest if Ginny suddenly laughed at one of his silly jokes? Would he like the real woman as much as the police officer who refused to drop her guard?

Would Mitch be disappointed in the real Casey? A crippled, solitary has-been was hardly a worthy match for a man with his credentials and energy and soul-melting kisses.

He stuck by his cheating wife when she was dying because he thought it was the right thing to do. Would he bow to duty once more and pursue a relationship with her, even if he didn't—couldn't—love her? The heartrending consideration soured her amusement at the battle of wills unfolding between her companions.

"Dreadnaught."

"What?" Ginny's irritation colored her accusation.

With all the panache of a skilled magician, Brett laid down the letters *R-E-D-N-O-T* after the *D* Casey had just played.

"That's not how you spell the word."

"Hey, you're surprised it's even in my vocabulary, aren't you?"

A high-pitched ringing sounded from the direction of Mitch's desk on the far side of the room. Ginny bounced to her feet. "Saved by the bell. Literally. That'll be Merle's fax."

Casey tapped Ginny's wrist and stood, denying her the avenue of escape. "I'll get it. I need to stretch my muscles anyway."

Ginny's eyes spoke immediate concern. "Are you all right? In pain?"

Casey made her own escape on a little white lie. She almost always felt some degree of pain. After either too much exertion or too little exercise, Casey's muscles tightened up and the nerves in her leg went haywire. She waved aside Brett's concerned frown, too. "It's not too bad, but if I don't move around soon, it will be."

"All right." Ginny's worry eased a bit. "I'll go make

us some coffee. Brainiac here can put the game away. Just leave the report on Mitch's desk.''

From the corner of her gaze, Casey saw Brett lean back in his chair and follow the blonde's exit with his eyes. The wistful expression on his face reflected her own feelings, and the futility of loving a man like Mitch.

Because she did love him, she admitted to herself. She wrapped her fingers around the sturdy oak back of the desk chair and thought of Mitch's strength. His unyielding courage. And she wondered how she could ever become the woman he deserved.

After the cover page of the fax had cleared, Casey waited for the succeeding pages of the report to print. Could Jimmy be involved in some kind of cover-up? She knew Mitch thought so, even if he refrained from coming right out and saying it. He didn't like her godfather much, and frankly, some of his recent actions perplexed her, too. Assigning Mitch to protect her, then criticizing him for doing just that. Politics was a funny game she'd often observed but never quite mastered.

A few moments passed before the fax machine's silence registered. She lifted the papers to check for a printing jam. Two stark lines and a familiar picture on the message page drew her focus, and triggered her scream.

The paper flew from her hand as if the machine had zapped her with a bolt of electricity. Brett was at her side in the next breath, pushing her away from the desk and shielding her with his body. Seconds later, Ginny had one arm linked through Casey's, guarding her other side with a sleek silver gun drawn in her hand.

A colorful oath preceded Brett's terse announcement. ''It's the fax.''

''What does it say?''

Through angry shock, Casey heard the curt exchange of words.

Burned into her memory, the words flashed in her mind as he read them aloud.

"'This is the man who kissed the maid who died in the house that Jack built.'"

She sensed rather than saw him show Ginny the paper. Mitch's newspaper photo had been crudely scanned or copied. But the extra details, a slashed throat and a bleeding heart, had printed with frightening clarity.

"How does he know Mitch kissed me?" Her mind raced with the nightmare of sudden knowledge. She'd dropped her guard and given in to her feelings. And now her worst fear was being realized. Because of her, someone else would be hurt.

Because of her, Mitch could die.

Her stunned whisper gave way to the vehemence of anger. "My God, he's been watching us all along. He knows I'm here."

Brett was already on his way to the door. He shrugged into his coat and pulled out a cell phone. "I'll get Josh on the line and we'll check outside. Nobody should have gotten closer than three blocks without being spotted. He knows everyone by sight."

"He wouldn't recognize Emmett," Casey gathered her wits and called after him. "He could be anybody on the street. Even a close friend."

"That bastard doesn't threaten my family. Or friends. And he's not making himself at home in my neighborhood. We'll find him."

When the door slammed shut, Ginny moved her toward the relative safety of the dining room. "He could just be trying to spook you," she suggested. "Maybe he hasn't seen you and Mitch together. What concerns me is how he knows you're here. This fax was sent from a copy-mart across town. He either has an accomplice or lucky timing. I'm guessing the Taylor boys aren't going to find anything out there tonight.''

Casey agreed. ''He's smart enough to figure out I'm here without actually watching the place.'' She rubbed her hands up and down her arms, warding off an inner chill. ''Everyone at my house on Thanksgiving, plus my staff, knows Mitch was assigned to protect me. Emmett could have watched one of them or tapped their phone line or...I can't believe one of them would betray me on purpose.''

She stopped and gasped for air to halt the shrill rise of pitch in her voice. On a calmer, saner note, she forced herself to admit a portentous truth. ''We're not safe anywhere.''

''We?'' Ginny sheathed her gun in the holster at her belt.

''Mitch. Me. You now. Anyone who tries to help me.''

''Not true.'' Ginny dismissed the idea with a vigorous shake of her head, then pulled a plastic bag from her purse and dropped the fax message inside. ''The old man's like a pit bull on this case. He'll die before he lets anything happen to you.''

Casey swept her gaze around the room, taking in all the things that reminded her of Mitch. ''That's not exactly comforting. I don't want anyone else to get hurt because of me.''

''It's our job.'' Ginny joined her at the table. ''And I think it's something a lot more personal with Mitch.''

As she struggled to control her fear, a brusque anger cleared her ability to see the real situation.

''You're not listening to me.'' Casey picked up the plastic sheaf and reread the words on the fax, ignoring the mutilated picture. "This has to do with Mitch, not me. This time the rhyme is different."

Ginny tilted her head at a wary angle. "I don't think I like this."

Tossing the evidence onto the table, Casey hurried to the hall closet to retrieve her coat. "I have to see Mitch."

"Now I know I don't like this." With a quickness that easily outdistanced her own gaited pace, Ginny blocked her path to the front door. "You can't leave here. Mitch would have my hide, not to mention my next promotion."

Casey looked down at the detective and explained her discovery. "Think about it, Ginny. Emmett isn't threatening me this time. He's threatening Mitch. *He's* the one in danger."

Ginny crossed to the wall phone and picked up the number Mitch had left on a note beside it. "Then I'll call and fill him in."

"If you don't take me to the banquet, I'll find another way to get there myself." She pleaded with the other woman to understand the fear in her heart. "I've seen what Emmett can do. I know the cold look in his eyes. I may be the only one who can see it. I have to get to Mitch before Emmett does."

"No."

She tried a cooler line of reasoning. "Emmett knows I'm here! Your security's already been compromised. Where else will I be safer than in a banquet hall full of cops?"

Ginny's blue eyes flickered with contemplation. "But Emmett's M.O. is to kill a man and take his place, isn't it? Can you trust that he's not one of those cops in disguise?"

"Even if he is, what's he going to do to me there? It's our chance to flush him out."

Ginny blocked the door. ''There are supposed to be nearly five hundred people in that conference center. How will you find him in that crowd before he gets to Mitch?''

''We don't have to find Emmett. If I show up, he'll find me.''

''MITCH TAYLOR.''

Applause filled the room. The hollow sound grated on his ears. *Twenty years. Big whup. These people have no idea what this means to me.* But Mitch knew how to keep a straight face in the interrogation room or under oath. He'd worked undercover a few years back. He knew how to change his outward demeanor to fit in with those around him. These people cared more about appearances than anything else. Maybe he did fit in after all.

The ironic thought put a smile on his face as he adjusted the silk lapels of his tuxedo jacket and walked toward the podium. The action knocked Casey's miniature silver medallion from its clasp and it fell to the floor. A twinge of awareness skittered down the back of his neck like an omen. But Mitch wasn't a superstitious man. He just wished he'd take better care of Casey's gift. He wished he could take better care of Casey.

Making a mental note to get the pin fixed before he had to return it to her, and wishing that thought didn't conjure up such a feeling of finality, he scooped up the treasure and pocketed it in his coat.

He shook hands with the mayor and accepted the walnut plaque. His gaze moved past him and locked briefly with James Reed, sitting to the left at the head table. Funny, Mitch thought, the commissioner clapped politely enough, but there was no pride, no appreciation in his eyes for his hand-chosen candidate. No, they darkened with something more like a warning.

Of what? That he make the commissioner look good tonight? That he stop giving voice to his neck-tingling suspicions that told him the commish was guilty of something? Like covering up a crime? Or maybe the commish was simply guilty of dropping the ball when it came to taking care of his own family.

The man could take a lesson from the rediscovered generosity of his friends and cousins. His aunt and uncle sat at Joe Hendricks's table, beaming with pride. Sid clutched Martha's shoulder while silent tears streamed down her cheeks. He'd once thought of himself as an outcast, and maybe, to a lot of the people in this room, he was. He came from the wrong neighborhood. But he loved that neighborhood. He loved those people. His people.

Did he really want to leave them and become assistant commissioner? Did the job really matter that much when it meant leaving his friends and family behind? When it meant abandoning his precinct to some desk jockey, groomed by the commissioner or another bigwig? How badly did he want to fit in with that crowd? Maybe those were Jackie's left over dreams talking, and not his own.

But would the position make him the man worthy to love Casey?

The room quieted in anticipation and Mitch bit his tongue, resisting the urge to give the rabble-rousing speech that had been brewing in the back of his mind since the festivities began.

"Mr. Mayor. Commissioner. Distinguished guests. It's a privilege to accept this award. But it's been more of a privilege to serve the citizens of Kansas City…"

He slipped into a rote recitation of his speech. Damn. It would have been nice if his parents could have lived to see this. His dad, especially, would have been proud of him, continuing the successful career that should have been his if it hadn't been cut short so senselessly.

Guests milled in and out the back of the room, bored with speeches, taking calls, powdering noses. A handful of waiters moved throughout the tables, freshening coffee and removing dessert plates. He followed the path one took back to the swinging doors adjoining the service area. The kitchen door swung open and Mitch caught sight of a tiny blonde, underdressed for the patrons of the room in a blazer, thermal vest and jeans.

His senses skidded back to life, and his words faltered. Ginny?

The door opened again, framing a big man with long dark hair wearing a Sherpa coat. Brett.

A raging spiral of fear forked though him. Who was guarding Casey? What the hell had happened?

His speech stuttered to a halt. Had Raines gotten to Casey somehow?

The idea of another message, much less the man himself, making contact with her was unthinkable. Unbearable.

He cut the last part of his speech and made his thankyous. He crumpled his notes and jammed the paper into his pocket, holding the plaque aloft to a hesitant round of applause. He had to get back to Brett and Ginny to see what was wrong. But the mayor stood to shake his hand. Then the chief of police. Then three city councilmen blocked his path.

Mitch shoved past them in a frustration that bordered on panic, wishing for telepathic powers to reach Brett or Ginny so he could know what had happened. He craned his neck above the throng of well-wishers, desperate to make eye contact. Desperate to know the truth. His heart slammed in his throat at what he saw.

Flame-gold hair spilling across the shoulders of a dark coat. Pale skin flushed with the cold of winter.

Casey.

Brave and sexy and smiling through the fear that shadowed her eyes. The congratulatory handshakes, pats on the back and words of appreciation around him faded into white noise, an ignorable buzz that cocooned him as he walked past his chair and headed for the kitchen.

Every other face in the room blurred as he cut his way through the crowd. He saw only her serene smile and the flicker of uncertainty in her proud posture. His initial rush of joy at sharing this moment with her faded, and an angry resentment took its place.

"Of all the reckless, foolish…"

"Mitch?" When he broke through the line of onlookers, Casey launched herself into his arms. He felt the frantic clutch of her fingers at the back of his neck. He cinched her waist to hold her steady and took a step back to keep them both on their feet.

"What's going on?" he asked, nuzzling the free fall of hair behind her ear.

Before he could savor her sweet smell, she was leaning back against his arms. Her fingers skittered across his jaw and down the front of his jacket and back up to frame his face in their gentle strength. "Are you all right?" she whispered.

His attempt at a reassuring smile tightened into one of the gruff frowns he usually wore when the clues of a case refused to fall into place. "I'm fine. Except for my blood pressure, which is shooting through the roof because you're not where you're supposed to be."

She blinked dove-gray eyes at him. The panic she'd greeted him with receded in opposition to the smile blossoming on her lips. "I had to come. Congratulations."

For an instant, Mitch succumbed to her classic beauty. He basked in the pride he saw shining in her eyes, felt his contention over the evening's events soften in her quiet words—sensed something more ominous than friendly support had urged her out of hiding.

"Cassandra Maynard…?"

"What's going on?"

"Did you see…?"

The murmur of curiosity from the people gathering behind him spurred Mitch more quickly than his own worried instincts. He closed his fingers around Casey's shoulders and pushed her back into the kitchen. He slammed his shin into her brace in his haste to get her away from the gathering crowd. The jolt of pain knocked loose the last of his romantic ideas and reminded him of just how dangerous a public appearance could be for her. A nod to Ginny moved her out of the door, and her bodyguarding duties quickly switched to crowd control.

"What were you thinking!" His raised voice snared the interest of the kitchen staff. Before any expressed their concern, he snapped at them. "Clear out of here. Now! Police orders." A few scattered immediately. Brett circled behind Casey, and the big man's protective movements disbanded the remaining onlookers.

Casey flattened her hand against Mitch's chest. "I asked to come."

Ignoring her soft-spoken urgency, he directed a punishing glare over the crown of her head toward his cousin. "Why the hell is she out in the open like this?"

Brett stood his ground, offering a voice of humor that irritated the hell out of Mitch. "You try talking to her."

He felt a tug at the front of his jacket, diverting his attention from a duel he didn't want to fight. He looked down to the stubborn tilt of Casey's chin and spotted the

lines of strain bracketing her mouth. "Don't blame them,
Mitch. I insisted Brett and Ginny bring me. We got another
note from Emmett."

"How...?"

He cupped the delicate strength of her jaw in his hand
and brushed his thumb along her cheek, trying to soften
the worry etched there. He wanted to take her in his arms
again, swallow her up in a shield of comfort and protection. But with Raines around, he needed to summon the
cop in him, not the man. It was just so damn hard to think
straight when he could feel her trembling beneath his
touch. He compromised by releasing her and asking, "You
okay?"

She rolled her shoulders in that elegant way of hers that
left her posture square and determined. A storm flashed in
her eyes. "I'm mad as hell. He's here. I'm sure of it."

"Then let's go." He snatched her by the elbow and
turned her toward the back exit.

But Casey jerked her arm away and sidled up to Brett.
"I'm not going."

"If Raines is here, you sure as hell are!"

Brett glanced down at Casey, whose crossed arms and
tilted chin denied Mitch the right to dictate her actions.
With a shake of his head, Brett wisely excused himself.
"I'll go out front and help Ginny."

Left alone together, Mitch had a sinking feeling that he
was going to lose this battle of wills. His streetwise survival skills seemed to be no match for redheaded stub-
bornness. "What makes you think Raines is here?"

Without blinking or looking away, she reached into her
coat pocket and pulled out a crumpled piece of paper
wrapped in standard-issue plastic. Mitch unfolded the note,
read the sick message and swore in a colorful phrase that

dissipated the last of his anger and left him feeling raw and humbled by Casey's courage.

"You're worried about me?" he asked, incredulous and heartened all at once by her foolhardy show of concern.

"I'm worried about us." The steel in her posture cracked, exposing the vulnerability beneath the surface. "I'm worried about all the other innocent people Emmett might harm. I want to stop him, Mitch. I want him out in the open so we can find him and arrest him, and put him away forever where he belongs."

Didn't she understand what she was suggesting? Didn't she grasp the risk involved in this dangerous game she wanted to play? Didn't she see what it could cost him to go along with her half-formed plan?

"Casey. Princess..." He pulled at a strand of hair that lay across her shoulder and tucked it behind her ear, willing her to understand. "I may not be able to keep you safe."

She reached up and captured his hand between both of hers. The pleading in her eyes was as hard to resist as her welcoming touch. "You once said that I was the bait to flush my parents out of hiding. Shouldn't it work the other way, too? Aren't I the bait that'll bring Emmett out into the open?"

In jeans and her charcoal-gray coat, nobody looked more like a lady. Nobody looked more resolute. Nobody had ever captured his heart like this woman had.

He shook his head and pulled her along toward the back door with him. "I won't risk it. There are too many factors I can't control here. I have another cousin with a cabin out by Truman Lake. I'll call her and get the key, then figure out how Raines tracked you to my place so we don't make the same mistake again."

She did a quick double-step and dodged in front of him,

stopping him in his path. "You'll have to come with me. He wants you dead, too. You can't stay here."

"Case…"

"I won't go without you."

A bright flash of light blinded him. "Miss Maynard, are you coming out of seclusion?"

"Are you and Captain Taylor seeing each other?"

"Is there any truth to the rumor…?"

Mitch spun around, his left hand automatically going to his right side where his gun should be—which he had left locked in his car outside. He cringed at the overwhelming futility of his task. If Emmett Raines was part of this mess, it would take a miracle to spot him.

A sea of guests and reporters surged around them, filling up the empty spaces between shelves and islands and entrances and exits in the tiny service kitchen. Casey's fingers clawed the back of his jacket as she huddled behind him. Every ounce of male, territorial defensive instinct in Mitch swelled to the fore.

"Back off!" His clipped warning silenced the onslaught of questions, but cameras continued to click and whir with the disturbing repetition of gunfire.

The stream of gawkers parted and Ginny Rafferty slipped through. "Sorry, Captain."

He overlooked her apology and snapped an order. "Joe's inside. Track him down. Get on the horn and get every available man here. I want Casey out of here ASAP."

"Yes, sir." She scuttled back into the crowd, eager to redeem herself in his eyes. She displayed the kind of loyalty he expected from all of his squadron, but he had neither the time nor focus to reassure her right now. His primary task was guarding Casey.

When the crowd parted again, he half expected Ginny

to return with more bad news. Instead, a tall, robust man broke through. He extended his big, beefy hand. "Captain Taylor. I had no idea you were harboring such a big surprise from us."

Mitch shifted his body between Casey and the mayor's jovial accusation. "We were just on our way out, sir."

But he ignored the honest excuse and peeked around Mitch's shoulder. "Cassandra?"

Mitch felt a shudder ripple through Casey from head to toe. "This could be our best chance," she whispered against the back of his neck. "I need to try."

"No." She didn't have to do this. She shouldn't have to risk her life to protect or please anyone else.

She never failed to amaze him. Despite his futile protest, she stepped to one side and held out her right hand. "Mayor Benjamin."

"Please. You must join Sylvie and me at our table at the dance."

Her left hand clutched the sleeve of Mitch's jacket. The five pressure points of her fingertips seared his forearm beneath the fabric. He realized her show of strength was barely skin-deep. How far could sheer nerve take her? He admired her conviction, but he had no desire to see her suffer if her little charade failed. "Sir, I need to get Ms. Maynard home."

But the city's boss ignored Mitch's protest. "It's such a joy to see you venture out. We have a lot of catching up to do." The mayor took her hand and slipped it through the crook of his arm. "Of course, Captain Taylor is invited to join us. I had no idea you were receiving company again, or Sylvie and I would have been over to call on you...."

The crowd Mitch hadn't been able to disperse parted, and the mayor walked off with Casey. The sea of press and curiosity seekers fell into step behind them, leaving Mitch alone—apart from the multitude of upper-crust acquaintances, old friends and the professionally curious.

Left alone while the woman he loved got swept back into the world in which she so clearly belonged.

Leaving Mitch alone.

To curse. And to pray.

The captain of the Fourth Precinct, cited only moments ago for his dedicated service in protecting the citizens in his care, followed anyway.

"LET'S DANCE."

Mitch's terse whisper brushed across the shell of Casey's ear, momentarily distracting her from Sylvie Benjamin's in-depth plans to refurbish the mayoral offices. Fixing an attentive smile on her face, Casey turned her head ever so slightly toward the man in the chair beside her. "It would be rude to abandon the mayor and his guests in the middle of a conversation."

"Who's doing all the talking?" The harsh impatience in his voice prompted her to turn in her chair and face him.

Boredom hadn't agitated him into the request for her company on the dance floor. Icy chips of something much more territorial hardened the usual warmth in his eyes. "What's wrong?" she asked.

"About tonight?" He slipped his arm along the back of her chair, pulling himself around her in a half embrace that thrilled her with its discreet protection. But his tight-lipped frown made it difficult to appreciate the gesture. "Just about everything."

He nodded toward the two flutes of untouched champagne that had been delivered to their table on a silver platter. They were the fourth gift presented by their husky waiter on behalf of family acquaintances around the room. "Every legal celebrity and politician is flocking to you like some kind of good-luck charm."

"The idea *is* to draw attention to me," she reminded him.

His shoulders heaved with a sigh that did nothing to relax his expression. "The idea *was* to keep you safe."

She tipped her chin to argue her reasons for drawing Emmett out of hiding again, but a curious, cultured voice interrupted. "Cassandra, is there a problem?"

Casey turned to make her apologies to the mayor's wife, but Mitch beat her to it. "Not a thing, Sylvie." He towered beside Casey's chair like a leviathan rising from the deep. With her hands firmly imprisoned within his, she had no choice but to let him pull her up beside him. "I want to steal Casey away for a few moments on the dance floor."

Mitch easily commanded the older woman's attention with an irresistible combination of sexy authority and a little boy's wistful pout. Sylvie shooed him away with an indulgent smile. "Here I am going on, and of course, you want to celebrate. You two go right ahead. I'll catch the waiter and order another round of refreshments for us."

"Thanks." With a firm grip that prevented Casey from lodging any protest, Mitch led her through the labyrinth of guests and tables toward the small orchestra across the room.

But when they hit the smooth paneled floor, a new fear assailed her. A phantom pain shot through her damaged leg into her hip. She dug in her heels.

The sudden stop shifted her balance and she teetered backward, bumping her shoulder against a passing waiter. For a precarious moment, the tray of empty glasses he carried tilted. But he saved it from disaster with the same quick reaction Mitch used to steady her. "Sorry," she apologized.

The waiter smiled. "I should watch where I'm going, Ms. Maynard." His gaze slid past her to the man closing in protectively behind her. "Mr. Taylor. What a pretty pair you two make this evening. If you'll excuse me."

"What was that all about?" Mitch asked, turning her. He clutched her elbows while her fingers settled nervously at the satiny lapels of his jacket. "Why did you stop?"

"Mitch, I haven't danced since…" She scrunched her face into an awkward smile, hoping he would understand.

But a devilish challenge danced in his dark eyes. "You didn't think you'd see the Plaza lights, either," he dared her.

He flashed the same expression that had swayed Sylvie Benjamin. "C'mon. Give me five minutes of privacy with you. Just five minutes out of the spotlight. I promise I'll go slow."

Somehow, while she got lost in the masculine intent of his gaze, he managed to lead her to the center of the floor. A poignant cello crescendoed into the theme from a popular movie, and Mitch swept his arm around her waist and pulled her close. He pressed her hand over his heart and swayed back and forth in a slow step she could follow without putting any strain on her leg.

How could she fall with this man's strength beside her? How could she fear inside the shelter of his arms?

How could she allow him to be hurt by the shortcomings of her past? "I thought Emmett would be here. I was sure he'd try something tonight."

"He's here."

The conviction in his clipped words sent a shiver of apprehension down her spine. "How do you know?"

She stopped the dance when he did. Mitch released her

hand and rubbed the back of his neck in a world-weary gesture. "Just a feeling I have."

The play of fatigue and cynicism across his face convinced her to believe his instincts even if she didn't fully trust her own. She reached behind his neck and pushed his fingers aside, massaging the sensitive point where he carried the weight of his responsibilities. Above the corded column, she swore his warm skin tingled beneath her touch.

His eyes widened with a surprise she imagined reflected in her own. Suddenly, the world shrank down to just the two of them, standing together against a madman, finding strength and comfort in each other's unique compassion.

He matched her hold on him, tunneling his fingers beneath her hair to caress her nape. With the gentlest urging, she closed her eyes and buried her face in the heated juncture of his jaw and throat. The evening stubble of his beard rasped against her nose, and she breathed in the clean, spicy scent of him. Anchored so closely, they felt the gentle beat of the string bass vibrate through them both. As couples passed them by in time to the music, they simply stood there, and Casey shielded her indomitable gladiator with her body and her heart.

"This is it, Taylor!" A familiar man's voice, unnaturally shrill, shattered the loving illusion. "I'm officially scratching you off the list."

Rough fingers snatched her arm and jerked her out of Mitch's embrace.

"Jimmy!"

Casey stumbled against her Dutch uncle, but his bruising grip jerked her upright. The sour combination of brandy and cigars fanned her face as he slurred more accusations at Mitch.

"How dare you do this to my family! I counted on you to be discreet."

A waltzing couple bumped into them and loosened Jimmy's hold. His curse sent the apologetic dancers scurrying away. Others on the dance floor missed their steps and stopped to form a growing ring around them. But Mitch's beautiful eyes hardened with a deadly focus aimed directly at Jimmy.

"She's not a secret you hide away in a tower. If anyone deserves to shine in the light, it's Casey."

With a gleam of something close to satisfaction on his face, he snatched Jimmy's wrist and twisted it. The commissioner's fist popped open, freeing Casey from his punishing grasp.

Jimmy's cheeks flamed to scarlet as he massaged his wrist. "I'll have you up on charges of assault."

Casey ignored the soreness of her own arm and tried to reason against the groundless threat. "You've had too much to drink. I'm here of my own free will. Mitch hasn't done anything."

As the crowd gathered, Jimmy took center stage. "Cassandra will do what I tell her. First, you allowed that monster into her home. Then you whisk her away to your apartment. And now you parade her in front of half the city. You're just begging for Raines to try something."

An eerie sense of déjà vu chilled her. But instead of trapping her in the middle, Mitch edged to her side and slid his hand to the small of her back, supporting her. "We've been here for two hours. It's just now starting to bother you that she's out in the open like this?"

Iris Webster pushed her way through the crowd. Her smile for the guests around them vanished once she reached Jimmy.

"Darling, please. I know you're concerned, but you're

making a scene.'' She put her lips close to Jimmy's ear and whispered a succinct warning. ''The press is here.''

''We don't want to make the commissioner look bad, now do we?'' taunted Mitch.

When Jimmy lurched forward in an awkward physical threat, Iris linked her arm through his and pulled him back. ''He's worried about Cassandra. Maybe you should do a better job of protecting her, instead of accusing James of something that's not true. You have no idea the good this man can do for this city.''

The glare in her violet eyes speared Mitch, but he never wavered. ''He needs to do it for his family first.''

Iris's efficient voice shook with an intensity that went beyond that of a faithful employee. ''James lost nearly everything seven years ago. His best friend. His reputation.

''Cassandra, he's guarded you all this time out of loyalty to your father. He commands respect and authority. In a year, he could run for senator.''

''And you could be the senator's aide?'' prompted Mitch.

The angry clench of Iris's hand on Jimmy's sleeve drew Casey's attention. The last time she'd seen her, Iris had worn long gloves. But tonight she noticed the too-large-to-be-tasteful diamond ring on the third finger of the secretary's left hand.

''I won't dignify that with an answer.'' Not one hair of Iris's platinum-blond coiffure moved when she cocked her head and turned, steering Jimmy away from Mitch. ''I'll drive you home, James.''

Three beats of silence passed before the crowd began to murmur about the scene they'd just witnessed.

''Darling?'' Casey repeated the endearment she'd heard Iris use. ''She plans to be the senator's wife, not his aide. I wonder where he got the money for that gaudy ring.''

''He didn't buy it on a cop's salary.'' Mitch shook his head. ''Something smells dirty to me.''

''I think she loves him. That could explain why she's so protective of her boss.''

''Maybe he needs someone that loyal to watch his backside now. She seems devoted to the task.''

Startled by the similarity of their situations, Casey glanced up at her own watchdog. But before she could question the difference between loveless devotion to duty and loving devotion, Mitch guided her back toward their table. ''C'mon. Before the cameras find you, too.''

When they reached their chairs, Casey shrank into hers, shaking with delayed shock over the confrontation with Jimmy and Iris, and torn with her love for Mitch and her doubts about deserving to feel something so powerful for a man like him.

''Looks like another fan.'' Mitch's wry announcement forced Casey to put aside her thoughts and reach for the silver platter waiting on the table in front of her.

A rose this time. A full bloom in deep blood red. Long-stemmed and wrapped in clear plastic decorated with sprigs of holly. ''It's not exactly my color.''

She picked up the card lying beside the flower and read it. When she opened her mouth to scream, no sound came out.

''Casey?''

She knocked the tray off the table, and the contents scattered at her feet.

Mitch patted the front of his jacket and swore. ''The bastard picked my pocket. Joe!''

On the floor, pinned to a piece of hotel stationery, glinted the tiny replica of her silver medal. Her gift to Mitch.

He pulled her up and wrapped his arms around her, encircling her like a human shield. A slough of detectives surrounded them in a second circle. Urgent voices pushed the crowd back.

Casey searched for a face she had failed to recognize.

Again.

The waiter. She spotted one white jacket, and then the next. But knew no one.

She tried to push her way past the human wall surrounding her, but the cinch of Mitch's arm wouldn't budge. "Dammit, where the hell is he?"

The broken talisman that had once given her a sense of security mocked her. Somewhere in the crowd, Emmett Raines was laughing at her, too. Somewhere in the crowd, he knew his words were ringing true.

This is the rose, rich and rare,
That lay on the grave of the pretty pair
Who will die in the house that Jack built.

Chapter Ten

"You can't hide, can you?" The wraith of a man watched the predictable chaos around the mayor's table from the shadowy recesses of the coatroom. Tonight's show proved even better than he imagined. Then he laughed, a muffled, mad sound from deep in his chest. "I guess you can't run, either."

So many of his old friends gathered around Judge Jack's daughter. Curious. Concerned. Afraid for themselves.

They thought they could beat him at his game. But they were wrong.

Tonight's events were playing out with all the drama he had hoped for. Soon. Very soon, his mission would be accomplished, and his sister could finally know peace. He felt her restlessness, even after he knew she'd been put into the ground. He could feel her pain, her betrayal. Feel it as if it were his own.

They would pay for taking Darlene away from him. They would pay dearly for cutting out that part of his soul. Then he could rest. Darlene could rest.

He removed the tinted contact lenses from his eyes, popped them into his mouth and swallowed them. He'd need new supplies for his next performance. A pair of lifts for his shoes. Hair dye. He shrugged out of the white jacket he'd borrowed and stuffed it into his duffel bag. The banker's convenient stash had dwindled to almost nothing. The tip money from the waiter's pocket would provide cab fare, but little more.

But he didn't panic.

He never panicked.

That's what gave him his edge over those simpletons who had so many secrets to hide.

He went to the back of the coatroom and selected the brown tweed coat he'd been looking for. How tacky to wear it with black formal attire. But it would suit his purpose.

Before he climbed up to slip out of the hotel through the ventilation system, he noticed the full-length mink on the padded hanger at the back of the coatroom. He turned back the lining to check the hand-sewn identification label.

He crushed the material in his fist.

So Miss Peroxide was wearing it now. Maybe she didn't think anyone would remember that this coat had been bought for Cynthia DeBecque, and that by rights—for just payment of a job well done—his sister, Darlene, should be wearing it.

But he remembered.

He remembered the letter he'd gotten just a few weeks ago in prison, too. Darlene was worried. She was getting out for parole by January 1. She should have been thrilled.

But she'd been scared.

He could feel it now the way he'd felt it then. They'd always shared such a special connection. Twins, even fraternal twins, usually did.

He sighed deeply and savored the adrenaline rush that heated his veins. Darlene had the nerve, the ideas. He was the one to plan, to think. To make her ideas work. They functioned so well together. A perfect team. A single being.

But then Jack Maynard split them up. The no-budge judge locked her away from him, while his own little brat walked around in the spotlight.

But he'd taken care of that. She'd been imprisoned, too. But now she dared to venture out? When his own sweet Darlene couldn't anymore? Miss Maynard didn't deserve the privilege of living when Darlene was lying in the cold ground.

He clenched his teeth and breathed heavily through his nose, consciously controlling his burst of anger. He couldn't lose his focus now, not when he was so close to having them all playing the game his way.

Very soon, he'd have them all.

The judge who sentenced Darlene. His former employer who had decided he and Darlene were expendable. And Judge Jack's daughter. Because hurting her was the most satisfying way to make them all pay.

With the extra bulk of the fur tucked under his arm, he pushed aside a ceiling panel and climbed into the air duct above. Darlene would understand why he had to pawn her coat.

And he very much doubted anyone would report it stolen.

His friend out there wouldn't dare.

Laughter shook his chest as he replaced the panel and crawled outside.

"STAY PUT."

Casey nodded at Mitch's brusque command and stamped the snow off her boots on the mat inside the door of his cousin's cabin. Using the big metal flashlight he'd pulled from the glove compartment of his Jeep, he moved unerringly about the interior of the rustic structure, checking window locks, turning up the water heater and searching through the set-back kitchen for matches. He lit a kerosene lantern and placed it on the counter that served as a table and room divider. The yellowish glow illuminated some of the corners of the studio-style layout. But she noticed only the shadows the light couldn't reach.

"Is there electricity out here?" she asked, not missing the amenities of the city as much as she despaired knowing Emmett Raines had reduced her to hiding away in a secluded cabin south of a crossroads in the middle of nowhere near Truman Lake.

"Yeah. But the fastest way to warm up this place is to light the fire."

He knelt in front of the prepared logs in the rock fireplace and struck a match. The scent of sulphur stung her nose, but soon the odor gave way to the more homey smells of cedar and smoke as the wood caught flame and burst to life. He laid the matches on the hearth and turned and held out his hand to her. "Come here."

She obeyed the husky request, walking into the open arms of the truest haven she'd ever known. She buried her nose in the collar of his jacket, inhaling the bracing smells of smoke and winter air and warm man that clung to the damp wool. He methodically rubbed circles around her back and shoulders, instilling warmth and support.

"You okay?" His whisper was a dark rumble in her ear.

If she had tears left, she might have cried. But all she had left were the clothes on her back, the weariness of coming down after an adrenaline high and an ache in her heart withered by years of neglect and abandoned in the wake of a cruel man's vengeance.

Mitch closed his hands over her shoulders, pushing

some distance between them. But his gentle grip never slackened. "You know, it scares me when you're this quiet. Whatever you're thinking, don't."

She blinked and looked up. His eyes transformed into golden embers with the flickering reflection of the fire shining in their depths. Casey reached up and traced the tiny lines of age and sun and life beside his left eye. "How can you be so strong?" she asked, not really expecting an answer. "How do you keep going?"

"Because I have to. Just like you. I have to keep going."

Casey shivered despite the warmth of Mitch and the fire. He made no protest when she turned away to face the flames, hugging her arms around her middle. "Maybe I'm wrong to fight this."

"You don't really think that, do you? If we give up, Raines wins."

"Isn't he already winning?" Her voice sounded desolate in the cold silence of the cabin. "I wonder if the waiter he impersonated tonight had any family."

She hadn't for one moment considered that Emmett had *not* killed the man to take his place. Apparently, Mitch hadn't, either. "There are cops combing the hotel from top to bottom. We may know something by morning when I check in. Besides my cell unit, there's no phone out here."

Casey had lived with pain for seven years. She'd endured the grief of separating from her parents. She'd even managed to make peace with the loneliness. But this guilt...

How the hell could she live with the blood of innocent people on her conscience? "If only I could have done a better job of testifying against him."

"His sister would still be dead. And Raines would still have a vendetta against your family. Your father put Darlene Raines in prison. Because of that, she's dead. I think Raines wants a life for a life." Mitch's words hung in the air with the finality of a death knell. She heard a rustle of sound behind her. "I'm going to bring in some more firewood. I'll get my KCPD parka out of the Jeep and make sure there's no one around out there but Mother Nature."

When the bitter wind swirled into the cabin and swept around her, Casey didn't move. She was already cold, as cold as guilt and fear and heartache could make a person.

Eventually, she summoned the energy to dig up a kettle, two mugs and a canister of instant cocoa mix. She removed her leg brace to ease its chafing support. But she still couldn't relax. The day's events had left her reeling, unsure of herself, unsure of her purpose, unsure of anything save the need to make amends for her mistakes.

By the time Mitch returned, the water had heated over the open flame, and though she had no appetite, the idea of something warm on the inside to chase away the mental and physical chill appealed to her.

Mitch bypassed the light switch, turned up the thermostat and walked over to stand in front of the fire, shedding his parka, jacket and cummerbund as he went. The black leather of his shoulder holster stood out in stark contrast against his crisp white tuxedo shirt. From the recessed kitchen, she marveled at the brute strength of him, watching the ebb and flow of muscle across his back as he rubbed his hands together, then held them, palms out, toward the fire.

His shoulders needed to be that broad, she mused. How else could a man carry the responsibilities he did without crushing beneath the pressure? He possessed the will to match that physical strength, and the keen intelligence and acute instinct to use those strengths to his advantage.

And she...she could do so little for him. The one way

she could be useful to him, helping to capture Emmett Raines, she'd failed. Casey pushed aside that debilitating thought and squared her own shoulders. They had once propelled her to Olympic glory. Tonight, she vowed, they would be strong enough to help ease the burden she was to Mitch.

"Here." She crossed the room and pushed a mug of cocoa into his hands. "That should take off the chill."

"You didn't have to do that." But he still wrapped his fingers around the mug and sniffed the chocolaty steam appreciatively.

"It's no trouble." She stood beside him and sipped her own drink, willing the warmth of the fire, the cocoa and Mitch to chase away the frozen knot of guilt inside her. "Aren't you going to say 'I told you so'?"

He drank in thoughtful silence before answering. "You want me to?"

How could he deny his frustration and disappointment? This morning, he had vented his anger. Why did he keep it all inside now? "I looked that man right in the eye. He smiled at me and I didn't know him."

"You were worried about me. You were worried about all the people in that room. That's a hell of a lot to deal with and still concentrate on recognizing a man you haven't seen in seven years. I read the guy's file with a mug shot, and I didn't recognize him at the bank." His dark gaze flickered over her, and Casey turned her head to be ensnared by the fire dancing in his liquid amber eyes. "I think you did a very brave thing tonight, going to the banquet to try and force Raines's hand."

"But I failed."

He set his mug on the hearth, then loosened his tie and unhooked the top two buttons at his throat. "I don't think so. A guy like Raines wants to play the game by his rules.

You didn't tonight. You left your ivory tower, whether to save me or face him, it doesn't matter. You're not as easy to intimidate this time around. Now he has to fall back on Plan B, if he has one. Maybe enlist an accomplice, alter his timetable. He's more likely to make a mistake now, to tip his hand before seeking his next victim.''

''I'm terrified, Mitch.''

He reached out and feathered his fingers across her cheek. Casey leaned into the sweet tenderness of the caress. ''So am I, princess.'' She tipped her chin up, surprised by his admission. He cupped her jaw to ease the tremor there. ''But we can't let that terror rule us. Or Raines *will* win the game.''

''So what do we do?'' she asked on a breathless whisper.

He took her mug and set it beside his. He straightened with his arms outstretched, his dark eyes beseeching. ''We had our dance cut short tonight. Will you do me the honor?''

''There's no music.''

''Do we really need any?''

His throaty promise hummed along her spine. It turned her knees weak and sparked a responsive rhythm in her pulse. Slowly, daringly, she folded one hand into his and rested the other at his shoulder, already matching the subtle sway of his body. He pulled her to him, close enough to hear the brush of his wool trousers against the hem of her sweater, close enough to feel his powerful thighs press against hers.

Giving in to his strength, Casey laid her cheek on the pillow of his shoulder and slid her fingers to the back of his neck, finding that sensitive spot of his. He shuddered at her touch and his arm circled her waist, anchoring them together. They moved to the silent tune thrumming between them, hip against hip. He pulled their hands to the pulsing beat at the base of his throat and dropped his chin to brush against her knuckles.

The gentle abrasion of his evening beard made her long to feel that same friction against her cheek. She adjusted her stance and pressed her face to his. A thousand tiny fingertips stroked her skin and she gasped, inhaling Mitch's woodsy scent. A chain reaction skittered through her, upsetting the cadence of their dance, waking her body to the need of something much more elemental.

She missed a step and snatched at his shoulder to steady herself. Her fingertips brushed against smooth, cold leather. "Oh, my God." A jolt of panic surged through her. She shook her head and straightened, disoriented by the glaring reminder of death and danger.

"Easy, princess," he murmured, his voice a ragged reassurance that chased away her fears. He moved her grip to his waist, and she held on as he shrugged off his holster and set it on the mantel above the fireplace. He slid his hands across her shoulders and down her back. "It's just us," he whispered, whiskey-dark eyes glimmering with a fire of their own. "Tonight there's nothing else. No one else."

Casey latched on to his open collar and met his kiss, understanding and wanting and forgetting, just as he promised. His lips closed over hers, hard and demanding. A symphony exploded in her head as she opened her mouth and welcomed him. A hint of chocolate mingled with the taste of man when their tongues met and danced to the fiery concerto that consumed her.

Her mind dulled to everything but Mitch and the rightful claim of his mouth on hers, the needy pull of his hands as they glided beneath her sweater to heat the cool skin of her back. Her fingers didn't need the direction of conscious thought; they tugged at the placket of his shirt, freeing buttons and slipping inside to explore the masculine contrasts of hard skin and the soft, curling hair on his chest.

She closed her eyes against the dizzy sensation of flying. With urgent ease, he picked her up and set her down the sofa in front of the fire. "Mitch?"

He blanked out her confusion by covering her body with his, and covering her mouth with his own. Fear was forgotten. Inadequacy was forgotten. All she knew was Mitch and a need to hold and be held, to touch and be touched, to love and for this one night, be loved in return.

He pushed her sweater up and off over her head. His hand skimmed over the satiny camisole she wore. His lips trailed along a shoulder strap and over the swell of her breast before capturing a rigid peak through the silken barrier. Casey moaned at the sweet agony of it, wanting his touch, wanting more. She tunneled her fingers into his hair and clutched him to her, twisting the pooling ache of her hips against the hard evidence of his desire.

A cool breeze swept in between them and she gasped, the sharp intake of air almost as painful as the loss of his touch. She opened her eyes and sat up to see him kneeling beside the sofa. The quick rise and fall of his chest matched her own staccato breathing.

"Tell me you want me to stop now." He rasped the words out in tortured patience.

"I'm only afraid you will." Her words sounded small, vulnerable.

But they softened his rugged features into a handsome smile. He leaned forward and his rough hands cradled her face. "Whatever the lady wants."

He kissed her hard, branding her with his taste, assuring her of his desire, reigniting a feverish étude inside her. He pulled back to yank his shirttails from his waistband. He muttered a frustrated curse when the tiny buttons didn't respond to his large, eager fingers. Smiling at the unique feminine power his impatience gave her, she reached out and helped him shed the offending garment.

He returned the favor, and soon they were skin to skin on the blanket he spread over the braided rug in front of the fire. He played her body like a rare instrument, and his husky, eager responses to her touches gave her a confidence she'd never known before.

"You're mine tonight." He rose above her like a warrior victorious and claimed her with his lips and body. She surrendered willingly, giving herself over to the needful hands and brave heart of the man she loved.

SOMETHING WASN'T RIGHT.

Casey felt reluctant to give up the delicious warmth surrounding her. Lying on her side, she faced the crackling flames of the fireplace. Mitch must have added a new log while she slept. And she had learned that Mitch himself was a living, breathing furnace. He lay behind her now, just as he had after making love, holding her close to his chest, spoon fashion.

Only he wasn't holding her now. She felt his heat behind her, but as she roused herself from the groggy contentment of sleep, she recognized a detachment in him. He still sheltered her with his warmth, he was too caring to do otherwise. But he held himself back from her. She sensed the tension in his muscles. She smelled the restraint in him.

Had she disappointed him? She'd wanted him so badly last night, needed him. She was so out of practice with relationships, so far out of her league with Mitch. In the heat of the moment, he might have found her desirable.

But in the cool dawn's light, her inadequacies must be giving him some serious second thoughts.

Oh, God. If he said something polite and then excused himself to check the perimeter or call in the troops…

That's when she felt the brush of his fingers on her leg.

Over a ridge of scar tissue, down into the indentation of puckered skin, up over the next scar, then down again.

Casey snapped her eyes open, remembering a similar touch, a stroking hand from another place and time, admiring its handiwork and the pain it had inflicted.

Payback time. Emmett's voice wheezed through her mind.

"Please don't," she begged, her words a harsh whisper in the still air. The man was different. The touch was different. But the need to escape was all the same.

She sat up. Her body, replete with the wonder of Mitch's loving, protested the sudden action. She pulled the blanket up over her breasts, hiding her nakedness. She tried to pull her legs in under the cover, but her muscles had stiffened from sleeping on the floor.

"I didn't mean to frighten you. Princess, I…"

She jerked her shoulder away from Mitch's touch and rolled awkwardly onto her left knee and stood up. "You didn't frighten me."

He ignored the obvious lie and stood with her, freeing the blanket from beneath them. She tried to wrap herself in it, to hide herself from his view. Hours earlier, the blanket had been a soft nest of comfort. Now it felt bulky and scratchy. She clutched it to her breasts and behind her back.

Mitch stood before her as naked and glorious as a true gladiator. She was plenty warm now as the heat of shame climbed into her cheeks.

He'd seen her. He'd felt her. He knew the truth and she

could see it reflected in the unforgiving granite of his face. Her body repulsed him; her actions angered him. She'd thrown up her habitual walls of fear and distrust and shut him out. She backed away from the glower in his eyes.

She stumbled over the corner of the blanket, but Mitch caught her by the elbows to keep her from falling. His grip felt cool and impersonal. With deft, detached speed, he straightened the blanket, then draped it around her and over her shoulder, toga style.

"You gonna tell me what's wrong, or do I have to guess?" He released her quickly, picked up his briefs and pulled them on.

What's wrong? Wasn't it obvious?

"You tell me." Casey snapped the challenge at him, her pent-up emotions exploding in a rush of anger. She turned away, humiliated by the tears stinging her eyes. "On second thought, don't."

She had known he might find her lacking in the cold light of day. Like a fool, she had no one to blame but herself for thinking he wouldn't notice her deformities and be repulsed. She hurried awkwardly toward the bathroom, seeking the refuge of the only locked door she could put between them.

"Don't even think about it, princess." A vise clamped around her upper arm, stopping her in her tracks. She looked down at the steel grip concealed by the velvet gentleness of Mitch's five fingers. "There's no place here for you to run and hide. You're stuck with me."

"Don't you ever go off duty?" Sarcasm crept into her voice, defending her actions.

"I'm not talking about keeping you safe. I'm talking about being honest with me. Being honest with yourself."

Casey tipped her chin to defy the accusation. They stood nose to nose, his deep, even breathing a mocking counterpoint to his gold-rimmed eyes, shadowy with pain yet ringed by flashes of anger. She ignored the clench of compassion in her chest, the weight of guilt in her stomach. The habits of shame and self-preservation proved a more powerful force.

"Honest about what? You want me to tell how I honestly feel about you seeing me like this? About you seeing this weak, shriveled excuse for a leg? I'm embarrassed. Humiliated. I'm angry that I don't measure up. That no matter how many times the doctors graft on a layer of skin or alter the shape of a muscle, you can still see seven scars and know how that monster spells *revenge*."

"You finished?"

At some point during her tirade, he'd released her. The brilliant play of light in his eyes muted, and the utter stillness in his voice warned her too late of the limits of patience to which she pushed him. She flinched beneath his unforgiving scrutiny and dropped her gaze to the jut of his jaw. He turned away to pick up his tuxedo slacks from the night before and began to dress.

Casey tried to apologize, tried to make him understand that *she* accepted the blame for hurting him. "Look. Last night was a mistake. It shouldn't have happened. I don't want you to think I expect any kind of commitment, or that I'll put any pressure on you—"

"Oh, no, we wouldn't want to think that. Heaven forbid you get involved with the likes of me."

She took a step toward his broad, bare back. "Don't mock me, Mitch. It's hard to maintain a little bit of pride and keep the faith when you've lost nearly everything and a madman's trying to take away what little you do have left."

He glanced over his shoulder as he shrugged into his shirt, the grim slash of his mouth as cold and damning as the rigid planes of his back. "So now you're going to retreat to your ivory tower so you can nurse your wounds and feel sorry for yourself."

Casey lifted her chin in defiance. "I do not live in an ivory tower."

"Don't you?" Mitch turned on her, an angry beast roused from his cage. She instinctively backed away as he advanced toward her with spare, deliberate steps. "Every time you let your hair down a little too far, every time you show some real emotion, you lock down tighter than a prison riot. You tip that pretty little chin in the air and look down your nose at us poor peons who struggle to live with the real world. We deal with our problems—we don't hide from them."

Her spine flattened against the cold pine door at her back. Cornered. Trapped. She lashed out with the only defense left to her. "You don't know what it's like to lose everything!"

"Don't tell me I don't know what it feels like!" His initial flare of anger cooled to a deep, gravelly whisper that chilled her to her very bones. "I buried a wife. I buried my marriage long before that. I lost my parents to a junkie too stoned to even know he had shot two people. At least you have a chance to see yours again. I have to go to Washington Cemetery to visit mine."

She caught her breath and held the punishing assault of his gaze, ashamed of being so small, so weak. Then, as if he couldn't stand the sight of her a moment longer, he broke away. He sat on the sofa and pulled on his socks and shoes. Casey's shoulders slumped in concession to his rightful claim.

"But you're strong enough to deal with it. To move past it."

"So are you." He concentrated on the laces of his

shoes. ''You're the stubbornest woman I've ever met. You can handle anything.''

He silenced her protest by standing up and refusing to hear it. He picked up his gun and holster from the mantel, strapping it on like a weary soldier returning to battle. The image didn't sit well when he finally turned to her again.

''When I look at you, I don't see your leg. I see your courage. And I see my anger at what that bastard did to you. And I think things that are not at all professional. Things that could get my badge trashed permanently.'' He pulled on his suit jacket, building up yet another layer of symbolic armor she didn't possess. ''I'm sorry he hurt you. I'm sorry he hurt your career. I'm sorry he hurt your family. But most importantly, I'm sorry he took away your ability to trust.''

''I'm sorry…that I love you. And because of Emmett Raines, you'll never believe that I do. And, sweetheart, that's one dragon I can't slay for you.''

He put on his parka and walked away from her in firm, purposeful strides that negated the regret stamped in his voice. He turned up his hood against the brisk winter wind and went outside. The tumbler in the lock snapped into place behind him, echoing with the secure formality of a jail cell.

As that ominous click faded into the silence, Casey huddled inside the blanket, with silent tears streaming down her cheeks.

Chapter Eleven

Casey fingered the set of Ellis Peters mysteries Mitch's cousin Jessie kept on the bookshelves in her cabin. Once she, too, had loved reading mysteries. She enjoyed the intellectual challenge, the triumphant feeling of a smart detective outthinking the bad guys. She'd read of little old ladies and curious monks who had solved thefts and kidnappings and murders.

She knew of broad-shouldered warriors and petite blondes and lanky youths who did the same thing in real life. Fictional or real, they all seemed to possess a courage of character that Casey lacked.

Courage.

Mitch said he looked at her and saw courage.

Physical courage, perhaps. She imagined she had that in abundant supply. She'd swum through pain, rehabilitated herself after injuries, learned how to walk all over again.

But emotional courage?

"I love you," he'd said. She *didn't* believe Mitch. She couldn't.

He cared. He sheltered her. He made sweet, passionate love to her. But she didn't have the courage to believe he'd pledge his heart. Not to her. He couldn't really mean that.

Sighing deeply, Casey left the books on their shelf and circled the interior of the cabin one more time. She'd cleaned the place within an inch of its life. She'd put together a lunch for Merle Banning and herself, and drunk her fill of hot chocolate. She was slowly driving herself crazy having nothing to do but think.

She'd dressed and put away their bedding by the time Mitch came back inside that morning. The only thing he'd said to her then was that he needed to get back into town to get work clothes and follow up some leads, once a replacement guard arrived.

Merle was a nice enough young man, but he sorely lacked conversation skills. The dim afternoon sun and the shrouded quiet of the secluded cabin were slowly driving her nuts. She'd trained herself to tolerate, even appreciate, the drafty expanses and relentless solitude of her home on the Plaza. But this isolation felt different.

She felt different.

She'd been dead before Mitch Taylor barreled into her life, a spiritless shell of the woman she'd once been. Now she was alive, full of emotions she couldn't keep buried anymore.

She felt restless. Guilty. Afraid.

Afraid to love. Afraid to be loved. Afraid that Emmett Raines would take away her chance at love before she could figure it all out.

Mitch was right. Maybe she didn't hide away in a tower of stone or ivory anymore. But she was still a prisoner of her fear, a damsel locked away from life by the cold, bleak walls constructed out of a paralyzing fear of loss. That was a demon she had to conquer herself, a risk she had to be willing to take. But how did she fight that battle? How did she win that race?

Casey ended up in the kitchen, searching through cupboards to keep her hands busy.

"Hungry?" Merle's polite voice broke in on her thoughts.

"There's no coffee here," she replied. She'd sought out a hot caffeine rush earlier and had been disappointed. Now it served as a ready excuse for her brooding silence. "Maybe I'm going through withdrawal."

The young detective grinned. He didn't have the years and experience on his face that Mitch had, but he had a winning smile that proved contagious. "I was thinking the same thing." He closed the book he'd been reading and set it on the stool beside him. "There's a convenience store at the crossroads. What say we load up on the cappuccino and head right back?"

Grabbing at the distraction, any distraction, Casey joined him at the coatrack. "Won't you get into trouble?"

"With this extra layer of snow, the place is probably as deserted as we are out here. I'll call in to let them know our location, and then we'll head back here ASAP."

"Sounds good to me."

Twenty minutes later, Casey shivered at a Formica-topped table opposite from Merle, cradling a steaming vanilla cappuccino in her hands. The excursion had provided a change of scenery, if not a true diversion. Merle had buried his nose in the daily paper and prolonged his contented silence while he waited for a return call on his cell phone.

He'd been right about the traffic at the remote location. They were the only customers in the building, and the clerk who'd waited on them had already returned to her crossword puzzle behind the counter.

Casey was considering giving in to the urge to buy a tabloid magazine to find out exactly how a woman in the

Ukraine had given birth to forty-pound alien twins when Merle set down his coffee and smiled at her. "Hey, you made the paper."

"No kidding?" Feeling as self-conscious as if her face were on the cover of that checkout tabloid instead of buried in the society column of a respected daily paper, she nonetheless smiled back and took the section of paper Merle handed her.

Olympic Star Turns Out For Awards Benefit.

Casey groaned at the headline. If only the writer knew what kind of threat it had taken for her to venture out into the public eye. In the picture, Mayor Benjamin swallowed up her hand in his, while Mitch loomed behind her in the photo.

She'd graced the paper many times, either in relation to her parents' successes or because of her own accomplishments. But as she studied the picture, she could see she'd lost the brash sparkle and athletic confidence of the college-aged hero she'd once been. Despite the pallor on her cheeks, she wore a serene smile on her lips, and her eyes reflected dark determination as she greeted the mayor.

Is that what Mitch saw? The mature woman in the photo? Her leg brace was hidden by her coat. She looked like any of the other women crowded into the kitchenette area. Whole. Strong. As if she belonged.

Not fragile. Not wounded. Not a pampered hothouse flower tended by a vigilante Dutch uncle and doting staff.

"Oh, my God," she whispered. Did the rest of the world see something in her she couldn't see herself? An inner strength that Mitch nurtured, challenged and admired. A perseverance that she herself had allowed to atrophy over the years by backing down from any emotional fight that came her way.

Something stubborn and brittle broke loose inside her.

A fractured self-image that she'd clung to beyond the point of healing. She'd been afraid for so long. She had every right to be afraid. But looking back from that newspaper photograph stood a woman with the means—with the courage—to confront her fear head-on.

Be it Emmett Raines, or Uncle Jimmy, or Mitch's love. "Oh, my God."

"Did you say something?" Merle asked, breaking through her introspective path to discovery.

Casey turned her focus on him and smiled. "No. I was just thinking."

Her lack of an explanation seemed explanation enough. Merle tapped the top of one page. "There's a bit about last night, too, back on the third or fourth page." He stood and reached into the pocket of his jeans. He set his keys on the table and fished through a handful of change, dumping three quarters and a dime onto the table. "You want something to eat? I'm gonna grab a candy bar."

"I'm fine, thanks." After he scooped up his change and crossed the store, Casey thumbed through the paper, looking for the article he had mentioned. She made a mental note to ask Merle if someone would contact the McDonalds. They'd be reporting back to work after their Thanksgiving vacation to find either a police barricade or an empty house. She felt bad enough to have raised their concern with Emmett's escape, but the stories in the Monday paper, combined with her unexplained absence, would cause a needless panic for the staff who had been like family to her for so long.

On the third page of the front section, she found the article Merle had referred to. Above stock photos of Jimmy and Mayor Benjamin, she scanned through the list of awards that had been handed out the previous evening. Beneath the photographs, she read a second article in more detail regarding the reception that had followed the banquet. She glossed over the references to her own grand entrance and exit, and focused on the comments Jimmy had given to this particular reporter.

In a room full of distinguished police officers, how could one escaped murderer manage to threaten the late Judge Maynard's daughter? Commissioner Reed had this to say: "Jack Maynard was like a brother to me. We worked together on my election campaigns. 'The house that Jack built' is the slogan I came up with to promote his tough stance on repeat and violent offenders. I still stand behind those promises."

A disquieting chill of almost awareness shivered along Casey's spine. She read on.

"A man like Emmett Raines must not be allowed to terrorize innocent people. Be assured that we are doing everything in our power to track down and recapture this man. My goddaughter was hiding at a safe house that was compromised. The leak to that location will be dealt with. She has a full protection unit with her now, in case Raines is foolish enough to contact her again. We'll get him."

The article included comments from the mayor and city councilmen on their crackdown on crime. But Casey's gaze drifted back to her uncle's words. A safe house? Did he know she'd been at Mitch's? Or had someone filled him in at the banquet?

The house that Jack built.

She thought of the escalating terror of Emmett's cryptic messages to her. *The house that Jack built will come tum-*

bling down. Jimmy built that house with her father. They led a team of law-and-order professionals who helped lower the crime rate in the metropolitan area. And if he was part of that team, then...

"He knows something," Casey whispered out loud. His strange, unpredictable behavior, Iris's overprotective machinations—both were signs she had overlooked earlier. If Casey had been threatened, then no doubt Jimmy had been threatened, too.

She needed to talk to her dear old uncle. Face-to-face where Iris couldn't screen the call or take a message that would never be delivered.

She crumpled the newspaper in her fists, weighing the possible excuses she could use to get back to the city. If she shared her suspicions with Merle, he'd just phone them in and someone else would try to talk to Jimmy. Nor would he go against Mitch's orders and drive her there himself.

"Merle."

He wadded his candy wrapper and tossed it into the trash can. When he sat down across from her, she lowered the paper and feigned casual curiosity.

"Is my house still cordoned off as a crime scene? Would anybody still be watching it?"

"No. We cleared out of there yesterday. With the old man involved, we're moving the investigation along pretty quickly."

Old man. She heard his respect for Mitch, even in the silly nickname. She hoped what she was about to do wouldn't get him into serious trouble with his commanding officer.

"Would it be all right if we drove back into town and I got a change of clothes and some makeup? I've been wearing these since yesterday morning."

He shook his head with a rueful smile. "Mitch would

have my hide.'' But then his expression brightened. ''I can call Ginny, though, have her pick up something.''

''That'd be great.''

He dug his cell phone out of his coat pocket.

''Could you contact Ben and Judith McDonald, too? I don't know if they'd be at the house or their home, but I don't want them to worry unnecessarily about me. Judith could pack my bag, too. She'd know what I need.''

''McDonald,'' he repeated, punching in a number on the phone. ''I'll have to call the precinct to track them down. Maybe Ginny can get that number for me, too.''

''I appreciate it.'' Casey stood and slid the paper off the tabletop as she straightened. ''I'll just go freshen up, then. If you'll excuse me.''

She clutched the paper in front of her and hurried to the rest room in the back of the building. She slipped inside only long enough to unroll the newspaper and let Merle's ring of keys drop into her hand.

She trashed the paper and breathed deeply, trying to calm her pounding heartbeat. She hadn't sneaked out of a building since before her training days at Kansas University. Getting past Merle required speed and stealth, two more abilities Emmett Raines had stolen from her.

But she had questions that couldn't wait to be answered. Questions whose answers could piece together motives and stop a madman from killing again. Answers that could return her life to normal.

She pushed the door open just far enough to spot Merle pacing back and forth at their table, arguing into the phone—on her behalf, no doubt. Swallowing a twinge of guilt along with a prayer for success, Casey slipped out the back service door and around the side of the building where the detective had parked his nondescript sedan.

The winter air seeped in through the half-closed door as

she struggled to find the release button that would allow her to turn the key in the ignition. She'd slam the door shut later, once she was on the road. She'd worry about answering for her actions later, too, about justifying to the police—and Mitch, especially—why she stole a car and took the investigation into her own hands. The only person who could really understand a family secret was family. She'd lost seven years of her life believing herself to be some kind of family sacrifice. It was a sentence she'd agreed to because she thought she'd been paying a debt to her family, protecting them, according to Jimmy. Protecting herself.

Protecting the house that Jack built.

The key turned and the engine roared to life. She angled her body to release the brake and hit the accelerator with her left foot. She didn't have her purse, her license or any recent experience behind the wheel of a car. She slammed the gears into reverse and backed out, then shocked the cold engine by shifting into drive without the benefit of slowing down. She barely missed the gas pumps and hurtled over the curb before Merle ran out of the store, chasing her only a few steps before getting on his phone once more. She heard his curses in the air, felt deserving of every last one.

But Casey was on the verge of discovering the truth. Her mind tossed together pieces of a puzzle her heart didn't want to complete.

She'd been protecting the world that her father had built.

But only now did she realize that more than one person wanted to destroy it.

"WHAT ARE YOU TRYING to cover up?" Casey dogged Iris Webster around her office workroom, shadowing the eerie efficiency with which the older woman retrieved files, shredded papers and packed documents into a leather attaché.

Normally, Jimmy's suite of offices was a bustle of activity, even at five o'clock when the other public offices closed for the evening. But this place looked as if it had been deserted for an hour or more.

"Go home, Cassandra," warned Iris. "We have everything under control."

"Under control? There's a trail of dead bodies from Jefferson City to downtown K.C." Casey pointed to the black bag on the desk. "It looks to me like you're leaving town. Does Jimmy know what you're doing?"

Iris finally stopped. Her shoulders rose and fell in a weary sigh. She shook her head. "If only you had stayed put."

Casey squared her shoulders against the accusatory look. "Mitch didn't think it was safe."

"Mitch." Casey bristled at the ridiculing laughter in Iris's voice. "Assistant commissioner. Not while I'm in office."

"You work for the office. You don't run it."

Iris's violet eyes narrowed to derogatory slits. Then she resumed her work at the same controlled, but manic pace as before. Casey picked up a fistful of paper from the shredding machine and made herself at home, refusing to be dismissed. As she pieced together the long strips of paper, an image began to form. Outrage made her crush it in her hand again, and she moved to block Iris's path to the briefcase.

"This is Mitch's picture from the newspaper. The one Emmett faxed to his apartment. Why do you have a copy of it?"

The older woman's bottom lip actually trembled before she pressed her lips together in a tight line and answered.

"Coincidence. We're shredding everything that has to do with that horrid case."

"How did you know I was at Mitch's condo?" asked Casey.

"I didn't."

"How did Emmett know I was at Mitch's?" She repeated the question with more force.

She heard the click of a closing door a split second before a third voice answered for her. "Iris doesn't know." Jimmy's smooth tenor voice cut through the room and stilled her questions.

The late-November air clung to his coat and briefcase, and tickled her nose as he crossed the rose-colored rug to stand in front of her. "Where's your guard dog?" he asked.

She didn't pretend to misunderstand his question. "Mitch is working."

Jimmy tutted his tongue against the roof of his mouth. "I specifically ordered him not to leave your side until Raines was caught."

"I've had around-the-clock protection. He's doing his job just fine." Never mind the falling-in-love part. Never mind dragging her kicking and screaming and loving back into the real world. She closed her mind to the growing realization of her feelings for Mitch. "He's gone above and beyond the call of duty."

Jimmy glanced around the office, his superior gaze making note of Casey's absent bodyguards. "Yes, I can see how well he's doing his job."

Casey shook her head, clearing her emotions from her thoughts. She wasn't here to defend Mitch, though she sorely wanted to wipe that superior smirk from Jimmy's face and remind him that Mitch was busy tracking down a killer while it appeared that Jimmy and Iris were packing up to leave town. She was here to confront her uncle. "I need to talk to you."

He purposely ignored her request and spoke to Iris. "Is everything ready? I don't want to be late." Then he looked at Casey and gave her a familiar smile that didn't feel so warm and indulgent anymore. "You have five minutes."

She followed Jimmy into his silver-and-black office. He set the briefcase on his glass-topped desk and picked up the phone. He eyed Casey across the coldly modern lines of his steel-and-polished-ebony desk. "Where are you going?" she asked.

The assessing look in his dark eyes felt equally cold. "Conference in Mexico City. Had it planned for weeks."

His glib answer left a bitter taste on her tongue. "Awfully convenient, isn't it? You sure you can stand to leave me, what with Emmett Raines stalking me and all?"

He lifted his hand as if he didn't have time to listen to the pain of betrayal in her voice and spoke into the phone. "Yes, Detective Banning. She's right here, and she's fine. I'll take good care of her. Don't worry."

"Merle?" Pain gave way to the dawn of understanding. "That's how you knew where I was. But he's part of Mitch's team."

Jimmy hung up the phone and opened his briefcase. "He's part of *my* team. I gave him a call when Mitch broke contact with me. He's young enough not to be completely swayed by Taylor's questionable charisma. Banning understands the chain of command and how to take orders. Not all of my detectives in the Fourth Precinct do."

Casey couldn't tell if the subtle dig was directed toward Mitch or herself. She wavered toward a chair but didn't sit. If she gave in to the shock of finding out more than she wanted to know, she might never be able to stand on her own two feet again. If she became that spineless shell of a woman she'd been before Mitch came into her life, she'd never be able to look him in the eye.

And suddenly, she wanted very desperately to see Mitch and tell him exactly what she thought of him. Exactly what she felt for him. Exactly what she hoped she could prove to be for him.

She breathed in deeply and steeled her nerves. She glimpsed stacks of gray-green numbers lined up in Jimmy's briefcase. "Just how much money is in there?"

"Enough."

He closed the briefcase and gave her a very clear view of the handgun he pointed at her. A brief clutch of fear gave way to an almost giddy feeling of relief that Jimmy had finally swept away any remaining hopes and loyalties she had invested in him.

"So Merle kept you apprised of where I was hiding. And you just let that information slip to Emmett Raines?"

The house that Jack built...the slogan I came up with.

A connection blipped into her mind, and Casey felt like an idiot for not seeing it sooner. "You've been sending me those horrible rhymes."

"Just the one at Taylor's apartment."

Shock drained the blood down to her toes and made her light-headed. She'd suspected the truth, but hadn't expected him to admit it so casually, as if he were discussing an interesting old case over a family dinner instead of holding her at gunpoint and confessing to threatening her life.

Casey fought to regain control of her emotions. She narrowed her gaze and tunneled in on the tightening fist of Jimmy's free hand. "I wanted to get the job done," he went on. "But Raines thrives on the thrill of the game. That was his problem seven years ago, too. All they had to do was get the pictures and eliminate Cynthia. But he just couldn't—''

''James!'' The hard-edged female voice silenced her uncle's tendency to vocalize his frustrations. But no further reprimand came. ''We're on a tight schedule. Remember?''

''Yes, the car's waiting for us downstairs.''

Casey tried hard to think straight, to keep her sarcastic responses in check. So much rage swelled up inside her, it was hard to control the need to lash out. The need to hurt the man who had done her as great an injustice as the man who had nearly taken her life seven years ago.

Right now, she needed to think of a way to get help, needed to find a way to escape. But until the inspiration came, she held her tongue and followed Iris out the door, the gun pointed at her back an almost tangible pinprick between her shoulder blades.

No one spoke until the three of them stood inside the elevator. When Iris reached out to push the ground-floor button, another piece of the puzzle began to take shape.

''Where's your mink?'' Casey asked, noting the black wool coat Iris wore over her suit.

The other woman's fingers stiffened for an unguarded instant, then pulled back in a classic catalog pose. ''I don't wear formal attire to work.''

''Why did you come here, Cassandra?'' asked Jimmy, distracting her from her study of Iris.

''I was worried about you.'' Casey smiled at her own stupidity. ''I thought Iris...I thought you might be in danger, too. I hoped you weren't involved with Emmett Raines. I wanted you to prove me wrong.''

''I would have done anything for your father.''

''Meaning he didn't return the favor?''

''Quiet. Both of you.'' Iris hushed them again. ''I have

covered your mistakes for more than ten years, James Reed. Don't go soft on me now." She nailed Jimmy with a look that allowed Casey to see a gray-faced man whose once distinguishing character lines seemed deeper than she remembered. Despite the gun in his hand, he was a poor copy of the vibrant Dutch uncle she had once cherished.

Three more floors passed in silence before Casey returned her attention to Iris. "You really do run the office, don't you?"

"He's a great man." Iris's assertion held all the warmth and sincerity of Dr. Frankenstein describing his monster.

"Where's your diamond ring, Iris? Don't tell me the engagement's off." Casey's sympathy sounded equally sincere.

Iris sent Jimmy a look that could have withered a redwood tree. His dark eyes glared back with a forced deference that didn't sit well on his shoulders. For a brief instant, Casey knew her presence had been forgotten.

Jimmy compressed his lips into a weary frown. "I'll get it back for you as soon as I can."

"If only you had listened to me when I said to…"

The two of them silently duked it out to see who was the controlling member of their twisted partnership. But any chance of slipping away vanished when the elevator dinged and the doors parted. Jimmy poked the gun into her ribs, hiding the weapon in the folds of her coat. They walked through the lobby and climbed into the back seat of Jimmy's Continental without exchanging anything more than a nod to the people they encountered.

Without a word, Iris pulled into traffic. "Where are we going?" Casey asked, the tension between her abductors nearly as suffocating as the fear choking her veins.

"Home, my dear," he answered. "We're taking you home."

On Jimmy's lips, the granite walls of the Plaza house she grew up in no longer sounded like a haven to her. She clasped her hands together in a silent prayer, not for hope of rescue, but for forgiveness. Forgiveness for not coming to her senses sooner, and hurting Mitch the way she had that morning.

"Two questions, Jimmy," she asked, feeling her time running out and wanting to know the truth. "How long has Emmett Raines been blackmailing you? And why the hell did you stick my family in the middle of it?"

Chapter Twelve

Mitch pulled open the front of his jacket, rested his hands on his hips and breathed deeply. He felt tired. Weary beyond the usual long, frustrating hours he put in supervising an unsolved case.

He watched the crime-scene team scour the loading dock for physical evidence. Ernie Hutchins, the missing waiter, had been strangled with a knotted napkin and hidden in a laundry hamper. Dead for nearly twenty-four hours, poor Ernie was yet another innocent caught up in a web of deceit and revenge that seven years and five dead bodies still couldn't satisfy.

"He lived with an Elisa Alvorado in Raytown." Joe Hendricks strolled up beside Mitch and pocketed the notebook he'd been reading. "I'll get one of the local boys over there to do the notification. Unless you think we need to do any kind of follow-up questions?"

Mitch scanned the connecting walkway off the kitchen, then looked back at the shrouded figure on the transport gurney. "Whatever we need to find is here. Let her grieve without us nosing in."

They stood side by side, two old friends comfortable with the silence between them. Yet despite his fatigue and Joe's company, a restlessness plagued Mitch. A prickle of uneasiness twitched at the base of his neck, and he rubbed the spot. Unbidden came the memory of Casey's fingers there, smaller than his, yet strong. Magical. His body tensed with the memory of her in his arms last night. Needy yet giving. And beneath that false icy exterior of hers, fiery to the touch and healing to the soul.

Yet he couldn't reach *her* soul. He couldn't open up his heart to her. She just couldn't—wouldn't—see it. After Jackie's betrayal, he thought it would be enough to be needed again. He knew he gave Casey a sense of security, that his presence, despite their battle of wills, strengthened her. He challenged her quick mind and eased the desires of her body and listened when she reached out. She needed him, all right. It was almost enough.

Being needed made him feel useful. It gave him an acceptance of sorts, a personal connection he couldn't get from the detectives who worked for him or the citizens he served or even the extended family who'd taken him in. But that connection wasn't enough to fill the emptiness in his long abandoned heart. He wanted something more than the need, something more than the desire.

He wanted the love.

He wanted her to accept his love.

Another twinge had him rolling his neck to relieve the sensation.

"Something not sittin' right?" asked Joe, eyeing Mitch with a knowing suspicion.

Mitch pretended his buddy couldn't read the current focus of his thoughts and speculated out loud about his impressions of the crime scene. "Why didn't Raines cut up the body?"

Joe shrugged. "Was it a spur-of-the-moment decision to do the waiter?"

Mitch shook his head. "He doesn't do things on the spur of the moment."

"Interrupted?" Joe's direct eye contact reinforced his idea on the scenario of the crime. "Something must have come up to change his plans."

"Casey." Joe nodded and followed Mitch over to the corpse. "He was going to impersonate someone else, but she showed up and presented an opportunity he couldn't resist."

"So what was his original plan? Who was his original target?"

Mitch didn't have the exact answer yet. "The commissioner? The mayor?"

"He couldn't pass as that public a figure. Too much scrutiny would give him away, no matter how good a disguise he has."

"It could be me. I left my coat here last night. It's not here today." It wouldn't be the first time Raines had targeted Casey's bodyguard to get to her. He reached into his pocket and touched the nickel-sized reassurance of Casey's broken pin. If Raines did have a scheme to replace him, at least he hadn't gotten his hands on the identifying medallion.

"It might have gotten bagged up as evidence." Joe's reasoning made sense.

"Check it out. It may be nothing, but I want to cover every angle."

"I'll send someone over to lost and found, too."

Mitch pulled out his notepad and reviewed the observations he had made on the investigation. "Get me a list of the banquet guests."

"That's over five hundred...."

"I don't care if it's five thousand. I want to know who Raines planned to kill."

A female voice entered the conversation. "I think I can narrow your list." Ginny often saw a crime scene from a different perspective than the other detectives, and Mitch was a smart enough captain to listen to more than one idea.

"What are you thinking?"

She held out a slim manila folder. "Here's the cleanup report on Darlene Raines's murder. She was stabbed by a lifer named Rochelle Jackson."

Mitch opened the file and scanned the contents. "The warden doesn't know who set it up yet?"

"He didn't make a connection. But I think *you'll* be interested in a visitor she had about a week before the hit."

"Darlene?"

"Rochelle." Ginny corrected him and pointed to a line on the report. "Read the name on the sign-in sheet."

Mitch read the registration, bit down on the surge of triumph that turned his frustration into a plan of action, then looked up to let his pride congratulate Ginny. "Iris Webster."

His mind raced to fit the missing pieces of the complicated puzzle together, finding concrete answers to back up the suspicions his instincts had known from the evening he'd first called on Casey. He thought back to the run-in on the dance floor after the banquet. Then, she'd noted the curiously personal connection between James Reed and his assistant.

He stuffed the folder back into Ginny's hands and pulled out his phone. "Get me IDs on those stolen items from Cynthia DeBecque's murder, and a search warrant for Iris Webster's apartment."

Aftershocks from the tiny spasm in his neck rippled all the way down his spine. Fear was an urgent thing. And suddenly, every cell in Mitch was deathly afraid.

"Who are you calling?" asked Joe, tensing along with him.

"Casey."

When Merle Banning answered the phone, he was in the passenger side of a county sheriff's car speeding toward downtown Kansas City.

"What do you mean she's not with you?"

Merle's concise report rocketed Mitch's blood pressure to a ballistic reading. Why the hell had the idiot taken Casey out for coffee? Mitch forced himself to breathe deeply. Merle was still young and impressionable, and Mitch knew how stubborn Casey could be when she set her mind to a thing. He clenched his jaw and did his damnedest not to reach across the airwaves and rip off the kid's badge.

"Do you know where she is?"

Later, he might commend the kid for not making excuses for his mistake. Right now, Merle's quiet response plunged Mitch into a heart-stopping chill a hundred times colder than the raw winter air outside. "I think she went to see the commissioner."

Mitch cut off Merle and punched in a second number. After four rings, he hung up and snapped an order at Joe. "Get someone over to Reed's office and find him and his damn assistant. I need their location ASAP." He vaulted down the steps from the loading dock and hurried across the parking lot.

Joe fell into step beside him, pulling out his phone before asking, "What's wrong with Casey?"

"She got away from Merle. He thinks she went to see her uncle."

"And that's bad because...?"

"I think Emmett Raines was here to see Iris Webster

last night.'' Mitch climbed inside his Jeep and placed the portable siren on the roof.

"You think the commissioner's in danger, too?''

"No.'' The strength of Mitch's conviction was based on instinct, a lot of circumstantial evidence and the observations of one very bright, very beautiful redhead. "I'll bet my badge he and Raines are in this together.''

Mitch gunned the engine and flipped on the siren. The woman he loved was diving headlong into an irreversible disaster. And he might not get there in time to save her.

CASEY STUMBLED along the path at Jimmy's side, half hopping, half limping, as he hurried her toward the pool house. Though the gun in her side never moved, his gaze darted from side to side, as if expecting to be discovered at any moment.

For the first time, she saw her home the way Mitch had seen it, a prison surrounded by granite walls and iron bars. If Jimmy worried about getting caught, she'd tell him to rest easy. No one could see inside the Maynard estate.

On that note of gloom, he pulled out the key to the pool-house door. He turned the key in the lock. Casey tensed when he did. The door was already open.

"Expecting company?'' she asked, worried at the way Jimmy bit into his lip. His desperation already made him unpredictable. Another surprise could push him over the edge, and he might accidentally find the nerve to pull the trigger before she could escape.

"Shut up.'' His breathing caught and jump-started.

She made her move before he panicked. "We should just turn around and get back into the car with Iris. You have plenty of money. You can leave the country now, and Emmett will be blamed for everything.''

"I said shut up!'' He jerked her arm, nearly pulling it

from its socket. She fell against him and he hissed into her ear. "I have a campaign to run. These loose ends should have been dealt with long ago."

The door opened and Jimmy froze. Off balance, Casey turned more slowly to see the source of his shock. "That's no way to treat the lady."

"Mitch." She breathed his name on a grateful prayer. He filled the doorway, tall and broad. Cold-eyed anger flushed his face.

"It's you." Jimmy's greeting reflected her surprise. "How…?"

"Let her go." Mitch's command was a simple one.

Jimmy's hand unlocked like a springing clamp. Casey took a tentative step forward. But Mitch's gaze pinned Jimmy in his place. She took a second step, testing her escape. Jimmy made no move, said nothing. She ran the last two steps, threw her arms around Mitch's waist and held on tight. She buried her face in the secure familiarity of his tweed coat as one big arm cinched around her shoulders and pulled her into his protective embrace.

He pressed a kiss to her temple. "You're safe with me now."

Her blinding relief evaporated in the rapid-fire sensations that shot through her. The odd rasp in Mitch's deep voice. The subtle difference of her forehead butting beside his jaw instead of beneath it. He had no gun beneath his coat.

She snatched at his collar, her fingers as frantic as a madwoman's. She flipped his lapels, pushed aside the front of his coat, checked the suit he wore beneath.

No pin.

"Emmett…" Even as she backed away, his arm dropped to her waist and tightened like a vise. She shoved at his chest and screamed. "No!"

She kicked at his shins with her good foot. He cursed and lifted her off the floor. "Dammit, Jimmy boy, you're late."

Casey twisted and scratched and screamed for all she was worth. She'd been a fool. Over and over. An idiotic fool.

It couldn't end like this. She wouldn't let it end like this. He carried her to the pool and dropped her onto a wooden deck chair. She struggled to her feet, but he pushed her down and knelt on her lap, pinning her while he tied her hands together.

"Snap out of it, Jimmy boy. Get this damn thing off her leg."

"No." She hated to hear herself plead, but she begged anyway. Without her brace, she'd be virtually helpless. As if she stood a chance against these two men anyway.

With Emmett blocking her vision, she could only hear the rip of Velcro, and grimace against the jolt of pain as Jimmy tugged off her brace. She swallowed her pain in a silent gulp as Emmett shifted his weight off her and her foot flopped to the tile deck.

She locked her gaze on his as he backed up a step. He picked up her brace and held it out, taunting her like a carrot before a weary horse. At the last moment, she succumbed and lunged for it. But Emmett pulled it back, out of reach, and flung it behind him into the pool.

He laughed as he knelt in front of her. She watched him pull out a knife and open it as carefully and reverently as a surgeon's scalpel. She tilted her chin against the obvious threat, and fought to even out her breathing and remain calm enough to think.

"It's fitting, isn't it? The scene of so many triumphs for you shall be the scene of your final defeat." The well-honed point of Emmett's stainless-steel blade traced the line of her jaw and pricked a tiny cut in the point of her chin.

Though tinted brown by contacts she could now see, the eerie lack of color gleamed in his unblinking eyes. She had expected to feel terror the next time she looked into Emmett's icy eyes, not the creeping calm that simmered in her veins as he stroked her with his deadly caress. She glanced over at Jimmy as he paced into view behind her, the heels of his shoes clicking a nervous staccato on the deck tiles. She felt no fear there, either. Only pity that he had sacrificed family loyalty to Emmett's vengeance. And anger that he had used her father and Mitch and countless others with as little remorse as he had used her.

Jimmy stopped and turned on Emmett, but kept Casey as a cautious barrier between them. "Quit the theatrics, Raines. You said you wanted her. When Banning called and told me she had bolted, I thought she might come to me. I delivered her ahead of schedule. Now give me the negatives."

"All in good time, Jimmy boy." Emmett smiled indulgently, his gaze following the trail the knife made as it grazed across her lips. "All in good time. It's nice to know I haven't lost my touch. I had both of you completely fooled."

"Only for a moment." She challenged his triumphant smile. "You don't sound like Mitch. You're not as tall."

With the knife, he flicked a tendril of hair that had fallen across her cheek. "I'll put higher lifts in my shoes."

Casey squirmed against the nylon rope that bound her wrists, but didn't jerk away from his touch. It gave her some small victory to deny him the satisfaction of seeing her flinch beneath his taunts.

He knelt close enough for her to smell the tan foundation he'd put on his face and hands, close enough to see the odd strands of lighter hair at the roots of his nutmeg-brown dye job. At a distance, even she'd been taken in by the broad cut of his clothes, no doubt enhanced by padding of some sort. He looked like Mitch. He threatened like Mitch...

Casey did flinch at the realization she made. Emmett had altered himself to look like Mitch. That meant he intended to replace him. If he hadn't already.

"Oh, my God." She collapsed in her chair, all the fight drained out of her by the knowledge that Mitch might already be dead.

"I suppose I'm ready to do business," said Emmett, noticing her slack in posture, and apparently tiring of toying with her. "I believe you owe me a little bit of money."

"That's not the deal." She felt Jimmy's heat through the back of her sweater as he leaned forward. "The money stays in the car with Iris until I see those pictures."

Emmett rose to his feet, puffing out his chest and pulling back the front of his coat. Mimicking Mitch's fingers-on-the-hips stance. All he needed was the silver-medal-replica pin and she might believe...

No pin.

The realization that had panicked her before now coursed through her with a reviving flood of hope. If Emmett didn't have the pin she'd given Mitch, then he might still be alive. Emmett hadn't gotten to Mitch yet. She still had time to escape. Time to warn him.

She sat up straight once more.

"Now, that's the man I remember," said Emmett, turning to Jimmy for amusement. "A decisive man of action. Tough. But as I recall, not very good at his word."

Casey used the distraction of age-old male posturing for authority to do a quick study of her surroundings. Night had fallen outside the windows. The reflection of the rising moon off the snow provided a dim haze of light throughout the pool house. A garish beam of artificial light from the dressing room sliced across the deck with narrow laserbeam intensity. The contrast was more blinding than illuminating. If she could get to the power box and switch on the overhead lights, the glow could be seen from the street. Would one of the neighbors see the lights of the pool house, and with the rest of the house so dark think something odd? Would they call the police? Would they call Mitch?

But sending such a beacon was a useless consideration since Emmett and his knife, and Jimmy and his gun, had no intention of letting her up to stroll over to the light switch.

"Twenty-five thousand dollars and Cassandra, just as you asked," said Jimmy. "Now keep your end of the deal."

"I kept my word seven years ago when I killed that hooker for you."

"You were to bring the pictures to me."

Pictures? Had Mitch and Ginny been on the right track with their suspicions of blackmail?

Casey stifled her need to ask questions, to find out the truth, and searched for Plan B. The outside door was a good twenty feet from the side of the pool where she sat. Would the two men ignore her long enough to get there? Either could easily overtake her.

"But Darlene got caught. And you didn't get her off like you promised."

Plan C. She prayed. As hard as she had the night Emmett had pinned her to the floor and carved his hideous message in her leg.

She prayed for a miracle.

"I tried every way I could to influence Jack Maynard. I even told you how to get to Cassandra."

"My God." Plans for escape derailed at the baldly stated confession. Casey stood and turned to the monster she had once called family. "You did this to me? You told him to do this?"

She had known this day would come. For seven years, she had waited for this reckoning. And as much as she had feared it, she now almost welcomed it. Because, even if every plan of hers should fail, it would be over. The fear and the shame and the loneliness would all finally be over. "Jimmy?"

He refused to look her in the eye, but Emmett seemed to take a strange delight in aligning himself with her against Jimmy. "That's why you're still alive, champ. Ol' Jimmy boy couldn't bring himself to have another death on his hands. So I just used you as a warning to your dad."

She took a step back, hating to side with either man. "My father would never bow down to the likes of you. I'm glad your sister went to prison for Cynthia DeBecque's murder. Even if she was a prostitute, she didn't deserve to die like that."

"That prostitute got thousands of dollars from me." Jimmy ground his teeth in disgust. "She threatened to send pictures of the two of us to the press. During an election year! She had to be silenced."

Emmett raised one brow and dared to give him a holier-than-thou look. "We took care of your mistake, Jimmy boy. And then, instead of paying what you owed me, you up and arrest me for murder and assault and extortion. Did you think that would shut me up? My Darlene is dead."

"Your sister knew where the negatives were hidden. Once she got out of prison, she would have taken up where Cynthia left off. She had to die."

For a brief instant, the facade of Mitch Taylor vanished from Emmett's face, leaving a venomous, cold-eyed killer in its wake. Casey withdrew into herself at the heinous expression, rounding her shoulders and lowering her chin to keep from drawing any attention. Jimmy, unfortunately, was beyond the sense to protect himself.

He turned his accusatory glare on her. ''I served him up on a silver platter. All you had to do was identify him in the courtroom. Put him away. Maximum security. But you screwed up. You got *confused* on the witness stand.''

Casey didn't try to defend herself. Didn't try to rationalize the convincing perfection of Emmett's disguise. Didn't try to explain her terror at seeing the man who had disfigured her glaring at her across a courtroom. Jimmy wouldn't listen to her.

He never had.

''If you care so little about me, why did you assign Mitch to protect me?''

''I can answer that one.'' Emmett twisted his fingers into a white-knuckled grasp around the knife handle. He slowly circled behind Casey, forcing Jimmy to turn with him, so he wouldn't have his back to the enemy. ''Ol' Jimmy boy here is afraid to do his own dirty work. So he puts his best cop on the case. Leads me right to you, and hopes that...''

''Mitch will kill you for him,'' Casey finished.

''Ooh. She's smarter than you, Jimmy boy.'' Emmett's mirthless laughter grated through the pores of her skin. ''Darlene was my sister, my soul. Jack Maynard put her in prison. And you killed her because you couldn't find a more respectable bedmate.''

''Damn you, Raines, I've had enough!'' Jimmy rose to the taunt Casey had been able to resist. He reached inside his coat and pulled out the same gun he had used to *escort* her to the pool house.

Her instinct to duck was thwarted by the arm that closed around her neck. Emmett hugged her to him, with the point of his knife pricking the base of her throat. The muscular bulk of his forearm blocked most of the air through her windpipe, turning her scream into a useless squeak.

"No, you don't, Jimmy boy." Emmett's voice was a low-pitched menace in her ear. "I'm in charge here. *I'll* tell you when we're done. Now throw the gun in the pool and call your secretary and tell her to bring me the money."

Casey zeroed in on the wavering gun barrel. Jimmy closed both hands around the grip of his pistol to steady his aim. "No. The money stays with Iris until you hand over those negatives."

The vise around her neck tightened. Clearly, Emmett had no interest in negotiating. "Call her, Jimmy boy, or I'll cut her right in front of you."

The blood drained from her head at the vile threat, leaving her dizzy. To one man, she was a bargaining chip— to the other, a human shield.

Courage.

The word echoed in her mind like a distant memory. A sweet caress.

When Mitch looked at her, he saw courage.

His husky voice, his whiskey-dark eyes, his endless faith swelled inside her like a reviving lungful of air. She stretched her chin above Emmett's arm and let her instinct to win take over. It was time to fight, or lose.

Spying the clench of Jimmy's trigger finger, she twisted her body and dug her heel into the instep of Emmett's foot. The next few seconds unfolded with the agonizing slowness of viewing a motion picture frame by frame.

She doubled over and the bullet struck Emmett. Blood spurted from the gash in his forearm as his knife clattered across the tiles. Clutching his wrist, Emmett lurched forward, knocking the chair and Casey to the deck. He hit Jimmy full force, and Casey rolled away.

Ignoring the punches and grunts and threats that followed as the two men grappled for the gun and vengeance, Casey crawled to the knife. She sat up and sawed at the rope binding her, scooting across the ceramic floor on her bottom. When her hands were free, she staggered to her feet and limped toward the door. She didn't want to try running and risk losing her balance; falling would put her at the victor's mercy.

Her hand was on the doorknob when a second explosion behind her jarred her to a stop. A morbid, hopeful curiosity made her catch her breath and glance over her shoulder.

"Dammit! Messy, messy, messy." Emmett rose to his knees beside Jimmy's prone form, mopping at the blood that spattered the front of his coat. He shrugged out of it and straightened his jacket and tie.

"Jimmy." She breathed his name, a prayer of sorrow for the man she had once loved.

Then her eyes locked on the icy hatred in Emmett's eyes. Her heart stopped, then sped into maddening overdrive. He heaved a deep, foretelling breath. Terror spread like molten adrenaline through her veins, overriding her shock. She spun back around and fumbled with the locked door. But her panicked fingers proved no match for Emmett's ruthless obsession.

She felt his wrath an instant before he grabbed her shoulder and jerked her around. With his own knife, she slashed at his face. She cringed as it sliced into skin and bone, but gasped in victory when he released her and clutched at the wound. She shoved him, hard, with her fists. Off balance, he stumbled back, giving her space to try for the door once more.

Her fingers found the dead bolt. Slipped it back.

"You bitch!"

He snatched a fistful of hair and yanked her off balance. A million knife pricks burned across her scalp as he dragged her away from the door. She tried to dig in and fight, but pain shot through her ankle and her leg crumpled beneath her.

The sudden action pulled her free, but Emmett was on top of her before she could escape. He tossed Jimmy's gun aside and pressed himself into her. "I prefer a more hands-on retribution."

He panted hard, his hot breath dampening her skin with its mad promise. The clammy fingers of one hand crushed her wrist, squeezing the sensation out of her fist. As her grip loosened from the handle, his other hand darted out with the coiled accuracy of a whip snake, snatching the knife from her grasp.

Casey twisted beneath him. He rolled his weight onto her injured leg, and she cried out. She scratched at his wounded face, cursed his evil smile.

From the corner of her eye, she glimpsed the shift in his grip, saw the knife coming toward her…

Felt him go still—the only sound in the world was her own heartbeat pounding in her ears.

"Let her go, Raines, or I'll put a bullet in the back of your skull." Her miracle had come. With the voice she knew for certain this time. Dark and deep—and full of such deadly intent that she herself felt chilled. "Drop the knife nice and slow, and lie facedown on the deck."

"Mitch?" She nearly sobbed his name, her relief was so intense.

When Emmett crawled off her and did as Mitch instructed, she could see his grim, tight-lipped, handsome face towering above her. He shifted the gun trained on Emmett's head from both hands to his left. With his right, he reached out to Casey. "You okay?"

She saw the reaction in Mitch's eyes before she saw the threat itself. With nothing left to lose, Emmett made one last desperate lunge. He kicked, catching Mitch on the knee and tripping him.

"No!" Casey screamed at the crunch of fist and bone that snapped Mitch's head back. With a madman's fury, Emmett wrapped his hand around Mitch's gun and the two men rolled toward the pool, locked in gladiatorial combat.

Mitch had saved her life. And now he would surely die. Because of her. She could not let him die.

With energy to do little more than pull herself to her hands and knees, Casey crawled toward them. Emmett was weakened from his previous fight, from his wounds. Mitch was bigger, stronger.

"Please, God," she prayed, changing course, pushing herself to her feet and scrabbling for Jimmy's gun. "Please don't let him die."

She straightened with the gun in her hands, aiming at Emmett. Or was it Mitch? One and the same, they rolled, broad shoulders and brown tweed. Suddenly, the other Mitch's back was in her sights. She lowered the gun. A fist swung low into one man's gut. He recoiled. She raised the gun again.

A shot rang out.

Casey flinched at the loud report. Her hands shook in the dead silence that followed. But she hadn't fired her weapon.

In the unnatural quiet, she heard a man's last breath.

More terrified than she'd been at the thought of her own death, her weary body quaked at the idea of Mitch dying.

She scarcely breathed in those out-of-time moments. But then something stirred. One massive shoulder shrugged. A broad back straightened. A large, abraded hand reached back and rubbed that corded, sensitive neck that bore the weight of the world with such practised ease.

"Mitch?"

She held her breath, not trusting what her heart wanted to believe. He reached into his pocket as he climbed to his feet. She raised the gun.

Between his thumb and forefinger, a tiny circle of silver reflected the light off the snow outside.

"Mitch!"

He was staggering forward by the time she reached him. She swallowed him up in a fierce hug. His muffled grunt registered a split second later. He tried to draw her back into the life-giving warmth of his arms, but she pushed away, berating herself for not seeing the blood at the corner of his mouth, the scrapes on his knuckles…

The knife sticking out from beneath his ribs.

"Oh, my God." She pulled him away from Emmett's body, and he dutifully followed. But when she tried to lay him down to prevent shock from setting in, he refused. "Dammit, Mitch, he stabbed you. Let me help." She pulled a handkerchief from her pocket and wadded it to press to the wound, but she hovered around the knife hilt, not wanting to aggravate the injury. "Do I pull it out? What do I do?"

Mitch caught her hand in his fist, stilling her efforts to help. "It's not that bad." He stroked her cheek with gruff, shaky fingers. "You're hurt, too. We need to get you to the doctor."

"Of all the stupid, asinine things to say." She tilted her chin, unshed tears burning her eyes as she glared defiantly at him.

His eyes reflected an unreadable liquid turbulence. She felt at once chastized and cherished. "Let's talk stupid," he said. "That was an incredibly crazy stunt you pulled, running away from Merle. I expect you to tell me anything you found out from Jimmy.

"But first, princess..."

She didn't know whether he was furious or exasperated or even, despite the horrible way she'd treated him at the cabin, overjoyed to see her again. "What?"

He bent his head and covered her mouth in a raw, soul-stealing, possessive kiss. Her head spun. Her heart pounded. She answered back with all the love in her heart.

Then he closed his hands over her shoulders and pushed her away. His face teetered back and forth in front of hers. Casey clutched at his forearms, steadying herself. Steadying him. "Mitch?"

"Second..."

A horrible suspicion spiraled through her. "Mitch!"

"Get the radio from my jacket and get Joe in here. I think I'm...I'm gonna pass..."

One hundred eighty pounds of Mitch Taylor collapsed on Casey and carried them both to the floor.

Chapter Thirteen

"Mr. Taylor! If you don't sit still, you'll rip the stitches. You wanted this change of clothes, so let me do it."

Mitch frowned and looked at the clock. Hell, it had been more than twenty-four hours since he'd seen Casey! Was she all right? He'd shot Raines dead, hadn't he? He hadn't passed out on her and left her alone with a man intent on killing her.

Had he?

The nurse who'd been on duty before Attila the Hunette here took over said only that Casey had been admitted to the hospital. The frustrating lack of details might be the staff's way of sparing him emotional pain until he was physically stronger. He'd lost a lot of blood. But fate had sent Emmett's blade through a band of muscle, and missed nicking or puncturing anything vital.

Had Casey been so lucky?

Attila pulled on his arm and commanded him to stand. He didn't obey so much as succumb to the nurse's stern will. She steadied him while he pulled on his pajama bottoms, and then batted his fingers away, taking over his clumsy attempts to gingerly tie the waist string around his surgical stitches with an IV needle and tube attached to his arm. She guided Mitch back into bed with swift, efficient movements. Mitch groaned at the combination of pain and frustration. Attila could run The Fourth Precinct office and whip all his men into shape. Single-handedly.

"There." She covered him up and rolled the tray table up over his lap. "You're lucky. The doctor said you could have solid foods." She uncovered the plate. "Enjoy."

Mitch eyeballed the oatmeal, juice and scrambled eggs. Not exactly his idea of solid food. But then, he didn't think the sour feeling in his stomach was related to either his injury or hunger. He gave his nurse and keeper his most apologetic expression, hoping charm might win some answers. "You're sure no one has asked for me?"

She folded her arms and shook her head. "There are a couple of reporters anxious to see you."

Mitch grit his teeth at the woman's obtuse response. "What about the woman who came in with me?"

"Mr. Taylor, you were the only one on that ambulance. After prepping you in the E.R., they took you straight to surgery and stitched you up."

"What about the redhead?" he snapped. The one with the singular color of hair and claim to his heart? "She's tall. Built..." He traced Casey's perfect curves in the air with his left hand, then curled the fingers into a fist. "Her name is Cassandra Maynard. She was involved in the same incident that I was. I need to see her."

"Will we do for company?" The door opened, and Mitch's flare of hope quickly faded with Joe and Ginny's arrival. His old partner looked as if he'd been living on coffee for the past twenty-four hours, and Ginny didn't look much better.

Mitch swallowed his disappointment and studied them thoroughly, gratefully. "How are you guys holding up?"

Joe smiled. "Hey, things are running smoothly with me

in charge. You *will* be out of commission for a while, won't you?''

Mitch extended his hand and grinned, understanding the teasing bravado and the subliminal get-well message buried in the words. Joe's grip was firm, reassuring. Mitch knew his precinct was in good hands.

''Merle?''

''I chewed his butt for letting Casey's location slip to the commissioner.''

Despite the dangerous chain of events that that little bit of knowledge set into action, Mitch felt his fatherly concern kick in. ''Rookie mistake. I can imagine what kind of pressure the commish put on him for the information. You think he can get on that computer of his and track down Casey's location now?''

Ginny exchanged a smile with Joe. ''You haven't seen her?'' she asked.

''I can't even get an update on her condition.'' Mitch considered ripping the IV from his arm and beginning a room-to-room investigation himself. ''You did bring her to the hospital, didn't you? She was hurt. Bruises and a cut on her face. I don't know what else.''

''I loaded her into an ambulance myself,'' said Ginny. ''Right after I rounded up Iris Webster and her twenty-five grand. She may be facing some serious time as an accessory after the fact. She's been covering up the commissioner's indiscretions for years.''

Mitch nodded. ''Casey suspected as much. And the commissioner?''

''Dead on the scene. Along with Raines.''

''And the McDonalds? Their granddaughter? No one else got hurt?''

''All fine.'' Joe laughed. ''It's all in my report, old man. Incidentally, I'm looking forward to reading yours.''

"I'm not writing anything until I find out about Casey. It's that bad, isn't it? That's why no one will tell me anything."

"I haven't had a chance to see her yet. I've been filling out paperwork and fending off the press—"

"Dammit, Joe…"

Nurse Attila touched his arm. "Calm down, Mr. Taylor. You can't afford the rise in blood pressure or the strain on those stitches."

The dull ache in his side wasn't nearly as painful as the uncertainty in his heart. He lashed out. "Dammit, lady, if you don't quit with the nagging and get me some answers…"

"Threats will get you nowhere, Mr. Taylor."

Mitch rose up in the bed, feeling justified to do some damage to this woman.

"Charming the ladies as usual, I see, cousin."

There was a knock at the open door, and Mitch fell back onto the pillows at the sound of Brett's voice. He sauntered into the room, followed by his aunt and uncle. Martha hurried over to the side of his bed. She kissed his cheek, then felt his forehead as if he were ten years old again and she was checking for a fever.

"Are you feeling better?" she asked, fussing over him in a more loving, though no less efficient, manner than his nurse.

"You had us plenty scared," said Uncle Sid. He stuffed his hands into his pockets and shrugged off the concern that must have been worrying him, as well.

Mitch felt the walls closing in. He'd known he had family, friends who cared about him. Maybe today more than any other time in his life, he consciously accepted that despite his parents' murders, despite Jackie's betrayal and death, he was loved. And he was grateful and proud to love every single person in this room.

Well, Attila would take some getting used to.

But he still had a big gaping hole in his heart. Casey might not want his love, but he loved her anyway. She might not need him now that Emmett Raines and James Reed were dead. But he needed her. She might not want him in her life anymore, but he wanted...

"Can anyone join this party, or is it a private affair?"

With the snap of magic fingers, the room fell silent. The others disappeared from Mitch's vision as he drank in the sight of Casey walking toward him. Supported this morning by a stainless-steel crutch with an arm cuff, she nevertheless crossed the room with her innate grace. Her cinnamon-gold hair fell in loose waves about her shoulders, and her eyes glimmered with the gray of the sky just before dawn. A set of pale bruises dappled the side of her jaw, and her pert little chin tipped upward ever so slightly, its proud angle marred by a white suture bandage.

While his heart marveled in the beauty of her spirit and body, his pulse calmed with the reassuring sight of her in one piece. The fear and impatience that had crowded his thoughts, his concerns about the case, his gratitude to his friends and family, all ceased to be important at that moment. He loved Casey Maynard. Fiercely. Forever.

And all he could think to say was, "You okay?"

She came to the end of his bed and assessed him from head to toe. He felt a twinge of guilt at causing the frown that creased the corners of her mouth. His black eye, perhaps. Maybe the bandages that wrapped his ribs.

"I'm okay, old man."

In his peripheral awareness, he saw Ginny nudge Joe, heard Brett laugh, saw his aunt searching her purse and Uncle Sid pull out his handkerchief and give it to her.

Nurse Attila shook her head and made a loud pronouncement. "We'd better clear out this room and give Mr. Taylor a chance to rest."

Everyone said their goodbyes and drifted out the door. "Not you." Attila put her hand on Casey's shoulder and nodded toward the bed. "I think you're the medicine he needs." In a rustle of surprising understanding and clingy support hose, she was gone.

Mitch glanced at the closed door and then at Casey. "I guess I'm not running things anymore."

He scrunched the corner of the top sheet in his fist, then smoothed it flat again. He hadn't felt this nervous since... Hell! He'd never been this nervous.

Casey spoke first. She fidgeted her fingers along the steel frame of the bed. "Looks like you're giving the nurses a hard time. You really should work on your people skills."

Mitch responded to her gentle teasing. "Nurse Ratchit there wouldn't give me any answers about your condition. Do you know where I wanted to wrap that blood pressure cuff?"

"I'm okay, Mitch." When he met her gaze, the lighthearted banter was gone. "Really. I'm alive, thanks to you."

"I've never been so scared as I was when I saw Raines holding that knife to your throat." He couldn't keep the bleak desperation in his soul from creeping into his voice.

Casey smiled, transforming her face into serene royalty. Leaving the crutch at the foot of the bed, she moved to his left side, pushed away the tray table, wrapped her arms around his neck and squeezed him in a tight hug. "Then let me be the one to hold you when you're scared."

Trembling with humility and overwhelmed by her generous action, he curled his left arm around her waist and pulled her onto the bed. He clutched her to his side, not quite willing to interpret her show of compassion as a declaration of love. But he could hold her like this forever, burying his nose in the softness of her hair, inhaling her unique scent, trading strengths until he felt composed enough to speak again.

"I thought I'd lost you, princess." He nuzzled the elegant shell of her ear.

"I'm a survivor, remember? You said we pick up the pieces and go on. Because we have to." Hearing his words on her lips sparked the first ray of hope he'd felt since leaving her at the cabin.

But hope was a precious thing. Once he hoped his parents had somehow survived that holdup. Once he hoped his marriage to Jackie could work despite the demanding time and pressure of the job that was so much a part of him. He had even hoped that his instincts were wrong when he knew Casey's life was the trade-off James Reed wanted to pay Emmett Raines.

Did he dare hope that Casey could one day learn to accept his love? To believe in the love he wanted so desperately to give her?

She snuggled closer, and he tried to convince himself that this was real trust. That this was more than just gratitude or shared relief that they had both survived the attempt on their lives.

Casey shivered despite the encompassing warmth of Mitch's body. She'd come so close to losing him. And though he felt strong and solid as she curled up against him, she couldn't help remembering the haggard shadows on his face when she'd walked into the room.

She held on as tight as she dared without touching the dressing on the right side of his torso. "Emmett wanted you to track me to the house with Jimmy," she whispered against the pillow of his shoulder. "He wanted to kill you and take your place. I can't even think of what he would have done to your body to hide it."

"Yeah. That was creepy when he rolled over. It was like looking in a mirror."

Casey shivered against him. "Then he could arrest Jimmy, take away his career and money that was always so important to him."

"Put him in prison where the commissioner of police wouldn't last too long. He could die just like Darlene Raines." Mitch sighed beneath her cheek. "I had a bad feeling about Jimmy from the start."

Casey shrank back. "I know. If only I'd listened to you."

She sat up straight to see his face, to confess her uncle's sins and show Mitch how sorry she was that he had ever been touched by her family's sordid secrets. "You were another pawn he used to cover up his affair with Cynthia DeBecque. He hired Raines and his sister to kill her and retrieve incriminating photos. When Darlene was on trial, he told Emmett…" She swallowed past the lump of tears in her throat, and tipped her chin to keep her composure intact. "He told Emmett how to get around the security assigned to protect me. He used poor Steven then the way he used you now. I'm sorry. I'm…sorry."

She couldn't think of anything more to say.

She'd sought out Mitch's room to see for herself that he was in one piece. To apologize. And to explain the understanding she had learned about herself under the threat of Emmett Raines's knife. But suddenly, her courage seemed far out of reach, her self-assurance an unsteady thing.

"Casey?" His dark, powerful voice resonated along her trembling backbone. He touched her jaw and angled her face so she looked up into his eyes. The true brown depths glittered with pride, hope and that blatant raw fire she'd seen there when he'd spoken of love. "You aren't responsible for Jimmy's actions, or anyone else's. Only your own. And I think you're the bravest, smartest, sexiest woman I've ever known. The past has finally been put to rest. The present will take care of itself. And the future…"

"Do we have a future?" Her words spilled out in a rush, falling into a yawning silence that hung in the air between them like an insurmountable brick wall.

"You tell me."

His challenge laid the first rung on the ladder that would carry her to the top of that wall. He'd said he loved her. Maybe her life required a similar act of courage.

She reached out and cradled the stubbled strength of his jaw in her hands, reaching the second rung herself.

"My handicap has never mattered to you, has it?" she asked.

His hands slipped to her waist and held her, but didn't pull her any closer. "About as much as the part of town I come from matters to you."

The third rung fashioned itself in their mutual acceptance of self-perceived shortcomings that weren't really shortcomings after all. She could see the top of that wall.

The phone beside the bed rang, leaving her stranded on the brink of the summit. Mitch reached over and picked up the receiver. The stretch made him clutch at his side, and he grumbled a pained oath about sadistic nurses and bandages that cut off circulation.

"Taylor." He sat up in the bed, almost snapping to attention. "Yes, sir." His gaze shot to hers. "I understand." The tense line of his mouth softened with the hint of a smile. "I'll tell her."

"Who was that?" she asked after he'd hung up the phone.

"An agent from the witness-protection program. Your folks are on a flight to the U.S. right now. They'll be at KCI airport by five this evening. I'll send Joe out to meet them."

"They're coming home?" An oppressive weight lifted from Casey's shoulders and she launched herself into Mitch's arms. She hugged him around the neck, tears of sheer joy blending with tears of relief on her cheeks.

"Much better, princess." His whispered words lapped deliciously against her ear. His arms tightened around her, and she grew achingly aware of the solid heat of his arms and chest, and how strips of gauze and hospital garb left very little to the imagination.

Instead of retreating, Casey snuggled closer.

This was it. Now or never. If she didn't give everything she had right now, she would lose this most precious race of her life. "Mitch. What you said at the cabin. About love and courage..."

"I was out of line..."

"No." She shifted quickly and pressed her fingers against his lips to silence him. "You were right. I was a coward. I took everything you offered me because I needed it—your warmth, your embrace, your protection. Even your love. And I treated you like you were just doing your job."

She bit her lip, hurting inside at the hateful memories of how foolish and cruel she had been.

"Look at everything that was going on around you. You had every right to doubt me."

Casey shook her head, loving him even more for the unending compassion hidden beneath his gruff exterior. "You are one good man, Mitch Taylor. I love you."

His shoulders sagged, and for an instant she wondered if he had changed his mind about her. If she had waited too long to accept the beautiful gift he offered her.

And then his arms were folding around her and his lips were covering hers. Branding her with his taste, claiming her with the promise of his love. His hands were in her hair, skimming down her back, lifting her onto his lap. She heard a little grunt of pain deep in his throat and tried to move away, but he pinned her firmly against his thighs and tucked the crown of her head beneath his chin.

"No way, princess. You're not going anywhere. Not this time."

Casey thrilled to the uneven huskiness of his voice. Her valiant gladiator had a weakness. Her. She silently vowed to protect him always.

"Mitch?"

"Hmm?"

His heartbeat steadied beneath her ear as she nestled into the treasured haven of his arms. "Would you like to meet my parents in person?"

He half laughed, half frowned into the billow of hair at her temple. "What made you think of them? All I can think of now is whether or not I'd rip any stitches if I made love to you right here in this hospital bed."

Her cheeks grew hot, and she made him suffer for the suggestion by running her fingernails along that sensitive spot on his neck and eliciting a feral groan. "Don't you think they'd like to meet the man I plan to marry?"

He eased away from her then, keeping one hand at the small of her back, and tipping up her chin with the other. The earnest frown creasing the corners of his eyes touched her heart. "You think the judge would take an old downtown boy like me for his son-in-law?"

Casey tunneled her fingers into his hair and reassured

him with a smile. "Did I ever tell you that my dad was an old downtown boy himself?"

"No kidding?"

"No kidding." She gave a gentle tug and pulled him closer. "He's going to love you, Mitch. Almost as much as I do."

His eyes blazed with the power of love that filled her, made her strong, made her his. "In that case, princess, I accept your proposal."

What can be stolen, forgotten, hidden, replaced, imitated—but never lost?

HARLEQUIN®

I N T R I G U E ®

brings you the strong, sexy men
and passionate women who are
about to uncover...

SEC**R**ET
IDENTITY

LITTLE BOY LOST
by Adrianne Lee
August 2000

SAFE BY HIS SIDE
by Debra Webb
September 2000

HER MYSTERIOUS STRANGER
by Debbi Rawlins
October 2000

ALIAS MOMMY
by Linda O. Johnston
November 2000

Available at your favorite retail outlet.

HARLEQUIN®
Makes any time special ™

Visit us at www.eHarlequin.com

HISI

THE SECRET IS OUT!

HARLEQUIN®

makes any time special—online...

eHARLEQUIN.com

shop eHarlequin

♥ Find all the new Harlequin releases at everyday great discounts.

♥ Try before you buy! Read an excerpt from the latest Harlequin novels.

♥ Write an online review and share your thoughts with others.

reading room

♥ Read our Internet exclusive daily and weekly online serials, or vote in our interactive novel.

♥ Talk to other readers about your favorite novels in our Reading Groups.

♥ Take our Choose-a-Book quiz to find the series that matches you!

authors' alcove

♥ Find out interesting tidbits and details about your favorite authors' lives, interests and writing habits.

♥ Ever dreamed of being an author? Enter our Writing Round Robin. The Winning Chapter will be published online! Or review our writing guidelines for submitting your novel.